THE ZEAL TRILOGY

BOOK 2

The Price of Redemption

THE ZEAL TRILOGY
BOOK 2

The Price of Redemption

Michelle Warren

Discover other titles by Michelle Warren:

THE ZEAL TRILOGY Book 1: A New Kind of Zeal
THE ZEAL TRILOGY Book 3: The Crux of Salvation
Yeshua

Statement:

This novel is a work of fiction. Any resemblance of a character to a person living or dead is a coincidence apart from the clear characters of inspiration from two thousand years ago. Likewise, in the slightly futuristic poetic interpretation, the organisations, positions, places, nations, ethnicities, religions, ideologies, and customs explored do not represent any current reality today but represent a fictional future. Those portions set in the past are also fictionalized.

No offence is intended in the writing of the novel. The opinions upheld by the characters do not necessarily represent the opinions of the author, and any criminal actions or acts of war committed by the characters are not endorsed by the author.

This novel is not intended to incite violence or warfare: quite the opposite, the goal of the novel is to evoke peace.

INTRODUCTION

This novel follows the events that took place in the novel
A New Kind of Zeal.

Contents

The final in The Zeal Trilogy: The Crux of Salvation

References

PROLOGUE

*R*achel Connor stood inside the gates of Parliament.

In front of her, four people lay shot on the ground. She rushed toward them, to help – to check their pulses – but was shoved away by army officers.

"Stand back!" they ordered.

Rachel stared at them. "I'm a doctor, for Christ's sake!" she said. "Let me pass!"

But they shook their heads. "No exceptions."

The army were surrounding the people; ushering them out of the Parliament grounds, back onto the street. Rachel was pressed back. She almost stumbled, but somehow kept her footing.

Through the black gate, Rachel saw a movement behind the army officers. A suited man was walking to the Hill Street gate.

Joshua stood in the intersection; Rachel's heart pounded in fear. He was alone, isolated out by the army. His white face was unreadable.

"You can't kill him," Rachel whispered to the army officers. "He has committed no crime."

"We're the army," an officer replied, "not the police. We act in times of war, to establish national security."

"We are not at war!" said Rachel, and now Joshua's eyes were on her.

War...

"He's done nothing," said Rachel. "He's a pacifist, for God's sake! You can't kill him!"

She looked over the street to John Robertson – the fear in his eyes, but also the gritty determination.

The Bishop of Wellington, Mark Blake, was standing in Anglican robes on the steps of Saint Peter's Cathedral, watching the crowd.

"Joshua Davidson killed our people," said Blake, pointing to Joshua. "He is destroying our nation."

Rachel tried to look to her left, down Hill Street – who was the politician? The man emerged on the street, opposite the steps of Saint Peter's, facing Joshua in the intersection. It was her father, James Connor.

His face was taut, his forehead creased with burden. This was the Prime Minister of New Zealand! This was his nation, going to pot!

"What the hell are you doing?" Rachel cried out to him. "The army, Dad? What are you thinking?"

An officer forced her down to her knees, pressing a rifle to the back of her head.

"Leave her," said Joshua calmly. "No one else needs to die today."

Rachel's body shook hard. She stared at her father – he stared back at her. Then his eyes shifted to Joshua.

"You are a curse," he said, spitting at him, "a curse that is bringing our people to ruin!"

Joshua faced him, but did not speak. Confused, Rachel searched his face. He was innocent! He was good, not evil! How dare Connor accuse him, and blame him, when Connor's own actions had precipitated the riot?

"You're a bastard!" Rachel shouted out to him. "An incompetent bastard!"

And now she felt a blinding, sharp, painful blow to the back of her head.

The Price of Redemption

She fell, gasping, on her face. Her vision blacked out, though she heard her father's voice.

"Stand down, officer!" he ordered. "I am your commander!"

A hand was on her head. The pain disappeared, and her vision returned. Confused, Rachel looked up. Joshua was standing over her, smiling. He reached out a hand and pulled her back to her feet.

"Don't argue any more," he said quietly to her. "Don't fight them. You'll get yourself killed."

The Governor General, Anita Mayes, stepped forward toward her father.

"Right Honourable Prime Minister James Connor!" she said loudly. "Do you really think this is legal?"

"The nation is under threat, Right Honourable Governor General," Connor replied. "I have taken the necessary actions to ensure our nation's survival."

Blake now shifted, on the steps of Saint Peter's. "Connor!" his strong voice called out. "Do something! Deal with this man, before it is too late!"

Connor lifted his hand toward the crowd, and Tristan Blake stepped between the officers.

He was carrying a rifle.

Rachel swallowed. "Oh my God..."

Tristan's face was hard, his eyes distant and far away...

"Tristan!" she whispered. "What are you doing?"

A lead weight was in Rachel's stomach now; a terrible twisting in her gut.

"Oh my God." Connor had organised the assassination of Joshua.

A strange girl was with Tristan, flitting about, dancing.

"Your majesty!" she said, bowing – and she put an ancient metal crown on Joshua's head.

Joshua's face turned a sickly shade of grey. His brown eyes fixed on her with agony. His head tipped back, he clung the crown firmly to his head, and began to stagger.

Rachel clenched her fists.

"Kill him, Connor!" Blake called out. "Do it now!"

"Not yet!" John cried. "Not yet! It's not the right time!"

Joshua was groaning, staggering, trying to keep his footing, his face pointed up to the sky; his hands still clutching the crown to his head.

Tristan stared at Joshua, his body shaking.

"Kill him!" Blake cried out. "Kill him, and we will all be safe! Kill him, and we will all find our peace!"

"The scapegoat..." Tristan whispered. "Oh my God – the scapegoat..."

Rachel thought the rifle might fall from his shaking hands.

"Kill him!" Blake repeated. "Execute him! Do it quickly!"

"Prime Minister!" The Governor General cried out. "Our state is a democracy! We have a Law! We have a court system!"

"To hell with the Law!" said Blake. "This is about our survival! Our survival, as a people – even as a race! What are you waiting for?"

He was staring at Connor.

Rachel saw reluctance in her father's eyes. He didn't want to execute!

"Do this," Mayes declared loudly, "and I will use the powers invested in me to dissolve the Government! This is not your role, Connor! You are way out of line here!"

Connor's eyes moved over the crowd.

"Let the people decide!" he said. "What is your decision?"

There was silence, and then a response.

"Oh, to hell with it!" someone cried out. "Get it over with!"

"Kill him?" Connor asked. "How many say 'Yes'?"

"Just kill him!" the people cried. "Get it over with! Kill him!"

Others struggled! Others shouted for his life! Rachel raised her voice, loud and strong.

"No!" she cried. "Kill him, and it will all be over! We will never be the same again!"

Joshua's eyes were on her now. He was suffering. His grey face was sweating, and bleeding! Bleeding...

The Price of Redemption

Tristan stood before Joshua. Rachel watched as Tristan looked at Joshua's staggering form and saw the blood. Tristan's face contorted. Joshua was looking at him! His eyes were clouded with pain, but gracious! Rachel was drawn into his expression. It was love! Tristan saw it, too; he looked stricken by it! Love.

Joshua reached out a hand to grasp Tristan's shoulder, and his body stiffened. He fell to his knees, his back taut; his face pointing to the sky.

"Father!" he cried to God. "Don't hold it against them! They really have no idea what they are doing!"

Blood dripped down his face. The crown fell off his head, and now he stretched his arms out wide.

"Where are you?" he cried to God, and his face now contorted with terror! "Oh, God, Daddy – I can't see you! Darkness! Darkness…"

Rachel's eyes filled with tears – she blinked them furiously away. Joshua! Joshua…

Tristan was rigid. Dismay flooded his face. Then he stepped back, gathered the rifle, and fired.

Rachel choked. Bullets landed in Joshua's chest; many bullets! They jerked his body backwards – they threw him to the ground.

She rushed forward to him. He was lying on the ground, his body jerking with pain, gasping. She tore away his blood stained white shirt, to find five bullet wounds – two to each lung, and one to the heart.

"Oh, God," Rachel breathed, shaking. "No…"

She reached for his neck, to his pulse. It was still there, but faint! Fading rapidly! He was bleeding badly from the chest – gasping for breath, bleeding from the heart.

Rachel took off her own jacket, and pressed it into his wounds. Pressure! But she knew it was useless. His heart had been penetrated, and his lungs! There was no way he could survive.

He grasped her hand. Rachel sobbed, as he met her eyes – as he struggled, on his last breaths.

"It's finished!" he gasped. "It's sorted!" And his face broke into a sudden beautiful smile.

Rachel grasped him, crying. "Don't go!" she said. "Don't go!"

Peace filled his eyes – and then his head fell back, and his hand fell from hers.

He was dead.

Rachel sank to the ground next to him. Resuscitate? She crossed her hands over his chest, and began to pound his heart. But then she felt a hand to her shoulder.

It was John. His eyes were filled with tears. He held her gaze, and shook his head.

"It's over," he whispered. "Don't try to bring him back."

She stared at his face, and began to weep. She shrank back away, from John and from Joshua's body. Then she looked at the crowd.

They were silent.

"Enough!" cried the Governor General's voice. "By the power invested in me, as the representative of the Queen, I now announce that the current Prime Minister has acted outside of his jurisdiction!

"I am dissolving Parliament! The Queen will rule directly, until time permits to allow for an election – until democracy is effectively established again!"

Democracy...Freedom, choice: they had gone! Fear had ruled – corruption had acted.

Joshua was dead.

"Dead."

Rachel jerked up. Dead. She stared out ahead of herself into the darkness, clutching a hold of the soft duvet covering her legs. The image of Joshua's body was still before her eyes – five bullet wounds, four to his lungs, one to his heart, bleeding…unstoppable.

He was smiling! Pain seized her chest as she looked into his brown, lit eyes, while his body struggled.

"It's finished!"

"Don't go!"

"It's sorted."

"No…"

His hand fell away from hers. Peace was in his eyes! Peace, and then death.

"No."

He was gone.

Rachel drew herself out of bed, sinking against the wall, pulling the duvet instinctively around her. In the bed John stirred, now uncovered.

"Rachel?" he whispered, while his hand stretched out to grasp the duvet back again.

"Can't," she whispered.

"Can't what?"

"Can't accept it."

She reached out to the handle of the wardrobe, and grasped her stethoscope. Tears filled her eyes. "Can't save him," she whispered. "Every time I see him in my dreams, I can't save him."

Now John was standing in front of her, his new blue pyjamas a little dishevelled in his haste.

"It's okay," he said, stifling a yawn. "He's okay."

"I know you believe…"

"I saw him."

"I know you believe what you saw."

"I know the wounds I touched, Rachel," he said, his green eyes gentle and patient as he repeated the same words once again. "I know the bullets I see and feel."

And now, again, he pulled the bullets out, always kept in a pocket close to his own body – five bullets, deformed and used…five bullets she could not explain.

"It's dangerous," she whispered. "Dangerous to claim such an impossibility."

"I know," he murmured. "I also watched him killed; I know the risk. But I can't hide the truth, Rachel – such a massive truth! I mustn't hide it."

"I can't grasp it," she said. "His wounds were fatal. I watched him die."

"I saw him alive again."

"I just can't bring myself to believe it…"

"I know."

"I'm sorry." Now tears filled her eyes again. Weeping suddenly took her, and she shook her head and turned away from him, clutching onto her stethoscope.

"I need to go to work soon."

"I know."

"After we go down to the waterfront."

"Okay."

And she held the duvet around herself and moved away from him, out of the bedroom and down the hall toward the bathroom.

Chapter 1

TE HARINUI

Tristan Blake stood on sand. In front of him, Rau Petera was balancing on one foot on a rock. Typical, Tristan thought, for a preacher on Sunday morning. Not bad for an old man, though!

Tristan grinned, and then looked over the faces gathered around his friend – Maori, Pakeha, Pacific, Chinese, Indian, and an African face amongst the crowd of two hundred.

"We're gathered today," began Rau, "because great things have taken place for all people, right here, in our own land! Right here, in the heart of Aotearoa."

Tristan lifted his eyes across Wellington harbour, behind Rau's back. Light was sparkling off the calm water. Rau almost looked alight himself, his gentle face a brown silhouette surrounded by a shimmering halo. Tristan rolled his eyes.

"Arohanui!" said Rau. "Te harinui. I have come to bring you great news of great joy, for all people. This day I say to you, death has been overcome! Darkness has been defeated. Light has broken forth, like the glorious blood red sunrise of a brand new day. Time for a new beginning! It's time for a new life."

9

A new life.

The eyes were all watching Rau, brown, blue, green, hazel, some lit up, as his, and some puzzled. There were four army soldiers watching behind them, standing just within the retaining wall to the beach. They were clad in olive green uniform, their arms folded across their chests, their rifles hanging unused at their sides; their foreheads creviced in concentrating frowns.

Tristan resisted the temptation to reach a hand into his own inner jacket pocket. The weight of the weapon remained by his left side – the army rifle he had used to shoot Joshua Davidson.

"Joshua is alive," called Rau. "I have seen him! I have touched him."

The soldiers shifted uncomfortably on their feet. One unfolded his arms to finger his rifle.

"One thing's for certain," muttered Tristan under his breath to Rau, "you sure have guts, my friend."

"I left him," said Rau, and his voice cracked, his brown eyes moistening. "I knew he was going to be shot, and I left him."

"You knew?" Tristan stared at him, and now Rau's eyes found his. "Did you know who was going to fire?"

"We all shot him," said Rau. "We all cried out for his death! We all abandoned him."

Tristan felt his body stiffening, his hands clenching.

"But his strength was greater than our weakness!" said Rau. "His life was greater than our desire for his death."

Tears blurred Tristan's vision. He closed his eyes, and then felt a hand to his shoulder.

"He planned it this way," said John's voice. "He chose to die."

"But why?" choked Tristan, his eyes flicking open to watch John join Rau, perched on the rock. "Why would he do this? Why would he let himself get shot? Why would he let me pull the trigger?"

Tristan suddenly felt the tsunami again, deep within, rising up! Threatening to break! Threatening to take him. John's green eyes came to him, even as he spoke to the crowd, his gentle face unassuming.

"He chose death so he could overcome it for us," said John. "Forgiveness! He offers us forgiveness. He offers us a kind of life which is stronger than death."

"Forgiveness?" choked Tristan.

"He takes our bullets," said John. "He takes them into his own body, into the grave, and overcomes the death of our crimes, so that we can live."

"Why?" breathed Tristan. "Why?"

"Arohanui," replied Rau. "The greatest of Love."

"Grace," murmured John, his voice soft, only loud enough for Tristan to hear. "The grace to accept, and forgive, and change the killer within us all."

"Grace," whispered Tristan.

"With grace," said John, "there is no need for a gun."

Tristan stared at his knowing eyes, stiffening again, but then he heard a harsh expiring breath. He turned to find Rachel standing next to him, arms folded stiffly across her chest, face drawn and wet.

"Grace?" she said, her beautiful face almost gagging on the word. "I watched it all – I was there too! I felt the bullets land in his chest! He's dead, Tristan Blake – he's dead, and you shot him!"

Her voice lifted loud and strong across the crowd. Horrified, Tristan stared at her as her words continued to pour out.

"Where's the justice?" she cried. "A murderer goes free? An innocent man is killed, and we all go about our business as if nothing has changed?"

A soldier was moving toward them. Instinctively Tristan reached toward his left inner pocket, but made himself stop.

"You speak of love?" said Rachel, her eyes moving to Rau. "What about love for Joshua? I loved him!" Now her body stiffened, and Tristan longed to comfort her but could find no words. "Does no one else here give a shit about him?"

Silence filled the crowd. The soldier approached Tristan.

"Is this woman bothering you?" he asked. "Any unrest must be contained."

"No," said Tristan, quickly shaking his head. "It's under control."

"No violence will be tolerated."

"She's only speaking the truth." Pain filled his body.

"If she incites a riot…"

"Please," said Tristan, "let her be. I vouch for her."

The soldier held his gaze, and then his shoulders relaxed.

"All right, Blake," he said. "Once army, always army." And he moved away.

Troubled, Tristan looked after him, then he turned back to find John standing before Rachel.

Husband and wife. It still hurt Tristan. Yet there was so much more to this moment than simply their young marriage. John reached out to take Rachel's hand, but she threw his down.

"I can't," she whispered, and John's kind face contorted.

"He's alive," he said. "That is the justice, Rachel, can't you see? Death is a pathway into greater life, if we can only accept it! If we can only trust beyond the pain."

"He was the greatest man I ever knew," replied Rachel, her face drawn, "don't you understand that, John? He put me to shame! He still puts me to shame, because he loved him!" Her hand flicked out in Tristan's direction, and Tristan swallowed. "He loved him, even knowing that he would shoot him! He loved him, even while he was being shot by him! When I…all I can do is hate…"

And now she choked, and grasped the stethoscope hanging around her neck.

"My ways are sticks and stones next to him," she cried. "I stumble on, trying to do good, when he was the Master of all things good, and now he's gone! He's gone! And all I can do is mourn for my own incompetence."

Tristan stared at her, and reached impulsively out to her pain, but now she was clinging to the stethoscope.

"I have to go!" she cried. "I have to work."

And she turned on her heel and ran away.

Tristan stared after her. Love! He still loved her! Fiery, passionate, her words like arrows penetrating to the heart of him with brutal precision; true precision. A surgeon! She was a surgeon, not a physician! Applying her steel with scalpel sharp accuracy most acutely on herself.

In Joshua she had found the one she had never known she had yearned for, and he, Tristan, had brutally robbed her of him. Words? Words as weapons? How could he deny her at least this? He had been army, when she had been physician. He had won – Joshua had died, despite all of her training. Rachel had lost the battle.

"I'm sorry," said John, and Tristan shook his head, looking at him.

"No," he said. "No."

"It broke her," said John, and Tristan closed his eyes. Two hearts shot...

"How can I ever fix what I have done?" he whispered.

"We killed him," called Rau to the crowd, over his head. "But does that mean everything is over? No! There are still choices to be made, still paths to take. We can turn back into the right way. Some burdens are too great to carry alone; some crimes tarnish us from within. Joshua has taken our bullets into himself – he has taken our crimes into the grave. Come, take a hold of innocence again! Trust in what he has done! The living example of a Greater Love: of the Greater One, beyond us, the One who made us – the One who wants us back."

Now Tristan watched Rau turning toward the harbour.

"The Spirit of te Atua is like the ocean," he murmured. "Pure, life giving, washing us clean."

Suddenly Rau was off the rock.

"Who wants to be made right again?" he asked. "I'll go first! I failed him! I abandoned him!" Tears filled his brown eyes again. "Aue te whakama! Shame! But with Joshua my mana is restored. With Joshua my honour is restored. Anyone who wants to be made right, follow me!"

And now he was wading into the water.

"Hey!" cried Tristan, before he could stop himself. A winter swim?

Was Rau serious? "You'll catch pneumonia, old man!"

But the Maori priest didn't notice. His body was shaking as he waded further in, until little waves lapped at the belt of his black pants. He lifted his arms and his face to the sky.

"E te Atua!" he cried out. "E te Ariki! I failed! I failed! Wash my shame away! Let me start again!"

And he lowered his body under the water, until his black curls had totally disappeared.

Tristan stared after him. He glanced at the crowd, at the silent army, at John's smiling face, and then back at the bubbles appearing in the spot where Rau's head had submerged.

"Oh, come on," muttered Tristan. "Don't make me go in there after you..."

But now John was laughing.

"Come!" he said, tugging on Tristan's sleeve.

"No," said Tristan, shaking his hand off. "I think I'll stay here."

"A bit of cold water scaring you off?" chided John, smirking. "I thought you were army!"

"It's not the cold I'm worried about!" chided Tristan back, but now John shrugged.

"Guilt cleared by an honest heart and a dip in water," said John. "Who could make it easier than that?"

"Who indeed," murmured Tristan, and John waded into the water after Rau.

"Come!" he cried out to the crowd. "Now's your chance!"

Suddenly a flood of people entered into the ocean.

"No way," whispered Tristan, and his eyes blurred, and he blinked the tears away. They were all dipping under! And yet, he could not! The gun! The gun in his pocket...

Rau's head popped up again over the water's surface, his face breaking into a radiant smile. His voice lifted: what was he saying? It wasn't English, or Maori...Tristan could recognise a few words of French from school.

The Price of Redemption

"Que Dieu vous benisse." *May God bless you.*

God...

With pain, Tristan closed his eyes again. God. He thought of his father, the Anglican Bishop, stood down for inciting murder...consumed by his grief at the loss of Tristan's mother, on the verge of suicide, now reinstated at Saint Peter's.

"Dad," he whispered. Then there was a movement before him.

"That was great," said Rau, and Tristan lifted his head to his dripping form.

"You're making a puddle," said Tristan, smiling.

"All of these just might make a wave," replied Rau, gesturing to the crowd emerging from the ocean. But Tristan noticed Rau's body stiffening and shaking in the light sea breeze.

"Here," said Tristan quickly, taking off his jacket and laying it around his friend's shoulders. "You're all crazy."

"Kia ora," said Rau, reaching his clenching hands into Tristan's pockets, his gaze shifting over the crowd with concern. But then Rau reached inside the jacket.

"What's this?" he said, and partially drew the gun out of the pocket.

"Oh, shit!" Tristan started, and now Rau's brown eyes were on him.

"You've still got this?" said Rau, and Tristan swallowed, trying to avoid his gaze.

"Well, yeah," he muttered.

"I thought the police..."

"It was an army job – not their jurisdiction."

"What?" Rau asked.

"An army job," repeated Tristan. "No one wanted to know, after the mess. No one followed up on the weapon."

Rau's eyes widened, and he quickly replaced the rifle into the jacket pocket and returned the jacket to Tristan.

"You should get rid of this," he said. "You have no need for a gun."

"Self-defence," said Tristan. "Who knows how mad it's going to get now we have a military state."

"Weapons are illegal," said Rau. "Why carry it, unless you are willing to use it?"

"I'm ex-army," said Tristan. "They'll look the other way."

"Tristan…"

"I only have it for defence."

"It's dangerous."

"So is our state."

Rau's eyes were fixed on him, even as his body began to shiver. "Did you not hear a word of what I just said to all of these people?"

Tristan smiled sadly at him. "I heard every word," he said. "I assure you of that."

"Joshua forgives you, Tristan," said Rau, and Tristan stared at him and then looked rapidly away, blinking away more tears.

"Told you, did he?" he asked.

"Something like that," answered Rau.

"That's nice," said Tristan, and Rau laid a hand on his arm. Tristan hesitated, squeezing his eyes shut, shaking his head, and then he made himself look back at his friend.

"Te whakama," murmured Rau. "I left him. I did worse than you."

"Bullshit," whispered Tristan, choking. "You don't know, Rau. You weren't there."

"I did know," said Rau. "That's why I ran away."

"You have no idea how it felt: how it still feels, to…to remember shooting him."

"He loves you."

"I know."

"He knew."

"I know he knew."

Tristan frowned, searching Rau's middle aged wrinkles for wisdom. "It's a strange thing," he whispered, "to be forgiven even in the midst of committing the crime."

"The idea is to change," said Rau gently, and Tristan swallowed again.

"I am changed," he said. "I'll never join the army again. My reasons were wrong."

"I know that," said Rau, "and yet the gun…"

"It's a lingering thing," said Tristan. "So much has changed, but everything, Rau? Can you really expect everything to change?"

Rau's face shifted into a gentle smile. "I can," he said boldly. "I have seen him alive again after death. For me, everything has changed."

"And yet not everything has changed for me, my friend," said Tristan. "A lot! But not all. I didn't see him again."

"What if he was here?" asked Rau. "What then?"

"Well then I'd tell him myself," said Tristan. "I'd ask him what the hell he was doing getting himself shot by me…"

Tristan remembered Joshua's face, then, in that moment – his brown eyes, his contorted face, clutching the crown to his own head, on his knees before him.

"I love him too," whispered Tristan. And then, with that sudden painful moment of truth, he drew his jacket around himself, reached to grasp securely onto the gun, and turned away from Rau.

"Tristan," Rau's voice followed after him. "The only difference between you and me is faith."

"I know," Tristan said back. "But that difference represents an entire different universe."

"Welcome to my world," said Rau, and Tristan glanced back to his beaming face.

"Thank you," he said, "but don't expect me to jump ship quite that easily, I quite like my universe. Rachel makes a lot of sense to me – I love her too."

He tipped his head to Rau, and then moved away from the sand.

Chapter 2

THE HOSPITAL

Hardwater Hospital. Rachel grasped the stethoscope around her neck and strode onto Ward Eight. She'd better quickly get onto the blood results, she thought, before catching up with her consultant, James Lester.

She slipped past the elderly ward clerk at reception to the crimson work desk behind, but James was already there, sitting in front of the computer, quickly tapping on the mouse. Rachel glanced quickly at her watch and back at his studious form. Eleven-thirty. No doubt he had pre-empted her at least by three hours.

It was Sunday. Didn't he have anything else to do? Rachel had told their House Officer Fatima to stay home.

"Doctor Connor," said James, still fixing his gaze on the results on the computer as she sat alongside him. "Nice to see you could make it."

Rachel grimaced and shifted slightly.

"Sorry," she muttered, and now he grimaced into the screen.

"I'm not interested in 'sorry,'" he said, "only in seeing the job done."

Rachel took in his slim form, in grey pants and a white shirt. He was conservative, and yet a little untidy. Rachel reached to grab the notebook from her white coat.

"What have we got?" she asked, and James shifted the mouse again to a graphic of the ward.

"Your programme?" asked Rachel, surprised, and he nodded.

"Of course," he said. "I did it while I was waiting for you. Now it's the intellectual property of the hospital."

"Aren't we all," muttered Rachel, and James threw her a wry smile as he rose to his feet.

"Come on," he said. "Let's do the ward round."

And she followed him into the first room.

"Doctor Lester," called out the first patient to James. She was a young slightly overweight woman with blonde curls. "My husband had to leave! You said you'd be in some time after nine o'clock."

"And so I am," said James, walking up to the bed. The woman frowned intensely as he reached for her pulse.

"Neurosis," muttered James under his breath, and Rachel flushed.

"My fault," she said quickly to the woman. "I was keeping Doctor Lester waiting."

"Rubbish," said James. "There's never any time for idle banter."

Now he reached into his deep right trouser pocket, and pulled out his stethoscope. Rachel suddenly noticed it was the new model, cardiology grade.

"What am I going to hear?" he asked. "When I listen to her chest?"

Rachel stared at the back of his slightly balding head. Three more years! She would have to train three more years to still attempt specialising as a Physician.

"You haven't told me anything," she stuttered, and knew he was smiling.

"Examine the patient, doctor," he replied. "What do you see?"

Rachel cast her eyes over the woman's face. What was her name? Sarah. She was in her twenties, European, and had a slight flush to her cheeks, mirroring Rachel's own.

"I don't see anything," she said.

"Look more closely," said James.

Rachel moved alongside him, next to the woman.

"May I?" she asked, and Sarah shrugged.

"Why not?" she said. "Got nothing better to do with my time."

Rachel searched her grimace: frustration!

"Sorry," she muttered. "We'll get hold of your husband…"

"Stop apologising," said James, "and just do your job."

Rachel reached out to Sarah's hands. Her palms seemed normal, her colour normal, her nails…Rachel looked more closely. She had fine red lines, at the tip of the nails.

"Splinter haemorrhages," she muttered aloud.

"The heart, doctor," said James. "Listen to her heart."

Rachel quickly reached for her own stethoscope, placing it in her ears and then putting the diaphragm on Sarah's chest. She could hear two normal heart sounds. She moved around Sarah's chest with the stethoscope, but heard no change.

She straightened, and pulled the stethoscope away from her ears.

"Nothing," she said.

"Oh," he replied, "those things are useless – use this."

And he reached to place his own stethoscope into her ears.

Rachel fingered the drum, and then placed the diaphragm on Sarah's chest. Clarity! She could hear the quality of the heart sounds – terms she knew in theory were suddenly becoming real!

"Oh," she whispered, and she searched for the other positions on Sarah's chest, and then, faintly, could hear a soft whooshing noise.

"I think…" she began.

"Don't think, just know," said his muffled voice.

"…I can hear a mid-diastolic murmur. I've never heard one…"

"Which means?"

"Mitral stenosis," she said, pulling his stethoscope from her ears.

"Of course," he said, his voice now clear. "But what else does it mean?"

"Bacterial endocarditis."

"And?"

"Rheumatic Heart Disease?"

"Or congenital. And?"

"Ah…IV antibiotics."

"Yes, yes," he said, "That's not what I'm getting at."

"Then what?"

"The stethoscope, doctor!" he said. "Yours is useless! Stop stuffing around: get one of these!"

And he reached to grasp his equipment back again, but Rachel lingered for a moment, holding his brown eyes.

"Beautiful," she said, and he shook his head.

"Not interested," he quickly replied.

"Not you," said Rachel, hurriedly quenching a smile, "the murmur! To actually hear it!"

Now his face lit up in a rare genuine smile. "Thank Christ you could hear it," he said, and Rachel shifted uncomfortably on her feet, made a few notes on the tablet, and followed him on to the next patient.

"This one," said James, flicking his finger in the direction of a young Maori man on the other side of the room. "He's got an interesting sign, can you spot it?"

"You know I'm not a med-student," said Rachel, and James smiled.

"Moving on from the Dark Ages now, are we?" he said. "Would have thought a medical registrar would be able to hear mitral stenosis."

"The tools, doctor!" said Rachel, smiling in return. "You said it yourself, it's the tools!"

"Then stop bloody well playing around," said James. "You have a keen mind, Rachel – don't let it atrophy for the sake of sticks and stones."

Rachel glanced down again at the stethoscope in his trouser pocket, and then back up at his face. His eyes were alert, focussed, but there was something about his manner… A slight tension in his shoulders, his movement around the bed a little stiff…he seemed on edge.

"Okay," she said quietly. "I'll look for the signs."

And she turned back to the Maori man, reaching out a hand.

"Kia ora, Tamati," she said, and his young brown face broke into a smile.

"Kia ora, Dr Connor."

"Rachel's fine," she said, reaching for his pulse. "How are you feeling today?"

"Much better, thanks." An IV line was running fluid into a vein on his left hand.

His pulse was eighty-four, with normal volume, and regular. She looked to his face: his colour was normal, and his hydration looked okay.

But his eyes…there was a subtle sign! The left eye was pointing in very slightly. She reached out a finger in front of his gaze. "Follow my finger, and tell me how many you see." Now she moved her finger in different directions, to his right, up, down, central, to his left…

The left eye couldn't move to the left. "Two fingers," he said.

"He has a sixth nerve palsy," said Rachel.

"How did he present?" asked James, and Rachel frowned, looking at the happy young smile.

"With a headache," she said. Shit – an aneurysm, ready to burst.

"Very good, doctor," said James. "A lot of people would have missed the sign without the history. The headache started this morning – he came in with asthma last night."

"MRI?"

"We did CT angiography this morning."

"A bleed?"

"Small so far," said James. "He's booked in for urgent neurosurgery, the reg is on her way. But if I'd waited for you for the initial assessment, who knows what might have happened later?"

Rachel stared at him. A massive bleed, with her delay, into his brain? Death? Another death she had failed to avert?

"Oh, shit," she whispered. And now, suddenly, Joshua was in front of her – his body being thrown back, bullets to his chest, bleeding. Now she was on her knees at his side, pressing her jacket desperately into his wounds to stop the bleeding.

She ran. Away from the room, away from the patient, she fled down the corridor into an unused single room, and hurriedly shut the door.

Joshua was grasping her hand! His face, smeared with blood, was breaking into a smile.

"It's finished!" he said. "It's sorted!"

"No!" cried Rachel. "Don't go!"

His hand was falling away from hers – dead! He was dead.

Resuscitate? She hovered over his penetrated chest with her hands crossing over each other in readiness. Resuscitate?

"Don't resuscitate," said John. "Don't try to bring him back."

"Resuscitate," begged Rachel. "Oh, please, let me resuscitate him."

And she sank down against the wall, wrapped her arms around her head, and cried.

In the distance she heard the sound of the door opening and closing again.

"What the hell was that?" said James's voice over her. "What just happened?"

"Post-traumatic stress," confessed Rachel into her arms. "A flashback! I've got PTSD."

James laughed. "You've got PTSD?" he said. "I'm the one who's been in the army!"

Rachel lifted her head in surprise to look at him. "You've been in the army too?"

"Sure," said James, shrugging, crouching himself down next to her. "A few years, in the Middle East."

"Peacekeeping?" asked Rachel. "Like Tristan Blake?"

Now she was seeing Tristan, standing there with his rifle, staring at Joshua on his knees before him. Tristan looked white.

"You know Tristan Blake?" said James, and Rachel swallowed.

"I wish I hadn't known him," she said. "It would have been easier."

"What would have been easier?"

"Watching…" Now she wrapped her arms around her head again,

hiding her face in her knees, and began to rock. "Watching him shoot Joshua Davidson."

She closed her eyes tightly, but the memory was still vivid in front of her eyes.

"I remember," said James's voice. "You tried to save him."

"Not a chance in hell," whispered Rachel. "Two bullets to each lung, one to the heart. Tristan was a very efficient killer."

"It was necessary," said James. "I'm sorry, but it was necessary."

Rachel felt her body stiffening. "You were there?" she asked.

"I'm ex-army, Rachel," said James. "I knew the uprising was coming."

"The uprising?" said Rachel, lifting her head in sudden anger. "It was a peaceful demonstration, for crying out loud."

"It shifted quickly enough. A hundred thousand people, approaching Parliament? What did you think the PM would have to do?"

"My father…" Now she rose to her feet, seeing her father standing outside of the Beehive – seeing him calling Tristan forward. "Oh God, it was my father."

Now James went silent. Then his voice was curt.

"It was necessary, Doctor Connor," he said. "For the survival of the nation."

"Bullshit," said Rachel, staring at him. "Joshua was never a threat to the nation. Dad knew he made a mistake."

"No," said James. "He did what any responsible national leader would have to do, in times of war."

"In times of war?" said Rachel. "What war, James? Who are you fighting?"

James's face flushed suddenly, and then his body stiffened.

"Take the day off," he said. "You're not feeling well. I'll finish the ward round."

Rachel shook her head. "I'll be all right," she said. "I'll tell you if I can't do the job, I promise you that."

"You look like you need some clonazepam," he said.

"No," said Rachel. Sedation? No. "If I start something like that, I'm seriously afraid I might never stop."

Again James was silent, looking at her. Then he turned on his foot, opened the door, and walked out.

Rachel quietly followed him, down the corridor and into the next room.

There an elderly woman was lying in bed, her eyes closed, her grey curls spread out on the pillow. Her wrinkled gentle face was slightly contorted.

"She's in pain," said Rachel.

A nurse hovered on the other side of the bed, reaching to check the leur in the back of her hand.

"I think it's blocked, Margaret," said the nurse. "I'll need to pop another one in, and then we can give you your morphine."

"That's all right, Kate," said Margaret, still with her eyes closed. "'The Lord is my rock and my salvation; the Lord is my fortress, I will never be shaken.'[1]"

"Sounds like she's already got morphine on board," muttered James under his breath, and Rachel threw him a foul look.

"Easy," she muttered. "My upbringing is Anglican."

"I like that Bishop of yours."

Bishop Mark Blake! Rachel stared at him. He was talking about Tristan's father, calling out for Joshua's death!

Rachel closed her eyes tightly, fleetingly. "Oh, please shut up," she whispered.

"Oh, I wouldn't worry about the Anglican Church," said James. "The Catholic Church is really the house of nutters."

And now he moved forward alongside Margaret, and took her pulse.

Rachel stared at the image before her: the middle aged medical consultant, atheist, scathing; the elderly patient, in pain, awaiting morphine, resting in Christian faith. She, herself, somehow in the middle – neither here nor there.

The atheist was taking the pulse of the Christian. The image felt surreal, caught for a moment in time. Rachel shook her head, and approached the bed.

"Metastasized breast cancer," said James. "She came in last night with a pleural effusion. I tapped it…" He gestured to the bottle and drain sitting on the ground on the left side of the bed, the tube still drawing fluid from her chest.

"Very good," muttered Rachel.

"…and her O2 sats are 95 per cent on air today."

"Hospice?" asked Rachel.

"Not yet," said James. "We should stabilize her first."

"They can…"

"Let's get on top of her pleural effusion," said James, "and then we'll transfer her."

"Okay," said Rachel. "And the pain? Seems more than the chest."

"Bony mets," said James, pointing to her left thigh. "Oncology's onto it."

"Okay," said Rachel. "We'll get onto the morphine then."

And she nodded to Kate.

Kate smiled, nodded back, and left the room, soon returning with a new leur and a liquid filled syringe.

"Morphine pump?" suggested Rachel, and James shook his head.

"Not yet," he said. "Let's monitor her requirements."

"Okay," said Rachel, and she reached over to Margaret's drug chart. Morphine had already been prescribed: five milligrams three times a day. One dose had been given the previous night.

"We are a bit late," said Rachel, and James nodded and turned to Kate.

"When you're ready," he said, and Kate nodded. Margaret's eyes opened, and Kate glanced at her then injected the morphine. The effect was almost instantaneous. Peace moved over her face like a wave. She closed her eyes again and promptly fell asleep.

Rachel stared at her. Tears pricked her own eyes, and she took a slight breath of relief.

"Peace," she whispered.

"Remember who the patient is, doctor," said James alongside her.

Rachel saw again Joshua before her eyes, dead, his face at peace.

Her dead patient – the Physician who had healed.

You were the Master of everything good, she thought to herself. *Am I a fool to wish I was just like you?*

She closed her eyes, and heard James shift impatiently next to her.

"Patients call," he said, and Rachel nodded, opening her eyes.

"All right," she said, as she followed him out of the room.

Chapter 3

THE CATHEDRAL

John Robertson stood in Saint Peter's Cathedral. The wooden altar stood in front of him, covered with white linen, with a silver chalice of wine and a silver plate with bread sitting on top. Behind the altar was the tiled image of Jesus, hanging on the cross. John noticed the crown of thorns pressed into Jesus's head, the drops of blood dripping down his face.

He remembered Joshua on that same gruesome day – on his knees, his blood-stained face contorting in agony while he clutched the ancient metal crown to his head…

"Master," he whispered. "You are the Master of everything good." Death! The death was necessary, to forge new life.

He reached out his hand to touch the smooth polished wood of the altar under the linen. He lifted his fingers to the silver cup, with the wine, sitting on top.

This is my blood, given for you – do this to remember me.[2]

Communion – it was a joining! A joining of one's depths to God; to the source of life, the origin of life.

"Forgive me," whispered John, always aware of his own flaws in joining with goodness – and he took up the cup in his hand, and drank.

The alcohol was warm on his tongue, and then warm in his chest. He sank naturally to his knees in reciprocal offering, pressing his head to the altar and closing his eyes.

Take my heart.

Joshua was in his mind's eye – his pain! The crown. The darkness of all, drawn to him as the scapegoat. The bullets, to his chest! The death, his willing death – his willing offering, to carry the shame, the corruption, of them all.

Rachel was on her knees next to him, longing to resuscitate him, but, no! John had felt it was right not to drag him back! He had found his peace! Peace in the willing death; relief from the agony of willingly bearing the crimes of all.

Peace...John drew his fingers again along the altar, still with closed eyes. The pain! John had felt the bullets, as to his own chest – had felt his choking. He had felt his death, as the sun going down on John's brand new life, his awakening joy quenched by horror. And yet there had been purpose – Joshua had always acted with purpose. Purpose had rooted John to that spot by his side, in the shared agony – purpose had girded him in the death.

Tristan. Pain seized John's chest as he dared to look at him, repeating his memory. There was a different kind of tearing agony in that white face, as he lifted the gun. John dared to watch Tristan again shoot his beloved best friend, and was astonished to find himself loving him. Tristan, John suddenly grasped: it was for him that Joshua had willingly died!

"There is no greater love than that a man die for his friends.³"

There was such a great cost, to love one capable of killing! Such a cost, to let him retain the gun! Such a cost, to appeal to his heart – to seek to have him make the right decision. What if he should not? Could not? What if he should fire?

Five bullets. John now reached into his pocket, and pulled them out. There were five deformed bullets. Head pressed still against the altar, he gazed down at them in his palm and again fleetingly closed his eyes.

Joshua was before him. Joshua! His coffin, behind his back, was open, the lid sitting neatly on top, no longer needed. His brown eyes were lit, his face breaking into his familiar smile, his warm hand reaching to pull John's fingers through the gap between the buttons of his white shirt, to the healed bullet holes beneath...

He was alive.

John remembered: shock had filled his body! He had collapsed. Joshua had caught him, and lowered him to his knees. Now Joshua was pulling out the deformed bullets from his trouser pocket – now he was laying them in John's palm.

"I'm alive," he said. "Pass it on! Death is overcome! The darkness is defeated."

John wept with the memory, seeing the white face of Tristan again.

"Good news!" he whispered to him. "Don't you see it, my friend? He has won! Joshua has won, and now all of us can win too."

But, remember, a voice said in his heart, *winning comes at a price.*

Fear whispered to him. He pressed more firmly into the altar, with his eyes closed.

"Have your way," he whispered into the wood. "Have your way."

And he rose to his feet, turned, and saw Mark Blake standing before him.

The Bishop's middle-aged face was quiet, his blue eyes, complex and deep, searching him.

"John," he murmured gently. "It's good to see you again."

"How was the service?" asked John. "Sorry I missed it."

"Good," said Mark. "Eun Ae does an admirable job."

"We did ours down at the waterfront," said John, smiling.

"With Rau," replied Mark.

"Yes."

"How was it?"

"Interesting." John grinned. "Two hundred people waded into winter cold water in the harbour."

Mark smiled. "Fascinating," he said. "Baptism. What will come next, I wonder, actual tongues of fire?"

John stared at him in confusion, and then glanced down to Mark's purple tunic and the rimu cross sitting on his chest.

"You've been reinstated," said John, and Mark's face clouded.

"I'm still not sure what to think about that," he said. "Personally, I would have chosen Eun Ae, not myself."

"Why?" asked John, looking back to his gaze. Mark might have actually refused the position?

Mark's eyes misted. "Of course, you know why," he said. "But since you think I need to say it out loud..." He hesitated, and pressed himself to continue. "I don't believe a man who incites others to kill should remain in the office of Bishop."

"It doesn't matter that the man was you," said John, searching him. "This is your standard."

"Absolutely," said Mark. "It doesn't matter that it was me: I would feel the same about anyone else also, and I also feel it about myself. I should not have been reinstated."

"And yet you were," said John.

Mark frowned, and looked up at the cross. "Don't misunderstand me," he murmured. "I grasp grace! I have received his forgiveness, truly I have." Now Mark's eyes moistened further, and John was drawn to his honesty. "He saved my life," he said. "He saved my soul. 'This is my body, given for you. This is my blood, shed for you.' I believe, John; I trust. But that doesn't make me fit to be Bishop."

"You are no longer a murderer," said John, and Mark closed his eyes tightly.

"No," he whispered. "No longer a murderer."

"I don't understand," said John quietly. "Haven't you just embodied the entire essence of the message the Anglican Church seeks to bring?"

"I have."

"You are changed."

"Yes."

"Then why not reinstatement?"

Mark's eyes opened, and John saw a new purpose infused in his gaze.

"Because," he began, "my position as Bishop has nothing to do with my own restoration: it is about the leadership of the Anglican Church in Wellington."

"Would you not lead them well?"

"Yes, but…"

"What more is there?"

"John, you're deliberately not understanding me!"

John smiled at the exasperation in his face. "I understand you," he said simply.

"Some boundaries must not be crossed."

"Yes, I get that."

"How can anyone possibly trust a man who has incited others to murder? How can anyone draw spiritual leadership from such a person? Perhaps some can, but others cannot, John, and fair enough."

"They would need to know the man," murmured John thoughtfully, "before trusting in one with such a journey."

"What would they need to know from the man, but what he had already done?" asked Mark.

"That the experience changed him," said John. "That it made him good in a way that transcended the bad."

"Redemption," said Mark. "But what are the signs of redemption, John? A life lived for self? A career forged on status? I have no desire for these things."

"Then you are redeemed, Mark," said John. "The Anglican Church has chosen well."

"It's not about me," said Mark. "It's about the Diocese. It's about serving the needs of Wellington."

"Yes," said John. "And maybe you, with all your flaws and background, are the most capable man to do that."

Mark silently watched him. "But how can that be?" he asked.

"Maybe it takes a saved wretch to know how to save the most wretched of people."

Mark stared at him, and now tears welled up freely in his eyes. "Yes," he whispered. "Yes, you are right."

John noticed Selena appear, her slim form slightly hidden behind Mark's back. Mark shifted slightly and reached out to take her hand, behind himself.

"I should go," he said, and John nodded.

"Congratulations, Bishop Blake," he said, and Mark smiled sadly.

"Thank you, John," he said, and he turned to his daughter, and led her down the aisle and out of the church.

Chapter 4

COURAGE

Tristan stood on the crest of the hill. At his feet, stretched out below, was the vast expansive view: Petone directly before him, Lower Hutt to his left, and the glistening light off the slightly choppy water of Wellington Harbour to his right. The motorway was still mostly abandoned, set in close against the hills beneath him. Tristan could see a military compulsory stop set up before the Petone onramp, checking those travelling toward the Beehive. He had managed to avoid the officers, catching the train out of the city centre and then walking up the hill.

Now he stood at the foot of his father's house.

The house towered above him: two floors of white, and wide, thick, full length windows exposing the lounge to the view. He swallowed. The last time he had seen this place had been nine years earlier, when he had walked out, when…when his father had…

Tristan closed his eyes tightly. It was ancient history now. His father was tall, but now middle-aged; Tristan was shorter but more solidly built, and twenty-six. Army training – he was more than a match now for any physical tussle. He reached his hand into his left inner pocket – the gun was still there. Self-defence…and yet…

He pulled out the rifle to look at it. He turned it over to look at the other side, and frowned. Why was he still holding onto it? Then, suddenly, he heard the sound of tyres, and hurriedly put the gun back into his inner pocket.

Now his father's hybrid Mercedes pulled up the drive, parking in front of the house.

Tristan felt his heart race. Why was he still afraid, now, after all these years? It was stupid, really! Stupid! And yet, what about his mother's death?

The driver door opened, and Mark Blake stepped out of the car. His father was turning to him – reaching out a hand. Tristan stared at it, confused, suddenly frozen: stupid! It wasn't as if they hadn't already spoken – hadn't already made up. But then, suddenly, his father pulled him forward; suddenly he was in his father's arms, against his chest.

Mark's arms were tight around him. Tristan closed his eyes, and let himself sink against him. Surely his father would feel the gun? Surely he would know? Yet Mark's voice whispered into his ear.

"I've been waiting for you to turn up for three months," he said.

"Sorry," whispered Tristan back. "I couldn't make it to your thing."

"It's all right," said Mark, "it was just a formality."

And Tristan found himself trembling in his arms.

Mark stepped back, and Tristan straightened and faced him. "So," he began, "back to being a Bishop again then?"

"Yes," said Mark, looking perplexed.

"I guess…" Tristan searched his face. "That's what you wanted?"

Mark frowned, and turned to cast his eyes across the valley. "I don't know," he murmured.

"You'll still be based at the Cathedral?"

"Yes."

"Next to the Beehive?"

Mark swallowed. "Yes."

"You'll have your finger on the pulse of all the happenings of our

'Constitutional Monarchy' then," said Tristan. "The Queen governing direct through the Governor General, the army presence…"

"Too many bad memories," muttered Mark. "Connor won't want a bar of me."

"James Connor?" said Tristan. "He's still there?"

"Back benches of the New Conservative Party," said Mark, "as they report to the Governor General."

"No democracy…"

"I destroyed his political career." Mark frowned again, now glancing to his right in the direction of the Beehive. "Only one of several lives I have destroyed."

"Dad," whispered Tristan, and now Mark's large hand came to his arm.

"Don't worry, my boy," he said, "there's still some use in your father yet. Or at least that's what the Archbishop tells me."

And he reached to open the back door of his car.

Selena stepped out the car, and Tristan shifted slightly on his feet. He hadn't seen her since…since the funeral of Joshua, when she had hidden constantly behind their father's back.

He glanced at her face, but her head was still bowed, her gaze lowered to her feet. Mark reached out a hand to her, and nodded to Tristan.

"Let's go inside," he said, and Tristan willingly followed his father and Selena up the steps of the little foothill and in through the front door.

Steps were before him, leading up to the upstairs hallway – then it was left to the bedrooms or right to the lounge. Tristan stood unmoving, watching his father's large form move upstairs, with Selena following.

His sister disappeared to the left, while his father looked down at him. "Tristan?"

Tristan stared at him, and swallowed. Fear was taking him: memories of his father's raised voice, of the call of their mother's death, of…of hitting…

Pain seized him: he saw, in that moment, his mother's body – a blood stained sheet over her face. His father was sitting alongside, the one who had driven her to her death.

"Tristan," said his father's voice, now soft; now gentle.

"Help," whispered Tristan instinctively. "I...I can't seem to do this."

Mark bounded down the stairs, his tear filled eyes before him, his hand reaching to grasp Tristan's arm.

"I'll help you," he said clearly. "I'll do what I failed to do the first time."

His father drew him up the steps, and now Tristan was standing in the lounge.

The view was before him: Petone, Lower Hutt and the harbour. A family photo was sitting on the coffee table – his mother! Tristan suppressed a gasp, looking at her. His mother? He had left with no photos, with no free memories. And yet there they were, down at Days Bay: mother, sister, and he himself, smiling! Joking, in front of the camera, before...before...

"Oh my God," whispered Tristan, and his hand shook, and he hurriedly returned the photo to the table before he dropped it.

Mark steadied his hand.

"She was beautiful," he said. "I am so sorry, Tristan."

"I know," whispered Tristan. "I know."

"I shouldn't have sped."

"It was an accident," said Tristan. "I know, Dad."

"I feel so useless, Tristan," said Mark. "But I know it doesn't help. I would beat myself up, but what's the use of that? Some kind of self-indulgence? As if that will help anyone! I...I want to start again."

Tristan nodded. "It's good," he whispered. "Good to start again. As Bishop I'm sure you'll..."

"I don't mean as Bishop," interrupted Mark. "I mean as a father."

Tristan trembled, holding his eyes. "As father?" he whispered.

"If you'll have me," said Mark. "If Selena will ever dare to let me in."

Tristan swallowed. He turned away to look out across the valley, across the choppy water reflecting light, and then turned back.

"Dad," he whispered. "There's something you need to know about me, if you still want to stick with me."

"What is it?" asked Mark.

Tristan hesitated, and then pulled out the rifle and laid it on the coffee table in front of his family photo. He glanced up at his father's face to see him staring down at the weapon.

"You still have it?"

"Yes," said Tristan.

"My God," breathed Mark, and he reached out to touch the surface, and jerked his fingers away. "Tell me, Tristan," he whispered, "why did you join the army?"

Tristan shifted slightly on his feet. "You know why," he said. "That's why you knew Connor would be able to use me."

Mark's eyes tightly closed. "Was I really that much of a bastard?" he asked.

"You were," said Tristan. "But I was the one who pulled the trigger."

Mark looked again at the weapon. "Why did you bring it here?" he asked, and Tristan smiled sadly.

"Not to kill you, if that's what you're worried about," he said.

Mark shrugged. "After all the hell we've been through, why would it surprise me?" he muttered. "But, no, that's not what I meant."

And now the blue searching eyes were upon him.

Tristan swallowed, and didn't speak. Tell him? Tell?

"The army," said Mark gently. "Was it my fault?"

Tristan suddenly felt tears again – he quickly blinked them away. "I was just a spindly thing at seventeen," he said. "Amazing what training can do."

"It was unacceptable, Tristan." Now Mark's voice shook, and Tristan instinctively looked at the naked pain in his eyes. "What I did: unacceptable."

Tristan felt his breath catch. "You were hurting," he whispered. "I was hurting too. I...I shouldn't have attacked you."

"What else could you do?" asked Mark. "I had just killed your mother."

The Price of Redemption

Now pain enveloped Tristan. He turned away, doubling over – he wrapped his arms over his head. He gasped, but now Mark's hands were reaching for him.

"I was your father, Tristan," he said. "Your only remaining parent. I brought death when I should have brought life – an assault in the place of love."

"You couldn't do it any other way," whispered Tristan. "You were lost."

"I was lost," said Mark. "But no longer."

Tristan straightened and turned to face him, and saw again the outstretched hand.

"I will help you," said Mark, "if you will accept me back again."

"I will accept you back again," replied Tristan instinctively, "if you will accept my gun."

Now Mark hesitated. Tristan watched him cast his eyes over the rifle again.

"I can't endorse it," muttered Mark. "It's illegal."

"I'm ex-army," said Tristan, and Mark hummed disapprovingly.

"The army is for true national defence," he said.

"Just my point," said Tristan. "Sometimes you have to shoot."

"I can't endorse it, Tristan," said Mark. "I succumbed to the worst of corruption in my own role, but I am still a priest."

Tristan looked at him, and back down at the gun. "What do you fear?" he asked.

"That you will be compelled to shoot," said Mark. "That you will go through the same hell all over again. You're not a true solider, Tristan."

"You'd be surprised."

"No, son." Now Tristan felt his heart suddenly, unexpectedly, gripped. "For all our hell, I still know you, Tristan. There is a time to shoot, I agree: but to have to do so all over again would kill you."

Surprised, Tristan gazed at him. "You're not afraid that I will kill an innocent?"

"No," said Mark plainly. "It would hurt you too much."

Tears filled Tristan's eyes. He reached up to cover his face with his hands – to be understood! To actually be understood again, after all these years...

"War must have been hell for you," murmured Mark, and Tristan shook his head.

"You have no idea," he whispered. "Peace-making? I was trying to make peace, Dad!"

"I know," said Mark. "I know."

"The screaming, the death..." Tristan caught his breath, and then lifted his hands away to confront his father, the priest. "How could God leave us in this shit-hole? Desperately wrestling it out, fighting each other tooth and nail: how, Dad?"

Mark frowned sadly at him, and then, again, looked out of the window.

"Do you see the chop?" he asked.

"Yes," Tristan replied.

"It's often choppy in Wellington," Mark said. "It's often windy."

"Horizontal rain!"

"Yes. But..." And now Mark's eyes came back to Tristan. "It's still home."

Now Tristan reached out a hand to finger Mark's face, suddenly caught in a very young memory.

"Home," he whispered, and Mark's eyes misted.

"I can't adequately account for God," whispered Mark. "I shot Joshua through you, Tristan, as surely as if I had been carrying the gun myself! You were only following orders..."

"Don't," pleaded Tristan, as his agony again was laid bare.

"But..." continued Mark, "I can say this: love somehow gains a much greater focus when it is set against pain."

And he gestured again out to the harbour, to the light reflecting off the choppy water. Tristan followed his point, and Mark murmured to him.

"Keep your gun if you must, Tristan," he said. "I trust you. I trust your judgement."

And Mark turned him, and lifted the rifle back into his right hand.

Tristan stared down at it, and then at Mark. His father guided his hand back into his left inner jacket pocket.

"We have been given the choice, Tristan," he said. "You must decide what you will do with your freedom."

"But what should I do?" asked Tristan.

"Only you can decide that," said Mark. "But let your heart be forged in goodness, as it once was."

Tristan looked down now at his father's golden cross, new, sitting on his chest, exposed by a casual white shirt.

"You have changed," he whispered, and Mark smiled sadly.

"I have only found again who I once was," he said. And he wandered over to the windows, stretched out his arms, and yawned freely.

Tristan watched his father, suddenly remembering his freedom – suddenly remembering childhood days, laughter, tickles, joy…

"Daddy," he whispered. "You're back."

Resurrected from the grave: a miracle! Death giving way to life.

He gazed at him – and then there was a movement.

Selena appeared at the entrance to the lounge. She glanced quickly at Tristan, her white face hidden by long dark curls, and then moved quickly away into the kitchen.

"Dad," said Tristan. "What's going on with Selena?"

Mark quickly turned back to him, his face turning serious. "I'm not entirely sure," he said.

"She looks…" Tristan hesitated and then continued. "She looks stoned."

"It's not drugs," said Mark. "I'm certain of that."

"Then what?"

Mark frowned. "Selena," he called out, and Tristan heard her resisting in the kitchen.

"What the hell happened to her?" asked Tristan. "She was circling around Joshua, almost as if…as if…"

Michelle Warren

"As if she was demon possessed?" asked Mark.

"I don't for a minute think…"

"How could you?" asked Mark, smiling slightly.

"But she was creepy!" said Tristan. "Like…like a psychopath."

He shuddered at the thought, while Mark watched him.

"Your sister is not a psychopath," he said clearly.

"What happened?"

"I…" Now he looked away and looked back. "I was a shoddy father."

"What did you do?" Tristan felt himself choking for a moment.

"It's not what I did," said Mark. "It's what I didn't do."

"Then what did someone else do?"

Mark's face whitened as he stared at Tristan. "Someone else?" he whispered. "In my absence?" Mark's gaze drifted toward the kitchen, and he wandered over.

"Selena," he said, and she suddenly appeared, shoving against him in her haste.

"I have to go," she said. "I have to study."

"No," said Mark quietly, reaching to grasp her arms. "Wait just for a minute."

She was desperately looking for anywhere else to set her gaze – she stared at his chest, almost writhing. Tristan remembered her face, white, dark, as she had pushed the crown onto Joshua's head, as she had circled around him while he had sweated blood on his knees – as she had cried out for his death.

"What happened?" whispered Mark, and Tristan felt his fingers reaching for the gun in his inner pocket.

"You know what happened," whispered Selena back, her blue eyes filling with tears. "Don't make me say it."

"Another father," whispered Mark. "Another kind of father."

Selena shook her head, tightly closing her eyes. "Don't make me."

"Show me," said Mark gently. "Please show me."

Selena's fingers were digging into Mark's arms. "It will hurt you," she whispered. "You will hate me."

42

"I won't hate you," said Mark.

"I can't."

"I will forgive you. I will try to forgive myself."

Selena's face lifted now, from within her black curls, and she turned over her wrist.

Mark stared down at it. He closed his eyes, and then opened them again.

"You know what I have done," whispered Selena, and Tristan watched his father sway before her. Then, suddenly, she ran; then she was gone.

Mark sank down to his knees. Shocked, Tristan stared at him. For a long moment Mark was silent. Then he lifted himself to his feet.

"What was that?" asked Tristan, and Mark grimaced at him.

"Only what I already knew," he said. "Selena…she went into a Shrine. It's a place in central Wellington, not far from Saint Peter's. She… joined with something in there."

"Joined with something?" asked Tristan.

"Something evil," replied Mark, his face contorting. "The symbol, tattooed on her wrist: the eye. 666. The meaning of 666, falling short of God's number, 7: fallen, fallen, fallen."

"You mean my sister has turned into a frickin' Satanist?" said Tristan, and Mark glanced curtly at him. "Don't beat around the bush, Dad, I know there's some weird shit out there."

"She's not a Satanist," said Mark. "And I don't know what to make of the whole demonic thing, Tristan – I'd be quite happy not to get it for the rest of my life. But…this Shrine exists. And I know she went there. And she gave herself in some way. And…the whole thing has wreaked havoc within her."

"What do you mean?"

"I don't know," said Mark, frowning. "She had some kind of power. She could read me, more than usual; she could taunt me, more than usual. She knew exactly what to say to get me to do what she wanted."

"What she wanted?" asked Tristan.

"Yes, but…it wasn't really her, Tristan."

Now tears filled Mark's eyes. "Something happened that changed her, and she changed me, and I changed Connor, and…and then all hell broke loose."

"A demon…?" muttered Tristan. "Some kind of spiritual power?"

"I don't know," said Mark. "I don't know anything about these things."

"I guess now's not a good time to mention that I'm kinda agnostic…"

"You should have seen me," said Mark. "I know atheists can be nice, kind, respectable people, but as an atheist I was a right bastard."

"And now?" asked Tristan, smirking.

"Now?" repeated Mark, eyebrows rising. "Not taking theism for granted in the reinstated Bishop?"

"No," said Tristan wryly, and Mark actually grinned.

"Very wise," he said, "judging from my own behaviour three months ago. But no," he continued, "I have found my faith again."

"I'm glad," said Tristan, and Mark's eyebrows went up again, but now with a warm smile.

"I'm glad you're glad," he said.

"So how do we help Selena?" asked Tristan, and Mark frowned.

"Yes," he said. "I'm praying for her, of course, but…I have a feeling it has to do with that boy I saw in the car park at Saint Peter's."

"Boy?" asked Tristan.

"Alex," said Mark. "I think his name was Alex. I think he took her to the Shrine."

"Bastard," said Tristan quickly, again reaching toward his gun.

"Who knows what his story is," said Mark.

"Better not be her boyfriend," said Tristan, "or I'll give him a talking to."

"Making up for lost time?" asked Mark, and Tristan flushed and looked away.

"Touché," he whispered, and Mark smiled sadly.

"Sorry," he said. "I'm the father, not you."

"Shoddy big brother," said Tristan.

"Brother," murmured Mark…and then, suddenly, he straightened. "Brother."

Tristan frowned. "Brother?"

"Same age," said Mark. "He was about the same age. Maybe a little older…"

"What are you talking about, Dad?"

Mark frowned, and stared out of the window toward the choppy water.

"He was never a boyfriend," he said. "I got it wrong."

"How do you know?"

Mark glanced at him. "I can't say," he said. "I just know. Alex is the key."

And now Mark looked down the hallway, toward Selena's room.

"He knows what happened to her," he said. "He knows everything."

"Where is he?" asked Tristan. "We could get him."

"No," said Mark. "We can't abduct him. He's a minor – he's not responsible."

"Bullshit," said Tristan.

"He's not responsible for her choices," said Mark. "There's someone else, someone more powerful."

Mark looked again out of the window, this time again in the direction of the Beehive.

"Something's going on," he said quietly. "I can feel it. And Alex has something to do with it."

"You're creeping me out now, Dad," said Tristan. "Starting to go all 'guru' on me."

Mark smiled. "What do you expect?" he said. "Miracles! I'm back from the dead, remember?"

Now Tristan stared at him. "I didn't say that out loud!"

"No," said Mark, "but you thought it." His expression changed, and he tilted his head.

"Tongues of fire," he said.

"What?" asked Tristan.

Mark grinned. "It's a mystery," he said. "A puzzle for you to decode. But it happened the first time: special spiritual gifts, of knowledge, and wisdom, and discernment of spirits, and healing. Spiritual insight. Maybe it's happening all over again."

"Like Joshua?" said Tristan.

"Yes," said Mark. "It's not all the same. It's only a picture of the original. But still fascinating, nonetheless."

"That's great," said Tristan. "You keep your theological fascination, and I'll just hold onto my gun."

"Be careful with that," said Mark. "That's all I ask."

"I'll be careful."

"Stay safe."

"I'll stay safe."

"I love you."

Now Tristan gazed at his face, and took a deep breath. His father! His father was back.

"I love you too," he whispered – and he reached out, and pulled his father to his own chest, and embraced him and then let him go.

"Let me know if I can help," said Tristan, and Mark nodded.

"I will," he said. "I will."

And he smiled, and Tristan cast his smile to memory, and he watched him, and finally dragged himself away, down the corridor, down the steps, and away.

Outside, Tristan gazed up at the house. His father was standing there, looking out of the lounge window at him, waving.

"Bye, Dad," said Tristan, and with tears he waved back, gathered himself, and moved down the drive.

Chapter 5

THE BLACK HOLE

A lex Kensington sat in Calculus class.

In front of him the teacher, Jones, taught mediocrity: the equation of a parabola, y equals a(x-h) squared plus k. Alex stifled a yawn, and glanced down at the tablet hidden on his lap under the desk. What was the velocity required to escape a black hole? To lift off from the surface? Even light itself could not escape from within the entrapment radius of the event horizon – what else could possibly break free?

"Care to join us, Kensington?" asked Jones suddenly, and Alex looked up at him. It was impossible! Impossible to break the speed of light; impossible to escape the crushing gravity inside the black hole. An implosion must follow! An inevitable implosion.

"I am with you," he said. "I can be in two different places at once." Laughter surrounded him.

"Explain," said Jones.

Alex looked back at the equation on the white board. "Two dimensions," he said pointedly. "All your teaching is in two dimensions. What about three dimensions? The paraboloid: z equals a x squared plus b y squared plus c. What about four dimensions?"

"You shouldn't be in this class," said Jones.

"I shouldn't be in this year," replied Alex, only to hear more muttering.

"Prick," someone said, and Alex shrugged.

"I say it as it is," he said.

Jones's eyes were on him. "Our school is too infantile for you?"

"The school doesn't matter," said Alex. "The curriculum's easy, it wouldn't matter where I was."

Now there was silence. Alex shifted slightly in his chair. The silence – that was the worst. Like the eye of a storm, anything might happen – anyone might act.

He kept his eyes down, and Jones's voice sounded.

"If that's the way you feel," he said, "then why are you here?"

Alex frowned. "I'm supposed to be here," he said. "Where else would I be?"

"The Principal…"

"I'm not talking about the Principal."

Now, involuntarily, his eyes went to Selena.

She was sitting a few seats away, leaning against the wall, her white face slightly hidden in her long black curls. She started slightly at his look, and turned her eyes away. Alex looked back at Jones.

"Cogs in the wheel," he said. "We are all just cogs in his wheel."

Jones shifted uncomfortably, and returned to the whiteboard.

Alex looked back down at his tablet. Now to the Theory of Relativity. Were all things truly relative? What of a Mastermind: One outside of the system, unconstrained by its laws, manipulating the laws, channelling the pieces to His own desired outcome?

For a Mastermind all was still Absolute: 'My Will will be done.'

Alex fleetingly closed his eyes. The bell went. There was movement all around – he was left alone. He took a deep breath of relief and opened his eyes, grasping his tablet, rising to his feet, moving through the door and toward the quiet of the library. Then, suddenly, Selena was in front of him.

Alex gritted his teeth. Her intense blue eyes were set on him with a challenge.

"Get out of my way," he said, moving around her, but now her hand was on his arm. He flicked it off.

"Don't touch me!" he cried.

"You took me there," said Selena, her voice cold, her white face fixed. "You bastard – you took me there!"

Alex laughed at her. "I took you there?" he said. "You are weak! Your thinking is weak! We are all cogs in his…"

"Bullshit!" said Selena. "We are all responsible! We are all responsible for what we do!"

Alex felt his face flushing. "You have no idea what you're talking about," he said.

"No idea?" she cried. "No idea, you prat? Didn't you see? Didn't you see what he…?"

Alex stared at her growing horror, and ground his teeth together.

"Shut up," he whispered. "Shut up."

"That bastard needs to be stopped," said Selena, tears filling her eyes.

"Yeah, right," said Alex. "And I suppose you're the one to do it? Sixteen-year-old feeble girl, crying, shaking at the knees witnessing a police officer killing – it was so easy, Selena, to corrupt you!" And now tears filled his eyes, surprising him, humiliating him, against his will. "Why was it so easy?"

The Bishop's daughter…draw her in, conquer her, reach her father and reach his high school friend – the seat of power in New Zealand: the Prime Minister, James Connor.

The plan…she was just a cog in the wheel…

But now she was hitting him.

Gasping, Alex took the blow to his face. "What are you doing?" he cried.

"That's for all your bullshit!" she said.

Now he lifted his hand to strike her across the face – but her eyes, wide, suddenly filled with fear, stopped him. He swallowed.

"I was only following orders," he said, lowering his hand. "This isn't part of the plan."

"I'm not just a bullshit part of your plan," said Selena.

"My plan?" Alex laughed. "You seriously think this is my plan?"

"You're the mastermind," chided Selena. "'I can be in two different places at once.'"

"Don't be a bitch," said Alex. "You know what I meant. You're the only one in that room who did know."

"I know what you meant," said Selena, "but I also know how you use your talents."

Alex flushed and turned away from her, looking back into the empty classroom, at the empty desks and chairs.

"You speak as though I have a choice," he whispered. "You should know better, Selena! After everything you have seen, you should know better!"

"I know what you can do."

"There is no other way."

"I'm just a pawn?"

"Of course, and he's the King."

"Then who are you?"

Alex stared at a desk in front of him. He felt his vision closing in – all he could see was the desk, everything else was in darkness.

"Who am I?" he whispered, his throat gagging. "I'm his Queen."

"Oh, Alex," breathed Selena, and Alex felt his body stiffening. He turned to run, but Selena's hand was on his arm, and now he wanted it there. He hesitated in his flight, and found her eyes.

"Understand," said Selena clearly, her strong gaze securing him, "the Queen is the most powerful piece."

"You're wrong," whispered Alex, reaching up to transiently touch her face, suddenly, for a moment, seeing beauty. "The Queen only does the bidding of the King. Her power is only used to conquer the enemy and defend him. She is strong, but she is a slave."

Selena's face contorted. "Her strength was not made for slavery," she said. "It was made for love – to defend her family."

Tears filled Alex's eyes. "In a dream," he whispered, "what you are saying is true."

"You are not the Queen, Alex," said Selena. "I am."

"Then who am I?"

Selena broke into a radiant smile. Alex stared at her, taken utterly by the light in her eyes. She was reaching now, slipping her fingers between his, taking his hand.

He trembled. Childhood. They felt like children suddenly.

"I read about a queen once," said Selena. "She was a twin: a twin sister to the king."

"Not married?" whispered Alex, staring down at their hands together.

"No," said Selena. "A twin. What use has a twin for marriage?"

"Quite," whispered Alex.

"But a King sometimes has a need for a sister."

"A King?" Tears blurred his eyes.

"I propose a different game," said Selena quietly.

"The rules are already set," said Alex.

"That's because you are still thinking you are on the same side as him."

Alex stared at her – he threw her hand away in shock.

"Treason," he whispered. "You are proposing treason."

"What is the goal, Alex?"

"The pieces are set."

"Yes: but you haven't yet chosen a side."

Alex frowned at her as she continued.

"Black, or white?"

"White?" he breathed. "There is a white?"

And now, instinctively, filled with fear, he ran.

People were all around him, with blurred faces, and scathing words. Conquer them – why not? Unseeing, unknowing, never understanding, always judging; they had no idea! No idea what a Black King could do –

no idea what the Black King was actually planning to do.

Alex reached the library. He ducked around the building, under the drooping leaves of a silver fern. He hid himself, away from the crowd, and covered his head with his arms.

Selena…he had led her into the lion's den. They had conquered her. He had watched her lay the cursed crown on Joshua Davidson's head. He had watched her dance around his suffering and incite the crowd to murder him.

She had taken on the very image of his father – Alex had led her to her fall. And yet, now she was speaking of treason? Of…of taking up a different side?

Something had happened in Saint Peter's. She had gone into that place to kill her father; she had emerged asleep in his arms.

Trust. Alex closed his eyes tightly. She actually trusted him, the one she had manipulated into arranging Joshua's death. And now the Bishop was reinstated at the Cathedral, and now she was speaking of a White King.

"It's dangerous," whispered Alex, "to change sides so thoroughly and so quickly, Selena: it's betrayal."

And yet, the light! The light in her eyes!

Alex felt a sudden yearning, a yearning he could not afford to entertain. He quenched it, briskly, violently. He flung the ferns aside and rose to his feet, quenching dead leaves at his feet.

The pieces were set. He set his jaw. The next phase was in motion.

He strode forward into the library. He closed himself away in a cubicle, and pulled out his tablet.

National security…The Ministry of Defence.

The army…it was only a matter of who to recruit.

Chapter 6

PAIN

James Lester sat at the computer. Rachel was sitting next to him, as usual, poised over her tablet. Who was she managing today, so attentively, as usual? He kept his eyes fixed ahead, on the blood count of Sarah. The white count was coming down, good. That woman had issues all right; the sooner she was discharged the better.

He kept Rachel in the corner of his eye.

"What have you got there?" he asked.

"Sarah's history," murmured Rachel.

"Chest pain," said James, clicking on to her liver function tests. "Shortness of breath, fever…" Her liver was normal.

"IV drug use."

James started. "What?" he said.

"The endocarditis: the source. She was shooting up," said Rachel.

James glanced at her troubled frown, as she looked down at the tablet.

"Have you tested for HIV and Hep C?" he asked. "Dirty needles."

"No," said Rachel, glancing up to his face. "Thanks."

"So, you'll arrange CADS then?"

"Okay," said Rachel. "But she must be detoxing on the ward."

"I'll bet," muttered James.

"Methadone?"

"Check with psych. Who knows what else she has going on."

He turned back to the computer, and clicked to the next result. Her kidney function was okay…

"That's the thing," said Rachel. "I think she's at risk."

"At risk?" said James, clicking on to her ESR. Still raised a bit…

"She was sexually abused as a child."

Now James shot up to his feet, logging out of his screen.

"Okay," he said, "enough banter: let's do the ward-round."

And he thrust himself down the corridor and into the first room.

Patients…so many patients. That was the problem, working in a hospital – all the eyes on you, as you enter the room. James resisted swallowing, and moved to the first bed.

"You do it," he said to Rachel, and she moved ahead of him alongside the young woman in the bed. What was she? Oh, yes, asthma. Easy.

Rachel reached for her pulse, and examined her chest. She did everything competently enough. James glanced his eyes over the patient's chart. The peak air flow of her lungs was good at 450, and the oxygen saturation of her blood was normal on air. She was ready for discharge.

Rachel was murmuring something with the patient, laughing. James shifted slightly on his feet. Then she nodded, and turned to James.

"Ready for discharge," she said, and he nodded back.

"Good," he said, and he moved to the next bed. Rachel was writing into the tablet as she moved. Where was Fatima? Rachel was carrying the House Officer role too much.

"What happened to our dogsbody?" asked James, and Rachel smiled sadly.

"She had something come up at home."

"Oh?" said James. "Kid has a virus?"

"No," said Rachel quietly, and James grimaced, looking at the compassion in her face. No one told him anything.

"Fine," he said. "It's just not fair on you, that's all. Twice the work."

Rachel's face brightened now. James was captured by her for a moment. Light! Light, in those eyes.

She was smiling at him. Then she moved on to the next patient.

This one had osteosarcoma. He would need to be transferred to the orthopods. James gestured to Rachel to continue, and listened to her voice: to her gentle laughter with the man who might die. He looked at the young man's face. He was Korean, worried, but reassured by Rachel's manner.

He liked her. All the patients liked her. James looked away – he reached for Rachel's tablet. She had light. She had…

He clenched his teeth, and moved on. Love – no. He wouldn't speak of it.

Sarah was next. James stopped himself rolling his eyes. The woman was out to get him, he was sure of it. Rachel followed him, and then went ahead willingly. She took Sarah's pulse, and murmured gently to her. She seemed to reach her. James watched her, sitting on the edge of the bed with the patient. She was a good doctor. She was…good. Tears pricked his eyes – he quickly suppressed them. What was goodness, anyway? Some evolutionary impulse? What was love, but a biochemical change in the brain?

Biochemistry…James swallowed. He set his eyes on Rachel's face. He took a slow deep breath. They moved on to the next bed.

This one was harder. James smiled slightly to himself, as he watched Rachel. He handed her the tablet. She scrolled through the history, and reached to take the woman's pulse. She frowned, and looked at him.

"Fibrosing alveolitis?" she asked.

"Maybe," replied James.

"I'll do the spirometry soon."

"That'll be interesting." He glanced over the patient's face – there was no blue tinge. He reached for her chart: the oxygen saturation was slightly down. "Do an arterial blood gas too," he said, and Rachel nodded, and they moved on.

James found himself watching her. Why? He took in the greenstone wedding ring on her left hand, as she sat next to another patient and reached for the pulse. Did he wish for this? There was no one at home, only isolation. He spent most of his time at work: work was his home. Was he ready for a wife? No. His seclusion suited him – the work fitted, like a familiar dressing gown. He was happy to let it be his life; he was happy to offer his mind to the task.

His knowledge was greater than hers, so he could teach her. He enjoyed teaching her. But she...she had something he didn't have. She intrigued him, with a sharp mind, but also...also a heart.

No. He swiftly pushed the thought away. He moved on ahead of her to the next bed. He cast his eyes over the patient's chart, and rigorously tested for anything he had missed. She followed him and joined his side, her smile complementing him. She was good with the patients, when he...he closed his eyes transiently...when he was not. They made a good team.

They actually made a good team.

Astonished, he looked again at her face. The light, the connection with the man in the bed, the connection with him, with his knowledge...Together they were much better than they were separate from each other.

Marriage? No. He had no desire for this, and he knew she had no desire for this. Then what? What was this thing? Collegial? Yes, of course. But...but there was something more.

He swallowed, before he thought to stop himself. Her manner, her smile, her...her beauty. It was reminding him of someone...of someone close.

Suddenly he saw her, in his mind's eye: suddenly another smile was in front of him.

"Oh, shit," he breathed, as he looked at his sister. Light! Light, in her blue eyes! Beauty in her sixteen-year-old face, before...

"Oh, shit!" he pleaded – and now he ran out of the room, into the corridor.

"James?"

Rachel was right there with him, at his side. Her face, her concern, her searching blue eyes...

"Stupid," James whispered to her. "It's just stupid. Let's keep going."

And he moved quickly into the next room.

Margaret was there, lying in bed. Her brown eyes were on him. The leur was still in her hand.

"How are you today, Margaret?" Rachel's voice sounded from behind him.

"Okay, Doctor Rachel," said Margaret, her face breaking into a smile.

Rachel reached for her chart. James watched her eyes scanning over the drug record, and then the blue eyes lifted to him.

"She's had her morphine dose already this morning," said Rachel, and she glanced across to Margaret's face.

"No pain?" she asked.

"No," said Margaret happily.

"Short of breath?" asked Rachel.

"No," Margaret said. "I'm feeling much better this morning, thank you, doctor."

Rachel moved alongside her, reaching for the stethoscope around her neck, and listened to her chest. Her face was bright as she flicked her stethoscope back over her shoulders, and reached for the bottle next to the bed.

"No extra drainage," she said. "I think we can take the chest drain out."

"Good," said James.

"She seems stable," said Rachel.

"Yes," said James.

"We could shift her onto a morphine pump and..."

"Not yet," said James.

"Not yet?" asked Rachel.

"We'll just monitor her use for another twenty-four hours, and then we'll put her onto the pump and shift her to palliative care."

Rachel frowned. "But why?" she asked. "A pump is more effective. The patient can control their own dosing."

"Let's just wait," said James quietly, reaching her. "Another twenty-four hours, and then we'll change her to the pump."

"Okay," said Rachel instinctively, as James knew she would. She trusted him.

"Take over," said James. "There's something I need to sort out."

"Okay," said Rachel, nodding.

He left her at Margaret's side, moving out into the corridor and then into the nursing bay.

Kate was hovering around the drugs. James moved alongside her, at the leur trolley. He reached for an IV kit, and brushed her side with his body.

She gasped.

"Where's the key for the Controlled Drugs safe?" he asked. "A patient is due for morphine."

"What?" she whispered, disorientated.

"A patient," repeated James. "I need the keys."

She reached instinctively into her pocket, and passed the keys to him.

"Thank you," said James. "Sorry about that."

And he took the keys into his own pocket.

Kate looked flushed. He leaned back toward her.

"Sarah in Room One needs her blood pressure checked," he said. "You're about the only competent nurse around here."

"Okay," she said, and she grasped her stethoscope out of her pocket and moved away from him and the medication, down the corridor and toward Room One.

The Controlled Drugs safe was before him.

James quickly reached up with the key and opened the safe. Morphine ampoules sat inside. He plucked one out, and reached for the record.

Margaret...her next dose was due in seven hours. He glanced over the other names...no one else in the ward needed a dose beforehand. Quickly he wrote Margaret's dose, and the time, in seven hours' time. Then he replaced the record, locked the safe, and returned the keys to his pocket.

Kate was in the corridor. She seemed to be hesitating, but she had no choice, he knew. Her role demanded her return.

She stepped back into the medication area. James handed her the keys.

"The blood pressure is normal," said Kate stiffly.

"Good," said James. "And what about your blood pressure?"

"Mine?" asked Kate.

"It must be high, knowing that I have the power to make or break your career."

Kate's eyes widened, staring at him, and her cheeks flushed. James was satisfied – she was in his control. He reached out for a saline canister, and handed it over to her.

"This is Margaret's three pm morphine dose," he said. "The placebo effect is a wonderful thing."

"What?" Kate breathed, staring down at the salty water. "But she's in pain."

"Aren't we all?" said James. "How much pain can you withstand?"

Now she looked horrified. James smiled within. As if he would inflict physical pain on her, stupid woman – didn't anyone understand a metaphor any more? But, still, her misunderstanding served his purpose. Fear was his greatest ally.

He walked away from her, and reached a hand into his pocket to grasp the morphine ampoule. He moved into the empty single room. He locked the door behind him.

His sister! He trembled, now, looking at her face in his mind's eye. She was still before him – he couldn't shake her. Beauty, and…and light, and abuse, and…and death…

"Oh God," he whispered, and he let himself sink under the constant pressure of the tide within. He reached for his pain relief, and felt the familiar woozy numbness as home, as he escaped against the wall into sleep.

Chapter 7

FORCES

Tristan stood at the waterfront, and drew his jacket more closely around himself. The sky was overcast and grey; there was a slight sea-breeze, and a few spots of rain were falling on his face.

Rain…There had been another time, on another waterfront, with a drop of rain. Tristan suddenly remembered the moment, up north, on Ninety Mile Beach, months earlier: Joshua, drawing stick figures in the sand, looking out to the horizon.

A storm is coming, he had said. Who had the figures been? Tristan stooped, and doodled with the sand at his feet. A man, a gun – he glanced up at the army soldiers, who returned every Sunday, and then looked back down at his art – another man. He dropped himself down to sit next to the drawing, and frowned.

The one man was shooting the other.

Tristan closed his eyes, and sighed. Why was he still carrying the gun? Why the hell had he shot Joshua in the first place? Recruited by the Prime Minister? Bullshit! He hadn't even been signed up – hadn't even been current in the army at the time. They had deliberately used him, off record, outside of normal constraints.

The Price of Redemption

And now he was remaining outside of normal constraints.

His colleagues were watching the crowd, carrying rifles, as if the ones following Joshua were a bunch of fanatics – as if they were criminals waiting to happen; a riot waiting to happen. And there was the irony, Tristan thought – all of these were actually innocent. It was he, himself, who had really committed the crime, but the army didn't care about this one vital reality.

The weapon was forgotten, as if it had never existed. Joshua also was forgotten, a New Zealand citizen, executed. But for this group of people, remembering him, deliberately lifting him up, he would fade fast into the obscure background of a military state.

Maybe that was why Tristan kept turning up. He didn't want Joshua to be forgotten. He didn't want the State to swallow up the individual generosity of this one man, who had shown himself capable of love and forgiveness, even in the midst of Tristan's bullets.

There was something very important about him; something that people needed.

"Don't hold it against them," Joshua had prayed to God, on his knees, in agony, *"they really have no idea what they are doing!"*

Tears pricked Tristan's eyes. No idea…never a truer word spoken.

A soldier taken by a pacifist, still carrying his gun. Tristan smiled wryly. Maybe he needed a shrink. Then again, maybe he just needed a minister.

He looked up to Rau, who was standing again in front of the crowd. That one would do.

Rau was talking, as always. Tristan walked toward him, and tuned in to the familiar sound of his voice.

"Don't be put off by cold wind, or rain," said Rau. "Bad weather is sure to come, but the sun is waiting to burst forth from behind the clouds…"

Tristan remembered his father's words: the chop, on the harbour, and the light. Home.

"Even death is only a gateway into greater life," said Rau. "A

61

transition; a new birth. Trust, and you will be delivered, like a baby is delivered into his mother's arms. Joshua has gone before us to God, to lead us into a greater life that is stronger than death."

Tristan gazed thoughtfully at his face. He liked listening to him, to his passion and certainty. Rau was starting to remind him of Joshua himself.

"If you trust then the Spirit of te Atua will come to you," said Rau. "He will strengthen you, and remind you of everything Joshua said, and he will give you new gifts."

New gifts…was this the tongues of fire his father mentioned?

"Knowledge," said Rau, "and wisdom. Healing."

"And discerning of spirits," said Tristan quietly.

Rau's eyes came to him, smiling. "Trust," he said. "Faith is the key."

"The key to what?" asked Tristan.

"To fullness of life," said Rau. "Both here and in the life to come."

Tristan watched him and then Rau stepped back from the crowd.

"Fullness of life," muttered Tristan. "What does that even mean?"

Rau looked at him. "Fullness of life?" he said, and he glanced around himself and back to the harbour. "The ocean," he said. "Our lives are like a puddle, but life connected with God is like the ocean."

"Oh," said Tristan.

"Joy," said Rau. "Like falling in love, only better."

"Okay…"

"There's hope…"

"Yeah," said Tristan, "I get that part."

"…and love…"

"Yeah, that part's good."

"…and peace."

Tristan looked at him. "I could do with more of that," he said.

"You'd have to give up your weapon first," said Rau.

"Why?"

"Well, it's hard feeling peace when you're still holding a gun."

Tristan suddenly noticed his hand was curled around the weapon in his left inner pocket again.

"Oh," he said, and he withdrew his hand. "Didn't even realise."

"No," said Rau. "I know. Lucky I trust you."

Tristan smiled slightly at him. "Sorry," he said.

Rau shrugged. "I'm starting to get used to…"

But his voice was interrupted.

A sudden strong gust of wind swept over them, throwing Rau off his feet onto the sand. Tristan gasped, for a moment unable to breathe, and then cries went up in the crowd. Tristan jerked himself forward, and reached out a hand to Rau to thrust him up to his feet.

French! Tristan could hear French again, in the crowd! Mon Dieu! Mon Dieu! Je vous adore! Then there was laughter, and singing, and, all in all, a scene that suddenly, weirdly, reminded Tristan of a bar.

Tristan laughed, looking at their faces, at the naked happiness in their eyes. And then, suddenly, they surged forward as one, like a wave.

A firearm sounded. Shocked, Tristan watched the crowd fired upon by the army. Three bodies dropped where they were.

"No!" cried Tristan. "God!" Agony seized his chest, and his hand instinctively gripped his gun, in his pocket. He fell to his knees. "Stop it! Stop it!"

Fire? Fire? He was gripped again by memories of the war. Of his firing! Of young bloody faces. But now, suddenly, he was seeing Joshua again.

"Don't hold it against them, they really don't know what they are doing."

"Don't fire!" cried Rau. "Peace! Peace!"

"Peace," pleaded Tristan. "Peace."

He unwrapped his hand from his gun, rose to his feet, and ran to stand between the army and the crowd.

The soldiers, still carrying their rifles, looked shocked. Tristan stared at their faces, with his hands up in the air; they stared back at him.

"Which side are you on, Blake?" asked one young man.

"I'm on New Zealand's side," said Tristan. "We are all New Zealand."

The next soldier over, the one who had fired, now threw his rifle forward onto the sand.

"I stand down," he said.

"We're not at war," replied Tristan.

"The crowd surged forward," said the soldier, his face flushing. "Just like on the day…"

"Understand me," repeated Tristan clearly. "We are not at war."

"We are at war," said the third soldier, a Major, with older entrenched lines across his forehead, "just not against each other."

Tristan frowned at him, confused, and now the older man laid his rifle down.

"Casualties," he said. "Let's attend to the casualties."

And he moved forward.

Tristan turned. Three lay on the beach, their blood soaking into the sand.

"Oh dear God," he whispered.

Rau was kneeling next to one of them, his eyes closed, his face contorted in concentration as he prayed. The older soldier moved to a Chinese woman, who was groaning. She was shot in the abdomen.

"First aid kit," ordered the Major, and the fourth soldier, who had been holding back, moved quickly back from the street and returned with a green bag. He crouched down, opened the kit and reached for a compression bandage. The Major had already stripped off his jacket and was plugging the wound with it.

The first young soldier had moved to the other casualty, a Maori man. He was sitting up, holding his shot arm. Tristan could tell at first glance he was going to make it.

But Rau…Tristan moved quickly forward to kneel next to him.

A young European child lay on the sand before him, her eyes closed. She had been shot in the chest.

"Oh, shit!" breathed Tristan. He glanced up to see the dismay and fear on the face of the soldier who had shot her.

"I'm going to get court martialled for this," he whispered, and Rau's voice sounded, next to Tristan.

"No," he said. "It's going to be all right."

Tristan stared at his tense concentration, at his closed eyes. Tristan reached out to the child's pulse, but there was nothing. He laid a hand on her chest. There was no breathing, or heartbeat. She was dead.

"Rau," he whispered, "she's gone."

Wailing surrounded him. Tristan looked up to see a woman, horrified, falling to her knees next to the child.

"I'm sorry," he said to her. "There's nothing we can do."

"No," said Rau. "It's going to be all right."

"Life after death, and all that," whispered Tristan.

"No, that's not what I mean," said Rau.

"My life is over," said the young soldier.

"You still have your life ahead of you," said Rau, his eyes still closed, his forehead still furrowed.

"In prison," whispered the solider.

Tristan reached out to the girl, to lay a hand over her face.

"Peace, little girl," he whispered. "Be at peace."

And then, suddenly, her eyes opened beneath his hand.

Tristan started, and pulled his hand back as if he'd been burnt.

"Holy shit!" he said.

The girl's eyes were hazel. She was staring up at him, looking scared. Tristan stared down at her. Blonde hair...how could she be alive? The chest...the wound had gone...

Tristan stared up now at the face of the young soldier. He had turned white. And now Rau was leaning into Tristan.

"Still don't believe that Joshua came back after death?" he murmured into his ear.

Tristan stared at his face, and Rau rose to his feet. He wandered over to the Maori man, and prayed for him. The man was relieved. He wandered over to the Chinese woman, removed the blood stained jacket, prayed for her, and then she was on her feet.

"I am mad, after all," muttered Tristan to himself. "Good job I'm not still in the army."

Rau faced the four soldiers.

"What you've seen here today," he said. "Are you going to report it?"

The soldier who had fired stared at Rau, stiff, unable to speak. The other two looked at the Major, who was frowning.

"There are forces at work here I do not understand," he said.

"Ae," said Rau. "That's true."

"Our role is to defend New Zealand."

"Ae."

"An enemy that cannot be defeated poses a significant threat."

"True," said Rau. "But do you really believe that we are the enemy of New Zealand?"

The Major glanced over the crowd and returned to Rau.

"No," he said. "I do not."

"Well…"

"However," continued the Major, "I still have a duty to report."

Rau held his gaze. He grimaced and then nodded.

"Do what you have to do," he said.

Tristan stared at the Major. He was reporting? Of course. Word would get back to the Ministry of Defence, to Parliament, to the Governor General, and to the Queen.

He looked at Rau as he reached down, grasped the European girl's hand, and lifted her to her feet. She was looking at her T-shirt, staring at the blood on her shirt, and Rau laughed with her, comforting her.

"There is no law for this," muttered Tristan. "There is no law against this."

"We are not the police," said the Major, "you know that, Blake. We are the army. We respond when challenges transcend the capacity of the law to maintain order."

"We are not the enemy," said Rau, looking back at him. "We are peaceful. We only want peace."

The Major nodded. "Noted," he said.

Tristan stared, between Rau, the priest, who had just brought a girl back from death, and the army. He shook his head slightly, to try to convince himself he wasn't dreaming.

"Return to your homes now, please," said the Major.

"We have done nothing wrong," said Rau.

"Understood," said the Major. "But I require you to disperse for now."

Rau held his gaze and then nodded.

"All right," he said, and he lifted his voice to the crowd.

"The Spirit of te Atua has come!" he said. "Life after death, if we trust in him! Remember: whatever happens, wherever we are, he is always with us!"

And Rau tipped his head to the Major, and walked off the beach.

Chapter 8

THE SHRINE

Alex stood outside the Shrine.

A few drops of rain were falling on his head. He lifted his face up to the grey, gathering, dense clouds. There was a light breeze. He closed his eyes. Let the rain come – let it come, and sweep him utterly away.

The image was in front of him, over the door: the all-seeing eye. Taking a deep breath, he opened his eyes to look up at it again. Go in? Go inside again? Clenching a hand into a fist, he strode forward and opened the door, closing it swiftly behind him.

It was dark. Alex swallowed, and waited for his eyes to adjust. He could hear sounds he did not want to hear. He could smell what he did not want to smell. He wanted to writhe, but rigidly stopped himself. Soon it would be over. Soon.

A dark shape was forming in front of him: a man, very tall, in black robes. The man was carrying a golden chalice. Alex gagged. One of the smells was coming from there.

"Drink," said Kensington's low voice.

"No," whispered Alex, and he was suddenly hit across the face. He gasped, and shook his head.

"Kneel," said his father, and Alex hesitated. Resist? He sank down to his knees.

"Drink," repeated the priest.

"No," he whispered again, and now he was hit across the other cheek. Stinging! Alex closed his eyes tightly.

"Do you have a death wish?" asked his father.

"No," whispered Alex, starting to shake. Stupid boy! Shaking, like a girl! "No."

"Then you will obey me."

Alex stared down at his father's feet, at the black leather shoes and black trousers, beneath the black robes. He could see nothing else.

"What do you want me to do?" asked Alex.

"Drink," said the priest.

"I can't drink," said Alex, and suddenly his father's fists were seizing his shirt – now he was being dragged along the floor and thrust up against a wall.

Alex stared into his face, at the dark penetrating eyes and rigid intense frown. Could he remember his father any other way? There had once been a man, hadn't there? A long, long time ago? There had once been a father.

The priest was gripping onto the chalice. Now his fist was gripping onto Alex's shirt.

"Don't make me drink," whispered Alex. "I brought Selena here – I killed Joshua Davidson for you. Don't make me drink."

"You are weak," said Kensington. "A pitiful girl."

"It must be my choice," said Alex, "to give myself. It must be my choice."

"You will follow in my footsteps."

"I remember your choice."

That day…that terrible day, years earlier, when his father had found his mother shot. Both parents! He had lost both parents that day.

"Don't talk to me about choice," rasped his father's voice, and he was reaching inside the robe and pulling out a gun.

Alex froze, staring forward. A black altar was behind the priest's robes, with more chalices sitting on top.

Now the pistol was at his temple.

Tears filled Alex's eyes, against his will. He squeezed them away. Death was always so near – always, always so very near…

"You will carry on my legacy," said his father.

"What do you want me to do?"

Kensington hesitated, and then, suddenly, he grasped him again, dragged him along the corridor, and threw him into a small room.

A single laptop was sitting on a plain desk. Alex stared at it and shook his head, as if he'd just been thrust out of a nightmare into an eerie imitation of normality.

"Here," said Kensington. "If you're too gutless to join me, show me what you can do without me."

Alex frowned, reaching out to the computer, pressing the on switch.

A programme was already running: searching, assimilating, building connections, penetrating…

Alex stared at the screen: Parliament, the Courts, the Reserve Bank, the Ministry of Health.

The Ministry of Defence.

"Shit…" whispered Alex.

"Use your genius on this," said Kensington. "Your spirit is useless, but maybe your mind can still keep you alive."

The programme was trying to hack, it was failing. But for what? For what?

"Make it live," said Kensington, "and I'll have no need for you to drink."

Alex stared at him, and then, suddenly, Kensington was gone, pulling the door shut. Alex frowned. He fingered the door handle. He turned it. It was locked.

Panic seized him – he was locked in! Tiny room, no windows, no toilet, no water…he banged his palms against the door and cried out, his voice rising closer and closer to a scream…

He clenched his hands into fists, and dug his nails into his palms. Pain! Physical pain! It calmed him! It distracted him.

Now he sank down against a wall, and he buried his head in his arms. Then he lifted up his head, rose to his feet, and moved to the computer.

This was his only connection with the outside world. How might he use it, to tell people of his imprisonment? They would not believe him, and he would get killed. Besides, who would care?

He fingered the keys…Parliament. His father's efforts were rudimentary, Alex was surprised. His fingers sped across the keys: access! Get access. He skimmed quickly through public knowledge: the Governor General was trying to move the nation again toward democracy. Two parties, Socialist and New Conservative. Changes to party lists.

Alex saw his own father's name under the Socialist Party. He skimmed the list, and saw sixteen names of his father's associates.

"What are you up to?" he whispered.

He would have to show his father something for his efforts. He would need to hack into something.

He glanced over the departments. Not the Governor General's office – hacking into the authority of the Queen would be high treason. Something small, something easy.

James Connor. Smirking, Alex looked at the name. It had been so easy to manipulate him once: Alex had brought the whole nation to their knees. Now? What could the man do for them now?

He hacked into Connor's emails, and searched out his communications. There wasn't much to see, the man was on the back benches of the New Conservative Party, humiliated, stripped of most of his power.

But he had a connection with Patrick Clarkson, the Leader of the Socialist Party. And a vote…a vote was coming.

The Socialist Party.

Alex stared at the names. A rigged election, surely that was his father's plan. To rule, through Clarkson: to rule under the guise of socialism – under the guise of democracy.

There was no greater slavery than to believe one was free.

Alex closed his eyes. He leaned his head forward, for a moment, against the computer. Cogs in the wheel…they were all just cogs in his father's wheel.

But why the Ministry of Health? Why the Ministry of Defence?

Alex lifted his head again. He tapped his fingers on the desk, hesitating, and then hacked into Connor's personal email address. Who was the previous Prime Minister trying to contact? Rachel Connor. James Connor had a daughter, a doctor working at Hardwater Hospital.

Alex tapped some more. Connor had emailed Rachel many times, but she had not replied. Was their relationship redundant now? Should he look elsewhere? He scrolled down Connor's inbox and searched for Rachel's name. Connor had sent twenty-one emails to her! When had been her most recent reply? There, six days after the death of Joshua Davidson.

'I can't believe you killed him.'

Alex blinked twice. He shifted with discomfort on his chair, and then clicked on Connor's reply.

'I didn't know what I was doing,' the PM wrote. 'Please call me. I know I was wrong.'

Alex stared at the words, and scrolled down.

'Please forgive me.'

Alex frowned. He tapped his fingers on the desk. Use this man again? Use his daughter? Kensington would soon return into the room, asking for his bounty.

Alex closed down Connor's private email account, and instead turned his attention again to his work emails. He found the new leader of the New Conservative Party, Matthew Scott. He scanned his details, and typed them on the notebook. He moved to his father's programme, scanned over the details, tidied it up a bit – heightened its efficiency a bit. Then the door opened, and his father entered.

"Well?" asked Kensington.

"Scott," said Alex, bringing up the notebook. "Connor talks with him a lot. Reach him, reach Connor, and reach Clarkson."

"Interesting," said Kensington. "But I think you have more."

"What?" asked Alex.

Kensington reached for the computer. His fingers sped across the keys, and now he was bringing up Connor's private emails.

"A daughter," he said, and Alex kept his face rigid.

"She's not in politics," he said. "They're not communicating."

"Connor is communicating," said Kensington, "and that's all that matters."

His face broke into an eerie smile. "This is what I need," he said. "Good work."

He closed the computer and left the room, and the door was left open.

Alex stared at it. He frowned. Then he tentatively rose to his feet and walked out through the door.

The service in the Shrine was over. The chalices were left, abandoned and clean. The smells had gone.

Alex stumbled through the Shrine and out of the door, feeling like his body was being controlled by someone else. He moved out onto the street. He walked steadily forward in driving rain.

It was Sunday morning. Vaguely he realised Selena would be in church. She was actually at Saint Peter's, with her father. He wandered vaguely in that direction, and then turned and walked down to the harbour.

A few people were scattered on the sand, at Oriental Bay. There was blood on the sand. Had his father killed them? Had he used their blood? Alex swayed a bit on his feet, and stared out to the water. He could walk in: just walk in, and breathe in the salty water, and end it all...but, no. He still wanted to live. Somehow he still wanted to live.

He picked up some sand, threw it into the ocean, and then turned on his feet and walked steadily away.

Chapter 9

AN AWAKENING

Rachel strode down the corridor of the ward. Fatima was back, chasing blood test results and setting up IV fluids. Now Rachel could set her mind more thoroughly to working out diagnoses.

She pulled out her own personal notebook, and searched under a medical textbook for shortness of breath, as she walked. Obstructive and restrictive patterns, yes, yes; fibrosing alveolitis, yes; sarcoidosis, amyloidosis…

Her cell-phone rang. Without thinking, she reached into her trouser pocket, inside her white coat, and pulled it out.

"Hello?" she said.

"Rachel!" said her father's voice. "Thank God you answered the phone!"

Tears filled her eyes. She stood, caught, in the middle of the corridor, with Kate passing by on her right.

"Dad," she whispered, "now's not a good time."

"No time is a good time," replied Connor through the phone. "Please, Rachel, let me speak with you! I'll call back if I have to, but please don't fob me off again."

She hesitated, rocking backwards and forwards between her feet. She glanced down the corridor.

"All right," she whispered, turning on her heel, and she launched herself in the direction of the single unoccupied room. "All right."

She opened the door, closed it after herself, locked it, and started to pace around the room.

"Fire away," she said.

"That's a very unfortunate choice of words, Rachel," said her father's voice wryly, and she broke into a grin, despite herself.

"I say it as it is," she said.

"Ain't that the truth," replied Connor.

"You killed him," said Rachel quickly to him. Seize the chance! "You killed him, and I watched it, and I can't get the thing out of my head, Dad!"

"I know," said Connor. "I'm sorry. I never expected you to be there."

"Where the hell did you think I would be?" asked Rachel. "I loved the man! You knew that! You knew I was with him!"

"You're right," said Connor. "I tried to get you to stay away. I should have known you wouldn't."

"He healed everyone, Dad!" said Rachel. "You should have seen him! Outside of North-East Hospital, all the cases we were losing – he took them in his stride! He showed me things…he…he even saved my life."

She remembered now, in Hell's Way, the burning water! Seeing her own body, floating face down, watching Joshua reaching into the water to save her. His voice, calling! Calling! Authority! She had followed his authority, back into her own body – an authority greater than death.

"You have no idea who you have killed," she whispered.

Connor's voice was silent on the end of the phone. Rachel wandered over to the empty patient bed, and sank heavily down on it.

"You don't believe me, do you," she said. "That he saved my life."

"I do believe you," said Connor. "It's just been a while since I've been in church."

Rachel laughed, and suddenly found herself crying.

"Rachel," breathed her father's voice, "let me come! I should come to you."

"No," she whispered. "I can't. Not yet! Not yet."

"There's so much, Rachel," said Connor. "So much I need to tell you."

"What?" she asked. "What more could there possibly be to say?"

"Things you need to know," said Connor. "Reasons why you needed him."

"Don't," whispered Rachel. "I don't want to go there."

"It wasn't my fault, Rachel," said her father. "All these years, it wasn't my fault, but now, with Joshua, it was my fault."

Rachel was silent, listening to his voice: listening to his confession.

"The grief," he said, "the loss, it has a much sharper edge, Rachel. This man, this Joshua, he gave you hope."

"Yes," she whispered, trembling.

"Hope beyond your own control."

"Yes." Tears filled her eyes.

"There's only one other person whom you have ever loved more than your own life, Rachel," said her father. "Do you remember who that person is?"

Rachel rose to her feet. Confused, she stared out of the window to the grey street below, to the people walking, under their umbrellas.

"Another person?" she whispered. "There was another?"

"For years you lost the memory," said Connor. "If this Joshua has affected you this deeply, is it possible…"

"Possible?"

"…that, at last, he's emerging again?"

Rachel lifted her eyes beyond the umbrellas to the street, to the pedestrian crossing…

"Oh my God," she whispered.

"I was never keen on naming a son after myself," murmured Connor, his voice now very gentle. "But your mother insisted. I got to choose Rachel, and she chose…"

"James..." whispered Rachel.

"You were both little, Rachel, when you were born. You both had a fight on your hands. You did better, he lagged behind...there was something different about him, but you didn't care. You were always protective, always helping, always caring, always..."

"...trying to save him," whispered Rachel.

"But you couldn't," said Connor. "And one day..."

Rachel stared at the pedestrian crossing. She closed her eyes tightly.

"A crash," she whispered. "Death."

"Crash?" said Connor. "No, sweetheart, not a literal crash. Probably it felt that way to you. Certainly it was a kind of death."

Rachel opened her eyes again, to look at the crossing – at a child, wearing a raincoat, walking across the road.

"What do you mean?" she asked, reaching her fingers to touch the glass, to touch the image of the child walking.

"He disappeared, Rachel," said Connor, his voice choking. "He disappeared, just like Joshua has disappeared. You always believed I should have been able to protect him! You always believed it was my fault. You shut him away, you shut the anger away. Until Joshua."

"Joshua made me angry?" asked Rachel.

"No," said Connor, "he made you real."

Rachel followed the child with her fingers until he had disappeared down the road. A deep, deep emptiness gnawed at her depths. A twin? A twin, lost? She remembered Joshua's face, the warmth, the love, the kindness. Lost.

"Why are you telling me all of this?" whispered Rachel. "Why now, Dad?"

"Because you're right about Joshua," said Connor. "It was unfair with James, Rachel, unfair for all of us! Most unfair for James himself! But Joshua? I've never regretted anything more in all my life. I'm stuck on the back benches, when I shouldn't even be in Parliament..."

"Anita Mayes..."

"It wasn't the Governor General who decided," said Connor. "It was someone else."

"Someone else?" asked Rachel.

"I shouldn't be here," said Connor. "It's humiliating enough, losing the top job, but why has my party kept me? I should resign."

"Surely you can help," said Rachel. "New Zealand's in a mess right now, and you were the PM just a few months ago."

"You sound like Blakey," said Connor.

"Blakey?" Rachel asked.

"The Right Reverend Bishop of Wellington," said Connor. "Mark Blake. Can you believe it? Reinstated at Saint Peter's. Met me for lunch one day, he did! Poured out his apologies about as profusely as the Hutt River floods. Never seen anything like it. Never will again. We talked politics…it was good to see a friendly face again. What, with how things are going around here."

"What do you mean, Dad?"

Now Connor's voice went silent. Then he spoke again.

"I'm sure this call's being monitored, Rachel," he said. "I'm sure everything is being monitored."

Rachel glanced again out of the window.

"I don't care," she said. "Why would I, after everything that has happened?"

"I want you safe," said Connor. "I will always want you safe."

"I know," whispered Rachel, and tears filled her eyes. "I love you, Dad."

"Please forgive me," whispered Connor's voice, and Rachel took a deep breath.

"Okay," she said. "I forgive you." Weeping suddenly took her, and her father's voice murmured comfort to her, and she felt, in that moment, a sudden weight off her chest.

"I'd better go," she said, turning away from the window, reaching out to unlock the door.

"Okay," said Connor. "Stay in touch."

"I will," said Rachel happily. "Goodbye, Dad."

"Goodbye."

She opened the door, and James was standing in front of her.

Rachel stared at him. He was staring back at her, clutching something in his trouser pocket.

Rachel dropped her phone. Hazel eyes! Her twin had had hazel eyes…James frowned, looking a bit agitated, and stooped to pick up her phone.

"What are you doing here?" he asked.

"I…" How to explain? "I was just going through some stuff."

"Nothing interfering with your work, I hope," said James, and Rachel stared down at his head.

"How old are you?" she asked.

"What?" he answered, frowning, rising to his feet and handing back her cell-phone.

He was balding: she had assumed he was mid-forties at least…

"Thirty-two," he said, and Rachel stared at him. She had done the Master's degree first! Biochemistry! He was five years ahead, but the army…had he raced through his training quickly?

"I'm thirty-two as well," she said, and he shrugged.

"I have some cases for you."

"I'm remembering some things."

"I'm not a shrink," he said. "I can't help you with your issues."

"I know, but…"

What had happened in his past?

Rachel stood before him, longing to ask but knowing, somehow, she must not. He was eying the door into the room.

"Do you need some privacy?" asked Rachel, and James shrugged.

"Sometimes I go in there to think."

"Me too," said Rachel.

"Hard to get space in a busy ward."

"Yeah."

"I…" Now he was looking over her face. Rachel held herself attentive. He hesitated, and then he spoke. "I have issues too," he said.

Rachel gazed at him, and then, suddenly, realised she was feeling for him.

"Go, then," she said. "Get your space." She stepped back, and he turned, and he was reaching his right hand into his trouser pocket. She watched him disappear behind the door, and heard him turn the lock.

Rachel frowned. She turned away, and wandered down the corridor. This was a feeling she hadn't had before, deep, foundational…Was it romantic? Quickly she thought of John, her husband…No, it certainly wasn't that. This new feeling was somehow more foundational than sexuality.

She swallowed. Love? Love for James? For what purpose? Certainly it would never be reciprocated. He would leave, she would leave: it would end. The ending would hurt, as all the other wretched endings had already hurt.

But there was something beautiful in the feeling, something pure, and releasing. It was self-less. It was giving. It was about family.

She chose it: she chose to continue in it. And now she walked into the medication bay.

Kate was standing next to the Controlled Drugs safe.

Rachel glanced up at her, as she reached again for her notebook, but the nurse's face, white and drawn, made her look twice.

"Kate?" she asked. "What is it?"

"Nothing," whispered Kate.

"Can I help you?" asked Rachel, and Kate's eyes set on her. She swallowed, and then she shook her head.

"No," she whispered. "You can't help me."

"You look sick," said Rachel.

"Yes," replied Kate, "I feel sick."

"Do you need to go home?"

Now Kate hesitated. She stared into the corridor and then looked back to Rachel.

"No," she said. "I'd better stay."

"Okay," said Rachel, frowning. "Just let me know if you need my help."

"Okay," whispered Kate, and she quickly moved away.

Rachel wandered up to Controlled Drugs safe. The keys had been left in the door by Kate.

"Oops!" said Rachel, and she quickly reached for them, but, instead of locking the safe, she instinctively opened it.

The record was there, next to the ampoules of morphine and pethidine. Rachel frowned, and fingered the record. She drew it out, and cast her eyes briefly over it.

"Tempted?" sounded James's voice, behind her, and Rachel started.

"Oh!" she said, and she quickly replaced the record, laughing slightly. "No."

"I know you've been going through some stuff," said James.

"Well, yeah," said Rachel.

"PTSD," said James.

Rachel reached to lock the Controlled Drugs safe, and drew the keys out.

"These were left in the safe," she said, and James's eyebrows went up.

"That's unusual," he said.

"I think…" Mention Kate? Instinctively Rachel let her words run out.

"Better get them back to Kate," said James, and Rachel nodded.

"Okay," she said, and she started down the corridor in Kate's direction.

Love…it preoccupied her thoughts now. She handed the keys back to Kate, and returned to the medication bay. Strange how familial love could be as unrequited as romantic love. Strange how it could take such a deep hold.

She sat herself down next to the computer; James sat next to her. They both attended to the results. It was natural, somehow, hand in glove. Unspoken connection.

James…

The memory whispered, from the past: a connection lost; a connection found.

A resurrection from the dead. An unseen shadow coming back to life.

Tears pricked her eyes. She longed to speak, but she could not speak. He continued with his work. She longed to ask, but she could not ask. He finished his work.

Joshua was before her again – the pain, on his face! The pain of his offering.

James was starting to doze at the computer. Rachel reached to log it off. She had a sudden impulse to lay him down and put a blanket over him. Instead she called his name.

He stirred. He looked at her.

"Better rest," she said.

"Okay," he whispered. And he lifted himself to his feet, and wandered down the corridor back to the single vacant room.

How many times had doctors slept on that bed? Rachel wondered, smiling. Night shift! James must have done an extra night shift, covering for someone else.

He'd left his stethoscope on the table. She reached to pick it up, putting it in her own pocket. Let him rest. She would cover the ward, now Fatima was around. She could take up the slack.

She rose to her feet, and wandered into a room. Patients awaited!

It was time for work.

Chapter 10

PAUL AND ALEX

John stood in Saint Peter's. The Cathedral was quiet, and peaceful. He stood in the middle of the nave, between the wooden chairs of the congregation. He looked forward toward Jesus, on the cross. He lifted his eyes to the stained glass windows lining both sides of the church. What figures were there, in illuminated colour? Jesus, in a white robe, healing the masses. Jesus, stripped and bloody before Pilate. Jesus laid bare on the cross. Jesus alive again, re-clothed, appearing to Mary, and Peter, and John, and many, all at one time.

Peter, the sturdy fisherman, was preaching to the crowd. Tongues of fire were resting on the people, on heads of dark curls. A wind was rushing around them. And, in the next window, there was another man. John peered more closely at him. He was a short figure, stout, blinded by a great light…

"Paul," sounded Mark's voice from behind him.

"Paul?" murmured John thoughtfully.

"The greatest missionary ever to walk the Earth," said Mark. "Or so we think of him."

"How so?" asked John.

"He took everything you see before you: the life, death and resurrection of Christ – he made them known across the Roman Empire."

John studied at the man. "Bet he got beaten up for that."

"Oh, many times," said Mark. "Called a spade a spade. Sometimes people don't like that."

"No," said John.

"He had the nerve to preach to Caesar himself, even in the midst of his captivity," said Mark. "That got him killed."

John frowned. Killed…

"Peter was killed too, of course," said Mark. "And eleven of the twelve disciples, after Judas was replaced. John lived to watch all of them die."

John stared at his face: Mark, the one who had cried out for Joshua's death, now restored as Bishop. Judas, redeemed.

"Do you think some of us are going to die, Mark?" he whispered, and Mark frowned.

"Death comes to all of us in time," he murmured gently.

"You heard about what happened at Oriental Bay."

"Yes," said Mark.

"The wind," said John. "It swept them up, Rau told me. It started a movement, and then three were shot."

"Fear," said Mark, grimacing. "The soldiers were afraid. Now word of it is buzzing all around Parliament."

John stiffened. He saw, suddenly, again, Joshua isolated out, in the intersection, between the Cathedral and the army. John was standing next to him, before the army. He wasn't going to abandon him – couldn't betray him.

"I'm not afraid to die, Mark," he said quietly. "Not for him."

"I know," said Mark.

"My life was nothing compared with what he was doing," said John, remembering the vision. The darkness! The darkness of all people, drawn to Joshua! The darkness, taken into the grave. "My life is nothing compared with his life."

The Price of Redemption

"He healed them, John," said Mark. "Through Rau, God healed the ones who had been shot."

"I know," said John. "But eleven of the twelve disciples died."

"Yes."

"Why?"

"'The blood of the martyrs is the seed of the Church.'" said Mark. "With every death, the movement became stronger. People could see they meant what they said. People could see that for the Christians, the 'little Christs,' their love for Jesus and God was more important to them than their own lives."

John wandered away from him, down the aisle, back to the altar. He reached out to touch the white linen lying over the wood.

"The blood of the martyrs," he said, and his vision blurred. "I always thought martyrdom was for show. For glory."

"What do you think now?" asked Mark.

John slipped his fingers beneath the white linen, to touch the wood.

"It's simply the necessary price," he said, "for doing what is right."

He fleetingly closed his eyes. Such a journey! His life in Whangarei seemed so far away: his business, in optical engineering, helping people to see...

"We are not alone," said Mark, "in the struggle."

"No," said John, looking up at the face of Christ. "We are not alone."

"Death is the gateway into greater life," said Mark.

"Yes," whispered John. "Only the gateway."

"Peace be with you, John," said Mark, and John nodded back to him.

"Peace be with you, Mark," he replied.

They grasped hands, and Mark nodded gently to him. Then he moved away, out of the nave toward his office, to attend to his duties as Bishop.

John looked down at the altar. He grasped a hold of it, lowering himself to his knees. Then, suddenly, instinctively, he crawled inside the structure, closing his eyes. A child – he felt like a child, in that moment. It was a deep offering. A full offering.

From his place inside the altar, he looked back up at the stained glass windows. Jesus, the disciples, Paul...John wondered about Paul. He wasn't like the rest, living with Jesus, eating with him, knowing him. He had resisted him! He had killed his followers! Such a swift change, within, from murderer to martyr.

John liked him. He smiled. Then he heard a movement.

A young man was walking up the aisle.

Hurriedly John removed himself from the altar and rose to his feet.

"Can I help you?" he asked.

The blue eyes penetrated him, partially hidden by blonde curls.

"I doubt it," he said. The eyes lifted to look behind John at the cross, and then to look up to the stained glass windows. His body seemed to stiffen.

"So this is all your bullshit," he said.

John shifted uncomfortably on his feet. The man brushed past him, striding up to the altar.

"Don't touch..." began John, but the young man was grasping a hold of the silver chalice, and now he was throwing it against Jesus, on the cross. The wine was spurting out all over the body of Christ.

"Hey!" cried John. "What are you doing?"

Suddenly Mark Blake's low voice was roaring out, filling the Cathedral.

"Alex!" he cried.

The young man started for a moment, staring at him. Then he broke into a wide dark grin.

"You!" he cried. "Reinstated! I didn't think even the Church could be so stupid!"

John stared at Mark's white face, as he stared at the youth.

"What are you doing here?" asked Mark.

"Just thought I'd check it out," said Alex. "The place where Selena almost made you kill yourself."

Mark's face hardened. "Don't talk about my daughter," he said.

"It was so easy," chided Alex. "So easy to change her, priest! So easy to change you!"

The Price of Redemption

Mark swallowed. "Stay away from her."

"Or you'll do what?" asked Alex. "Kill me?"

And now he laughed, loud and hard, his voice rising to equal the power of Mark's own.

"That'll be the day!" he cried. "You don't have the guts! Get Tristan to do it, that's the way! Use your son, get his hands dirty – I knew you'd kill Joshua that way, high priest! I know you! I know how you think! Pretty robes, pretty windows, but nothing but total shit inside!"

John stared at him, astounded. Who was this man? Alex? The one who had led Selena into the Shrine?

"I planned it all!" boasted Alex, sweeping his arms around the church, dancing in the aisle. "It was so easy! Kill Joshua Davidson: recruit Selena, you, Connor, Tristan – all of you!"

"You bastard," whispered Mark, but John frowned.

"It doesn't make any sense," he said. "Why would you want to kill Joshua?"

Alex shrugged, smiling. "Why not?" he said.

John searched him, and shook his head.

"No," he said. "There's something more."

"Shut up," said Alex swiftly. "You don't know me."

"Something brought you here," said John.

"Bullshit!" said Alex.

"You didn't just come here to boast."

Alex was staring at him. Then he strode back up to the altar, grasped the silver plate with the bread wafers, and smashed these against the image of Christ.

"Mark," whispered John, as Alex reached for another chalice. "Do something."

Now Alex was smashing the next chalice against Christ.

"Do what?" asked Mark. "He's a teenaged delinquent!"

"No," said John, tears filling his eyes. "Help him."

"Help him?" said Mark. "He sent my daughter to hell!"

John glanced at Mark, to see his body stiffening and darkness crossing his face.

"No," said John quickly, reaching out to grasp his shoulder. "No."

Mark stared at him. His body eased, and his face lightened.

"Okay," he whispered. And he walked up to the altar.

Now Alex was grasping another silver plate. Mark grasped his arm.

"Stop," he said.

"No," replied Alex, jerking his arm away from him, reaching for another chalice. "This is for all the bullshit!" And he threw it against the face of Christ. A tile cracked, and wine seeped into the crack.

"You'll destroy it," said Mark. "Is that what you want?"

"Yes," whispered Alex.

"Why?" asked Mark.

"Because it's all lies," said Alex, and his voice lifted again to fill the Cathedral. "It's all lies!" he cried. "Joshua claims to be a King, carries out bullshit healings, raising people from the dead – it's going on again, even with trying to get him out of the way!"

Now he turned to confront Mark. "There is no life," he proclaimed, "only death! There is no heaven, only hell! There is no love, only hatred!

"There is no light!"

Now tears welled up in his eyes, as he stared at Mark.

"Don't you understand, you bastard?" he cried. "You were weak! Do you think I wanted to corrupt Selena? Do you think I wanted to succeed? You were weak, and he was strong! Even Joshua Davidson succumbed to his power! There is no real light, it's all a façade! All pretty stories, and bullshit lies! The truth is, there is only darkness! Only darkness!"

And now Alex hit Mark across the face.

Mark gasped. John moved quickly forward, but Mark stretched out a hand to stop him, turning his face back to Alex.

"What's happened to you?" he asked. "Whose power do you mean? What kind of darkness?"

Alex's face contorted, watching him.

"You know whose power!" he cried. "You've tasted it yourself! You know what kind of darkness! Don't you even read your own text?"

Mark's forehead furrowed. "Satan?" he asked. "I'm not talking about him, Alex – there's someone else."

Alex stared at him. Then he suddenly tightly closed his eyes.

"Don't play with me," he whispered. "Don't manipulate me. I get enough of that at home."

"I'm not playing," said Mark.

"You have no idea what you're up against," whispered Alex.

"I have some idea," said Mark.

"I've seen shit that would make your hair curl," said Alex. "I know what he can do. I know what he's planning to do."

"Your father," said Mark.

Now Alex's eyes snapped open, and naked fear filled his face.

"No," he whispered. "Don't say that. He's not my father."

"Kensington," said Mark, and Alex shuddered.

"Oh, shit," he whispered. "What have I done?"

He backed away from Mark, and John moved slowly forward.

"Why did you come?" asked John, and Alex wrapped his arms around himself, staring up at the windows.

"So far away," he whispered, as if to himself. "He is so far away! Trapped in your sanctuaries, hidden in your constructs…"

"He is here," said John. "He is right here."

"Death is so close," whispered Alex, turning to look at Jesus on the cross. "Always so close. Hell is always so very near. I've crossed the line! I've angered him."

"No," murmured John. "There is still forgiveness."

"There is no forgiveness," said Alex. "Forgiveness is an illusion. There is only retribution: there is only judgement. There is only condemnation."

"There is no condemnation," said John, "for those who trust."

"There is no trust," said Alex. "Only slavery."

"There is love," said John.

"There is obedience," said Alex. "Only obedience, otherwise death – only hell, forever."

"There is life," said John. "Life after death. Life instead of hell. Life after your death."

Now Alex was staring at him, his face naked before him.

"At least in this we can agree," he whispered. "I am a dead man."

John gazed at him, captivated, and now Mark shifted alongside him.

"You have information," said Mark. "Knowledge that is important for our nation."

"I do," said Alex. "But I don't know enough to act, not yet."

"You have the ability to stop him," said Mark. "You have the choice."

Alex laughed quietly. "If you call this choice," he said, "you have rocks in your head."

"No one else can reach him," said Mark. "No one else is close enough. You are the only one who can truly overcome him."

Alex stared into Mark's eyes. "You are asking me to die," he said.

Mark swallowed, and held his eyes. "No," he said. "I am asking for your soul to begin to live."

Alex closed his eyes tightly. "My soul?" he whispered. "You think I have a soul?"

And he opened his eyes to stare up again at the windows. "They are stuck," he said, as if to himself. "They are all stuck up there."

And then, suddenly, he turned and wandered out of the church.

John stared at Mark's face. "What just happened?" he asked.

"Choice," the Bishop said. "The boy has just been given a choice."

"The boy?" asked John. "Or us?"

And now Mark frowned at him. "All, I suppose," he murmured in response, and he wandered up to Jesus, on the cross, reached for white linen, and wiped the wine off Jesus's face.

John wandered up, and fingered the cracked tile in Jesus's cheek. There was something that drew John to the young man. He liked him. How could that be possible? Something profound in his instinct.

"I choose him," said John, and Mark's eyes were on him as he turned to kneel at the altar, and closed his eyes to pray.

Chapter 11

THE UNVEILING

Alex walked out of Saint Peter's. The Beehive rose above him, with Parliament House alongside.

Shifting on his feet, he frowned. His father was there, planning. Should he go in? Find out the truth? He swallowed and then moved forward.

About twenty army soldiers were guarding the entrance to Parliament. Alex smiled at them, and they grimaced back. Two fingered their rifles.

"I have a meeting," he said.

"See security," one answered, and Alex moved forward into the building.

He walked through X-ray and was frisked, but was carrying no weapon, and so passed through. Surprised, Alex wandered up the steps to the first floor.

The circular hallway of the Beehive was before him, the full length windows looking out to the courtyard. No one was there. Alex hesitated, looking up at the grey clouds in the sky. Then he compelled himself forward.

He entered into the lift, and pushed the up button. The Prime

Minister's office was on the ninth floor. Surely he couldn't reach it, he thought. Surely he would be stopped.

The doors on the opposite side of the lift opened. He walked out. The corridor was abandoned.

Alex shivered, this wasn't right. No one around? No one in the Governmental offices? He walked forward, glancing at the names on the abandoned office's doors, and then, finally, reached the office of the Prime Minister.

The door was slightly ajar. He pressed on it gently, and it opened further.

James Connor was standing at the window, staring outside.

"Sir?" whispered Alex, and the man turned to look at him, his middle-aged face looking astonished.

"How did you get in?" he asked, and Alex shook his head, feeling bewildered.

"I don't know," he said.

"Who are you?" asked Connor.

"Alex Kensington," he instinctively answered. Honesty? He was choosing honesty?

"Kensington?" said Connor. "His son?"

"Yes," whispered Alex. Connor frowned then gestured Alex to a seat, and sat at his own desk.

"Do you see this place?" asked Connor, glancing around the room at the plain walls. "It's all redundant now."

"Redundant?" asked Alex.

"There is no democracy any more."

Alex stared at the desk in front of him, empty of papers and purpose.

"It's like a ghost town," muttered Connor. "This place, like…"

"…a graveyard," finished Alex.

He could feel Connor's gaze on his bowed head. "That's right," said Connor.

"There are some who believe in life after death," muttered Alex, staring into his own hands. "What do you think?"

"Life after death?" asked Connor. "I doubt it."

Alex shifted on his seat and then rose to his feet, wandering over to Connor's window, staring at the empty streets outside.

"Why are you here?" asked Connor.

"I don't know," replied Alex. "It just felt right to come."

"Your father seems to be making inroads into the Socialist Party."

Now Alex's throat tightened. "Yes," he said quietly.

"Clarkson trusts him implicitly," said Connor. "Should he?"

Alex frowned. A child was walking across the street outside. Drops were starting to fall out of the sky. Suddenly Alex realised why he had come.

"Do something for me," he said, turning; trusting Connor's perplexed face. "Do something, and you will know the truth."

"And will the truth set me free?" asked Connor wryly. "Will the truth set us all free?"

"Sometimes we have to die first," whispered Alex, feeling his body stiffen, "before we can truly live."

Connor's brow furrowed and then he nodded, and Alex led him out of the office toward Parliament House, where the Governor General was enthroned.

Connor passed Alex as he strode across the inner bridge from the first floor of the Beehive to the first floor of Parliament House, taking back the lead. He stopped at the four officers guarding the way, gesturing to Alex.

"He's with me," he said, and they nodded. Then Alex followed him where he had never explored, turning corners, walking through chambers, until they walked into the Debating Chamber.

The room was deserted.

"Get Clarkson," said Alex.

"Clarkson will be with Kensington," said Connor.

"Get him," said Alex. "Bring him here, and you will know the truth."

Connor held his gaze, his expression troubled, and then turned and left.

Alex wrapped his arms around himself. Death! He was inviting death!

He looked up at the plaques surrounding the Chamber, the images of New Zealand soldiers at war. This was the army, in true defence of New Zealand; in true defence of freedom. Now there were bugs behind the images of heroism. He looked at the Throne of the Speaker of the House, and the abandoned golden mace sitting on the desk in front. He looked across all of the seats of Parliament – the place where different voices had debated, where the views of every day New Zealanders had been upheld.

"God defend New Zealand," whispered Alex, and now the doors into the Chamber were thrust open.

It was his father. Alex stared at him, at his towering height and penetrating blue gaze. Alex had expected rage, but he saw no rage. Instead he saw cold calculation.

"Do you really think you are in control?" asked Kensington, striding toward him. "Now, after all these years?"

Alex swallowed. Speak? No, don't speak. Just stand and take it: take it, and take it, and take it…

His father's fists were on his shirt. He was being dragged along the Chamber, and now Kensington was pushing him back down onto the Throne.

"Do you think you are the King?" he asked.

Alex stared up at his face, starting to writhe beneath him. Silence! Keep silent!

"You are not the King," said Kensington. "You are not God. You are just a worthless piece of shit that needs to be flushed down the toilet."

Kensington pulled out a kitchen knife, and Alex shuddered. It was from within Parliament! His father had secured the weapon from within.

The doors to the Debating Chamber sounded again.

"I couldn't find Clarkson…" Connor's voice trailed off as he strode inside, the doors closing behind him. Now he stood a few steps away, staring.

Alex longed to cry out for help, but he bit his tongue.

"No," said Kensington calmly to Connor. "You won't be able to find him."

"Why not?" asked Connor.

"Because I am the one in control," said Kensington. "That is the truth you both must learn, right now."

And he thrust the knife into the left side of Alex's chest.

Blinding pain! Alex cried out, against his own will. He desperately, instinctively, reached out – he erratically grasped at his father's shirt. Something was punctured, inside! His breath! His breath was collapsing from within him.

"What are you doing?" cried Connor's horrified voice.

"Playing chess," said Kensington.

"You'll go to prison!" said Connor.

"No I won't," said Kensington, smiling. "Because you love your daughter more than you love truth or justice."

Alex stared up at his face, sucking in breath. His vision was darkening. Their voices were sounding hollow.

His father pulled out his cell-phone. Alex heard the tone, 111.

"Please come!" said Kensington into the phone. "It's my son! I think he just tried to commit suicide…"

There would be no police, only the ambulance! There was no need to hide evidence, let it be readily visible – seen, but not understood. Remove the recording: re-record it. Suppress it.

Alex glanced over at Connor. Was he surprised? Yes. He hadn't known the truth. Now he knew! Now it was up to him. They both could testify! If only…if only he could overcome the fear…

Connor's eyes were on him, his dismay. Had Alex's trust been justified? He could see the pain in Connor's eyes. His daughter? Risk his daughter again? Try to save New Zealand again, only this time from the real threat?

Alex held his eyes.

"Is there life after death?" he whispered. "What do you think, Prime Minister?"

Then darkness took him.

Chapter 12

PRECIPITATION

James sat in the Emergency Department. Fatima was sick, so Rachel had been landed again with the dogsbody job. They were on call, so he was needed. Good job, too, some of the ED House Officers were looking way out of their depth.

He scanned his own typed notes for the patient just seen. It was a pretty straight forward admission: pneumonia, IV antibiotics, and straight onto the ward. House Officer material. Where was Rachel? Floating about somewhere, seeing someone else.

How many had they admitted so far? James looked at the crinkled piece of paper in his hands: nine. Ridiculous! Winter. Soon they'd be having patient beds in the corridors again...

They must discharge more...that woman, upstairs! The neurotic one. But not Margaret, not yet. He needed another patient on morphine first...

Swallowing, he pushed away the thought. It wasn't his fault! It was the hell his damned father...

Suddenly the doors into ED thrust open, and a stretcher was pushed through.

James glanced up at the case. It was a youth, unconscious, with respiratory distress. His mind worked quickly: airway, breathing, circulation…

Where were the ED docs?

"Chest perforation injury," said the ambulance officer.

"I'm not…"

"I think the lung's collapsed on the left side."

"Tension pneumothorax?"

"O2 sats were 82 per cent on air, 91 per cent on high flow oxygen."

"Okay," said James.

"Take him in there!" said a nurse, and the boy was wheeled into a resuscitation room.

James pored over him. His breathing was laboured, his pulse about one hundred, regular.

"Blood pressure?"

"Stable," said the nurse.

James reached for his stethoscope. The right lung had good air entry, but the left lung had no breath sounds. He frowned. The puncture wound, what was it – a knife?

"Attempted suicide," said the ambulance officer. "He was in the Debating Chamber of the Beehive."

"Fitting," muttered James wryly. But suicide? Seriously? A knife into the left side of the chest?

"Like shit," he said under his breath, and then Rachel was there, on the other side of the bed.

"What happened?" asked Rachel.

"Stab wound," James said, pointing. "It punctured his chest wall and lung."

Rachel frowned, looking at the boy's face under the oxygen mask.

"What do you think?" asked James. "Suicide?"

Rachel smiled at him, looking bemused. "Suicide?"

"Yeah," muttered James. "That's what I thought, too."

"Isn't this an ED case?" asked Rachel.

James shrugged. "Looks like it just became ours."

"Well, he can tell us what happened when he wakes up."

"Damned right," said James. "In the meantime, get an urgent Chest X-ray."

"Okay," said Rachel.

"And…" James hesitated, looking at her face. Start morphine? No. No, he mustn't, the oxygen level was down. "Nothing," he said. "Just get onto the Chest X-ray fast."

"Done," said Rachel, and she quickly left the room.

James reached again for the boy's pulse. One hundred. Too fast, but understandable. He was stable enough: one collapsed lung wasn't enough to kill, only to incapacitate.

To incapacitate. James frowned. A puncture wound to the lateral aspect of the left chest. It had missed the heart, almost deliberately. Clearly it was not self-inflicted. Had the police been called? He tucked the thought in the back of his mind, and Rachel returned with the radiographer.

They wheeled the mobile X-ray machine in, took the X-ray, and wheeled the machine out again. The boy was starting to stir. Rachel reached out to lay a hand on his shoulder. The nurse turned up with a chart and stickers: his name was Alex Kensington.

The patient gasped, and Rachel murmured something over him. She was good that way, at calming the patients. Soon the radiologist was back, handing him a large yellow envelope with the film. James put the X-ray up on the light box, and turned the light on. The right lung was black with the normal white shadowing out to the ribs, but the left side showed black with a dense white shadow to the left of the heart.

"What do you see?" he asked Rachel, and she looked up.

"Collapsed lung," she said, "left side."

"Tension pneumothorax?" he asked.

"No," she said. "The left side of the chest isn't over-inflated."

"Better watch the dressing is right," said James, "or we might just give him a tension pneumothorax. A doctor-induced one way valve, sucking in air into the chest, collapsing the lung further – it would be embarrassing, not to mention life-threatening."

Rachel grimaced at him, and smiled, and then the patient's eyes were open. Rachel turned back to him.

"It's all right," she murmured. "You're in hospital. You'll be okay now."

"No," he whispered, reaching to grasp onto her white coat. "I won't be okay."

James looked at him, suddenly caught by his manner.

"You're safe here," he repeated. "Murderers aren't allowed in hospitals."

"Murderers?" asked the boy.

James smirked. "Think we were going to buy the suicide story?" he asked.

Alex's eyes were on him, blue and intense. His breathing was laboured. Rachel's hand was still on his shoulder.

"What happened?" asked James.

Alex swallowed. He looked between them, and then replied.

"Chess," he whispered.

James straightened, frowning at him. "Shit," he said.

"What?" asked Rachel, looking between them.

"What kind of mental illness leads to this kind of surgical precision, Doctor Connor?" asked James.

"Doctor Connor?" whispered Alex, and now he was staring at Rachel.

"You said chess," continued James. "Which piece are you?"

But Alex's eyes were on him, and James felt uncomfortable with the stare.

"That's not the right question," he said. "The real question is, which piece are you?"

James shifted on his feet. "I'm not a piece in someone else's game," he said.

"That's what you think," said Alex. "We're all cogs in his wheel."

"Whose wheel?" asked Rachel. "Who did this to you?"

Alex looked at her again, and reached out his right hand to touch her face.

99

"I hope you never find out," he whispered, and he gasped with the pain of his movement.

"Morphine," said James instinctively, without thinking. "You need pain relief."

Alex's eyes widened in fear. "No," he whispered. "No morphine."

"No morphine?" asked James, perplexed. The young man would refuse it?

"I have to think," said Alex. "I can't be groggy, or sleep. I have to be able to think."

"Think about what?" asked James intuitively, stirred by some hidden memory. "Your father's bullshit?"

James clenched his teeth. What had just come out of his mouth?

Alex stared back at him. "Don't," he whispered. "Don't."

Then someone else strode into the room.

James stared at him. He was tall, with blue penetrating eyes, rather like Alex's, only with a harrowing intensity.

"Excuse me," said James, "this area is off limits."

"This is my son," said the man. "You will discharge him right now."

James felt himself bristling. He clenched his fists slightly.

"I will not discharge him," he said coldly. "He will be admitted and cared for."

"I am his guardian," said the man.

"What is your name?" asked Rachel, and the man turned to her and smiled.

"Kensington," he said. "That's all you need to know, Doctor Rachel Connor."

Rachel's face looked a little flustered.

"Leave her alone," said James. "You are this boy's father?"

"Yes," said Kensington.

"What happened?" asked James, and the cold stare penetrated him.

"Shouldn't I be asking you that same question?" he said.

James shifted on his feet. He felt his teeth clenching again, and forced his jaw to relax.

"I'll ask you a second time," said James. "What happened?"

"I fell from a great height," said Alex, from the bed.

"What?" asked James, looking at him.

"It was an accident," said Alex.

"That's what they all say," said Kensington.

James looked between them, frowning, and Rachel's eyes were on Alex.

"Discharge him," said Kensington. "I'll sign the papers."

"No," James said, staring straight at him. "He's not stable enough to be out in the community."

"He has one collapsed lung," said Kensington. "He will live."

"Not if he develops a tension pneumothorax," said James.

"Leave the dressing off then."

"Pneumonia! A pneumothorax. He needs to be monitored. He needs oxygen."

Now Kensington reached over and pulled the mask off Alex's face.

James watched as his breathing became more laboured. His body stiffened.

"I will not discharge him," he said.

"I will put in a complaint," said Kensington.

James shifted again on his feet. "I won't discharge him."

"I'll complain to the Medical Council."

James swallowed. He looked at Rachel's face; her forehead was creasing.

"He makes the decision," she said. "Alex is legally old enough to decide."

"You already have had two complaints before the Medical Council," said Kensington to James. "One more complaint would end your career."

Now James flushed. Rachel was staring at him.

"Alex makes the decision," she said firmly. "This isn't about any of us, it's about him."

"I choose to self-discharge," whispered Alex, and James looked at him. He was struggling, in pain, with no pain relief, sucking in breath.

101

"You need care," whispered James, and Alex shrugged, and was silent.

James looked at Kensington. "Give us five minutes," he said. "We need to arrange the paperwork."

"All right," said Kensington, and he smiled and left the room.

James stared at Rachel. Her face looked white. He looked at Alex; his face looked resigned.

"Abuse," said James. "Abuse!"

"I'm not a minor any more," said Alex. "I'm eighteen. You have no duty to report."

"No duty?" said Rachel. "He is criminal!"

"Don't!" said Alex, grasping her arm. "Listen to me, there are bigger forces at work here."

"Bigger forces?" asked Rachel, frowning.

"Your father," said Alex. "You don't realise how important he is."

Rachel shook her head in confusion. "What do you mean?" she asked. "His career is over!"

"No," said Alex. "That was one of the reasons for the killing of Davidson, to get Connor out of the way."

"The killing of Davidson?" cried Rachel.

"There are bigger battles, Rachel Connor," gasped Alex. "Joshua knew that. Don't you?"

James stared at him. "Kensington's in Parliament?"

"Yes," whispered Alex.

"And Connor, too."

"Yes."

"Clarkson is the opposition. Set up humiliation for Connor, and then enhance the alternative side."

"Yes," said Alex.

"A hidden take over," said James. "Manipulation, control: victory."

"There is no democracy," said Alex. "Anita Mayes wants what is right. She will not achieve it."

James grimaced then walked over to a cupboard, pulled out a form, and returned to his side.

"Here," he said. "The self-discharge papers."

"If you do this," said Rachel, "you might die."

"I'm already dead," whispered Alex. "At least this way no one else need die."

James shook his head, while Alex signed the form, pulled the drip out of his hand, rose to his feet, and gathered his unbuttoned shirt back around him.

"A dressing," said Rachel, and hurriedly reached for some gauze and tape, and attended to his wound.

"Thanks," whispered Alex, and he walked unsteadily out of the room.

James walked out, with Rachel behind him, and watched Kensington put a firm hand on Alex's shoulder as they walked out of ED together.

"Bastard," whispered James, staring at Kensington, and he felt, within, a rising torrent of rage. "You utter bastard!"

And now he strode out of ED, into the corridor, and toward the stairs.

Rachel was suddenly behind him. "Where are you going?" she cried. "What's wrong?"

"He's a bastard," said James, "that's what's wrong!" And he strode up the stairs, two at a time.

Rachel was running after him, panting, to keep up. "We can't do anything!" she said. "We should call the police."

"We can't call the police!" said James. "He'll kill him before the police arrive!"

He stopped, in the stairwell, and suddenly punched the wall.

"James!" cried Rachel's voice. Her hand came to his arm, and he threw her off. Pain! Pain, in his hand! He might have broken a metacarpal!

"Shit!" he said, and he kept striding up the steps.

He reached Level Eight, and moved out of the stairwell toward the ward.

"James!" cried Rachel. "You can't go in there like this!"

103

"Go to hell," he said, and he launched himself into the ward and down the corridor.

Rachel was still there, fluttering after him. He tried to shove her away, but she continued.

"Go and see some patients!" he said. "Go!"

But she wouldn't go.

His hand was aching, and fury consumed him. He strode forward into the medication bay. Where was Kate? She was there, arranging an IV line. The keys were on a strap around her neck.

He strode up to her, with his hand outstretched.

"Give me the keys," he said. Kate was staring at him, her face white. Now Rachel was alongside, and Kate was staring at Rachel.

James drew Kate's eyes back. "You will give me the keys," he said, "and you will do the injection yourself."

"James," whispered Rachel's voice. "What are you doing?"

James blocked her voice out. His vision was becoming a tunnel, focussed on Kate.

"Give me the keys, woman," he said, "or I will end your career."

Now the nurse looked caught with tears.

"Don't," whispered Rachel's voice. "Don't."

Kate handed him the keys, and then ran away.

James turned to the Controlled Drugs safe, and turned the key.

"James," said Rachel's voice. "Don't do this. Don't."

He pulled out a morphine ampoule, and reached for needle and syringe.

"Oh my God," said Rachel's voice. "Oh my God, don't."

And now, in front of her, he drew up the morphine, changed the needle, and injected himself.

Now, with the morphine on board, he dared to look at Rachel's face. She looked pale. He watched her sink back against the wall, sliding down to the ground. She was staring ahead of herself, as if in shock; as if shocked that he could dare to do such a thing.

He couldn't feel. His vision was becoming a haze. He swayed, on his feet. He staggered down the corridor. He somehow found the isolation room, opened the door, closed it, and locked it.

The bed…it was right there. Sleep! Sleep, and never wake up…

He collapsed on the bed, and sleep took him.

Chapter 13

CONFLICT

Rachel sat against the wall. There was no one else around. No one else had seen what she had just seen.

Stunned, she stared out ahead of herself. Where was Kate? She leaned her head back, and closed her eyes tightly. How could it be possible? It wasn't possible, was it?

She was a doctor, on call. Her consultant was incapacitated. She had to work, she had to see the patients. They were sick! She had to ensure their safety.

She shakily pushed herself to her feet, and reached out to lock the Controlled Drugs safe.

"Oh my God," she whispered. Then she tucked the key safely into her own white coat pocket.

Where was he? In the isolation room. Go to him? Go? Her legs were still shaking. Confront him?

"Oh," she whispered. "No…"

Kate, what had happened to her? She had run away. Tears filled Rachel's eyes, and she blinked them rapidly away. Think! Hold it together.

Kate's face appeared at the entrance to the medication bay, her eyes wide, her forehead creased. Rachel grasped her arm and drew her into the office, closing the door.

"Kate," she whispered, "what the hell just happened?"

Kate was staring at her. She looked on the verge of collapse.

"I don't want the keys," she whispered. "I don't want the keys any more."

Rachel stared back at her, and then looked down at the keys in her pocket.

"How long?" she asked, choking. "How long…?"

"A month," replied Kate. "That I know about."

"And before you?" asked Rachel. "Nurses resigning? Resigning over him?"

"I don't know," whispered Kate.

"Does the Charge Nurse know?" asked Rachel.

"No," said Kate.

Rachel swallowed. "Does Fatima know?"

"No," said Kate.

Rachel closed her eyes. "Then it's just you and me?"

"Yes," said Kate.

"Shit," whispered Rachel, and she covered her face with her hands.

Kate's hand came to her arm. "It's all right," the nurse said. "It's not your fault. It's not your responsibility."

"Bullshit," whispered Rachel into her hands. "Now that I know, it is my responsibility."

"Don't report him," pleaded Kate. "I don't know what he'll do! He scares me, Rachel!"

Rachel heard her trembling voice. She lifted her hands away from her own face to grasp Kate's shoulders, holding her eyes.

"Leave," she said. "Resign."

"What?" asked Kate.

"Leave now," said Rachel. "The others will be able to cover. Get an off-work certificate."

"He'll find me," whispered Kate. "He'll end my career."

"No," said Rachel, holding her eyes. "I'll handle his reaction. Your part will become redundant, Kate, now I've seen it with my own eyes. I have much more power than you: I am his colleague."

"Will you testify against him?" asked Kate. "Will you testify?"

Rachel swallowed, and found herself holding her breath.

"I'll do whatever I need to do," she whispered. "Whatever I need to do to keep the patients safe."

Tears welled up in Kate's eyes. She grasped a hold of Rachel's arms.

"You're a good doctor, Rachel," she said. "Don't ever forget that, whatever he says, whatever happens. The patients need you to act."

Rachel felt her body begin to shake again. "Go," she whispered through tears. "Go now. Find a good place to work. Find a safe place."

"Thank you!" whispered Kate, grasping her hand tightly. "Thank you."

Kate reached for her bag, and Rachel watched the relieved tears spill down her face as she hurried down the corridor and out of the ward.

Rachel was alone. She reached up a hand to lean against the doorframe. She closed her eyes tightly, feeling giddy. Then her locator beeped. She looked: it was ED. Another patient. Taking a deep breath, Rachel gripped her stethoscope and strode down the corridor. Then she heard moaning coming from Room Two.

She glanced inside to see Margaret on her bed, with her eyes closed and her head lolling on her pillow.

Rachel stood quietly at the doorway. Margaret was feeling bony pain, gnawing, from the metastasized cancer. Rachel hesitated and then moved forward, reaching for her chart.

Morphine. Her second dose had been signed off just thirty minutes before: five milligrams. Rachel looked from the chart to Margaret's face.

"Bullshit," she whispered. "You gave her water, you bastard."

And she reached to cross out the dose and write another.

"Stop," said James's voice from behind her. Rachel stiffened. Margaret's eyes opened, and she smiled gently at her.

"Hello, Doctor Connor," she said.

"Hello," replied Rachel. "How's your pain?"

"I can manage," said Margaret. "'The Lord is my refuge.'"

Rachel stared at her, and then grasped her chart and stiffly left the room.

"What are you doing?" asked James's voice.

"I'm being her doctor," replied Rachel stiffly, briskly returning to the Controlled Drugs safe and reaching for the keys in her pocket.

"She has a set regime," said James. "You'll fuel an addiction if you add to what we have prescribed."

"Yeah, right," said Rachel under her breath, reaching to unlock the safe. "An addiction for a cancer patient? Like shit!"

She reached inside and grasped an ampoule of morphine. James's hand came to her arm.

"You can't do this," he said.

"Move your hand," replied Rachel, reaching with her left hand to the drug record.

"You have no proof," said James, and Rachel flicked his hand off.

"No proof?" she cried. "I saw you! I saw you with my own eyes!"

"And I saw you," said James smoothly. "With the safe open, and the keys in your hands. Kate was nowhere in sight."

Rachel turned to stare at his controlled face. "Step aside," she whispered. "I'm treating our patient."

"No you're not," said James calmly. "I'm the consultant, and I say 'no'."

"You're incapacitated," said Rachel. "You're under the influence of opiates and unfit to perform your job."

Now James's face flushed. "That's defamation," he said, and Rachel stared at him.

"Are you serious?" she asked.

"You're mentally unstable," he said. "You have PTSD, and it's incapacitating you in your job. I saw you collapse just now against the wall."

"I collapsed because I had just witnessed a colleague I care about shooting up on the job!" she cried. "Putting his patients in danger, leaving one in pain, and crucifying his own career!"

"I won't let you crucify me," whispered James, his face tight. "I won't let you destroy my future."

"I'm not going to play these games, James!" said Rachel. "You must know that! You must know that about me!"

"I'll take your career, Connor!" said James. "Just as your father's career was taken before you!"

Rachel stared at him, and tears filled her eyes.

"Do you think I care about my career?" she said. "What use is a career, when our profession is turned on its face? Patients existing for the sake of the doctor? What of the integrity of our profession? I care about our shared vocation! I care about the patients! If I have to risk my own career, I will do so!"

And she strode down the corridor.

"You have no evidence!" he called out to her. "Your word against mine, Rachel! I will tear you to pieces in court!"

Rachel stopped, staring out ahead of herself, and then she turned to look at him.

"I don't care," she said, and his face whitened as she felt her voice becoming stronger and stronger. "It's not just your word against mine, James," she said. "It's the truth! And I'll stand by it, even if I lose my career! I'll stand by it, James!"

And with this she turned, and took the morphine to Margaret.

Chapter 14

EXPOSURE

Alex stared up at the Cathedral. It was early, before the service. He swallowed. Selena would be in there, with Mark Blake, before the others. He hesitated. Then he propelled himself up the steps.

The Cathedral was quiet. Alex stood for a moment just inside the glass doors, looking up the aisle to the tiled painting of Jesus on the cross. There was a crack in his cheek, where he'd thrown the communion at him. Alex frowned. He looked over his body, stretched out – at the wrists nailed to the horizontal plank, and the feet nailed to the vertical plank – and tears pricked his eyes.

He took a hesitant deep breath, and noticed another wound in the figure of Jesus: a piercing, in his side. Alex started, and reached to finger his own wound, on his left side. He looked back at Jesus, to see the blood dripping down his face from the crown of thorns, and the blood pouring out from the wound in his side.

This is my blood, given for you.

"My God," he whispered. "The heart! They stabbed you in the heart."

He stared at the one who had offered himself willingly: the one he had assaulted. He remembered Joshua, on his knees before Tristan, the blood dripping down his face from under their cursed crown, as he was lifting his face to the sky.

"Father," he had cried, *"don't hold it against them! They have no idea what they are doing!"*

"No idea," whispered Alex, and he swayed on his feet, and now Selena was moving down the aisle toward him.

"Alex!" she said. He stood staring at the face of Christ. He lifted his eyes to the stained glass windows. Peter, John, James, and images of Jesus: they were all stuck! All stuck, high up, pretty, out of reach – contained! Contained in the container of the church, away from the carnage; away from those going through hell...

His eyes settled on a short figure, sturdy, surrounded by light. Who was that? Paul? The one responsible for spreading word of the resurrection beyond Israel?

Alex gazed at him, and now he felt Selena's fingers passing between his own.

"Alex," said her gentle voice, and he trembled, and dared to look at her face; her kind warm blue eyes, generous black curls, and quirky smile. She was beautiful. He gasped, and reached to grasp at the pain in his side. What had he and his father done to her? How had she turned back from their assault? Innocence! She looked innocent, like a child.

He closed his eyes, and found himself leaning into her. Her arm was around his shoulders, and now her arms were moving fully around him. He was being held! Gently, she was holding him! He had never been held, not since...not since that terrible day.

Now she was drawing him up the aisle.

He followed her, like a child, and she drew him onto a seat, near the front. He sat next to her, closed his eyes again, and leaned against her shoulder.

How long did he have, in this sanctuary? Just a few minutes? Just a few minutes to rest, before the crowd arrived? Before he must escape and return to hell?

"I'll take care of you," whispered Selena, holding tightly to his hand.

"I'll love you." He gasped, and drew his knees up to his chest. Love? A sister's love? Why did it hurt so badly?

"I'm loving too," he confessed, and pain engulfed him; need engulfed him.

"You could stay," said Selena. "You could stay here, with us."

"No," pleaded Alex, still keeping his eyes shut. "No."

"I'll talk to Dad," said Selena. "He'll make it easier for you. He'll help you to adjust."

"No!" cried Alex, and he launched himself to his feet, and now Mark Blake was standing in front of him, in purple, black and white.

His blue eyes were searching him, inviting him, like…like a father.

"Don't," whispered Alex, and he shook his head and turned away, and tried to brush past Selena, down the aisle and away into safety. But now Mark was grasping his arm, turning him back. His eyes! His eyes were reaching him.

"Join us," he said gently. "Make your home here."

Alex shook his head vigorously. "Can't," he whispered. "I can't."

"You need to escape from hell," said Mark quietly, his forehead creasing. "You need to find true life."

"Don't you know your own theology?" asked Alex, smiling wryly, reaching out to grasp Mark's shoulder as a sharp stabbing pain again pierced his side. "I can't find my own way out of hell, Father! I need to be rescued!"

Mark was smiling gently back at him, holding him up by the arms, as he swayed.

"You have a Christian background," he murmured.

"Catholic," whispered Alex. "My father was Catholic."

"And your mother?" asked Mark, and pain grasped Alex's chest again. Now he found himself clinging to Mark with both hands.

"Dead," he whispered. "Shot in the head."

Mark's face paled. "Dear God," he whispered, and Alex shook his head.

"Not 'dear,'" he whispered, "because how could God ever be 'dear'

113

after that?"

"Was it...?" Mark hesitated, and seemed to make himself continue. "Was it your...?"

Alex rose fully to his feet and shoved Mark back.

"No, you bastard!" he cried. "It wasn't my father who shot my mother!"

"I'm sorry!" said Mark quickly. "I'm sorry, Alex! It's just..." Tears filled the priest's eyes.

Alex stared at him, at the father crying. "What are you doing?" he whispered.

"I understand now," said Mark.

"Understand what?" asked Alex.

"How..." And Mark turned his face away, closing his eyes tightly, but made himself turn back again. "How you knew how to corrupt me. And...why you would want to."

Alex searched the man. Why corrupt him? Mark had accidentally killed his wife! Twist the knife! Use the daughter!

"But why did you want to kill Joshua?" asked Mark.

Alex found his eyes drawn to Jesus on the cross. He swallowed.

"The lies," he whispered. "I couldn't stand the lies."

"What lies?" asked Mark.

"That God is good," said Alex. "That he gives a shit. That there is anything in this Universe more powerful than evil and pain."

He cast his eyes over the wounded man pinned to the tree.

"Strange," he whispered, tilting his head, "how the answer can be right in front of you all the time, and still you cannot see it."

"You have such insight," said Mark, and Alex glanced back at him and shrugged.

"Doesn't seem to matter," he said.

"For evil or for good," said Mark. "That is the battle for your soul, Alex: whether your great insight will be given over for evil or for good."

"You've forgotten," muttered Alex, "I don't have a soul."

"Bullshit," said Mark, and Alex gasped, gazing at his face.

"I'm so sorry, Alex," continued Mark, and now, before Alex, his eyes filled with tears again. "You needed me to be strong, and I was weak! I was weak."

Weeping grasped Alex. He clung again to Mark's robes as his chest was racked with pain.

"I'm sorry too!" he cried. "I'm sorry."

"I know," whispered Mark. "I know."

Mark was grasping his shoulders, and now Alex reached out to the man out of his own choice. Now he instinctively reached up fingers, like a child, to touch his face...

A bell chimed. Mark straightened, looking surprised.

"Oh," he said.

"What?" breathed Alex.

"Quarter to ten," said Mark. "The call to church."

Alex stared at his eyes, and clenched his teeth. "Oh, shit," he whispered.

Mark gazed at him, his forehead creasing again. "I have to go," he murmured.

"So do I," whispered Alex.

Mark's face turned grave. "Stay with us," he said. "Leave that Shrine behind. Join our one instead."

"That would be a death sentence," said Alex. "You know that."

Mark grimaced, and reached out a hand to grasp Alex's face.

"Courage," he said firmly to him, and the eyes reached him; the eyes fortified him. "Have courage to do the right thing."

"I can't save myself from hell, Father," whispered Alex back to him. "The question is, can you?"

Mark stared at him. "Dear God," he whispered, "you are actually asking." And Alex shook his head.

"Not 'dear' God!" he insisted. "You keep getting that wrong!"

Mark smiled, and Alex found himself smiling, and he shook himself and made himself turn.

Selena was grasping his hand again, and now she led him down the aisle and out of the Cathedral.

Alex stood on the steps of Saint Peter's. The sky was grey. He looked across the street to the Beehive beyond. His father was infiltrating! And Connor was there in the backbenches, humiliated, trampled upon by Alex's own design at the desire of his father, but still there. He was armed with the truth, but could he use it? Would he?

The army was still carrying rifles in the courtyard, facing outwards toward the street.

Ironic, Alex thought: the true threat was within.

Kensington had directly threatened Connor's daughter. He had deliberately injured Alex to put him in the path of Rachel, and had deliberately provoked James Lester.

He was taking a grip around Connor's heart.

Would Connor speak with Clarkson? Would he inform him of what he had seen? He would risk defamation charges, and from this an entire ending of his career. He would risk endangering Rachel.

Alex had used Connor once, putting him in harm's way. But this time it was Connor's choice. This time it must be his choice.

Alex frowned. Choice. It was risky! Risky to start trusting other people.

Selena squeezed his hand. Startled, he looked at her. He had forgotten she was still there.

"Are you going back?" she asked, and he reached to touch her fine face.

"I am," he said. "I have to."

"You could leave," said Selena. "You're quite capable of leaving."

"How did you leave?" asked Alex, touching her black curls. "How did you recover, Selena?"

She smiled slightly and tears filled her eyes, somehow making her look prettier.

"Dad," she whispered. "Dad."

"Makes sense," said Alex with pain, "but I don't have a 'Dad,'

Selena. I don't have any family. Kensington is the only home I have."

"It's not a home, Alex!" said Selena. "It's a tomb!"

Alex grimaced at her candour. "I know it's not a home, Lena!" he said. "But it's the only thing I have! It's the only thing I ever did have, since Mum…"

And now he closed his eyes again.

"How can I blame him for anything?" he asked. "We were both thrust into hell together!"

"You have to let him go."

"I can't abandon him," said Alex. "I remember, Lena! I remember how he was. How he used to be."

And now Alex saw him again, ten years younger, face warm, eyes gentle…Alex laughed with him! Reached out his seven-year-old fingers to touch his face…

Now the face was rigid. Now the eyes were deathly cold.

"No," whispered Alex. "Oh, God, no."

"Both parents lost," murmured Selena, by his side. "I understand."

"No, you don't," said Alex. "You wanted your father dead: I want mine to live."

Selena gasped, and Alex turned to her and shook his head.

"I'm sorry!" he said. "I'm a bastard! I'm sorry. Your father was right, there was a reason why I knew how to manipulate you both! There was a reason."

"For evil or for good," murmured Selena, "a reason."

"I want to save him," said Alex suddenly, and Selena shook her head.

"You can't save him," she said.

"If anyone can save him, I can," said Alex.

"Alex." Selena was grasping his arm now, as her father had done before her. The eyes were finding him. "Do not try to save your father," she said. "He has given himself over, Alex! He's given himself fully over."

"Given his soul to Satan?" whispered Alex. "Didn't we also?"

"Some people have gone too far!" said Selena. "Some people are

117

beyond our reach!"

"No," whispered Alex, shaking his head. "I can't believe that. I won't believe it."

"Alex!" Now Selena was shaking him. Surprised, Alex stared at her. "You can't stay in that place!" she said. "You're not stronger than him, Alex, not alone! He will swallow you up, and your soul will be taken, and...and..." Now she started to shake her head. "I don't want to lose you."

Alex reached his fingers now to touch her face. Tears? Tears, on her cheeks, for him? He stroked the tears away.

"Don't worry about me," he whispered. "I still have strength within me."

"He stabbed you, Alex," whispered Selena, her face contorting. "How much longer until he kills you?"

Alex stared at her and swallowed, grasping her hand into his own.

"He won't kill me," he said. "It's not part of his plan, and he always sticks with his plan."

"What if we disrupt his plan?" asked Selena.

Alex gazed at her, and touched her face again. "You have guts, Selena," he said. "I've always admired that about you."

And he turned on his heel, set his jaw, and walked down the steps of the Cathedral to the street below.

Chapter 15

CATHARSIS

Alex stood outside the Shrine. He was late. He swallowed, looked up at the all-seeing eye, and compelled himself to enter.

It was dark. He could smell blood.

"Where were you?" asked his father's voice.

"Researching," whispered Alex.

"How is Selena?"

Chills went up his spine. "She is with her father," he replied.

"The wayward Bishop, reinstated," said Kensington, and his voice was laced with sarcasm. "But Mark Blake is no King."

Alex stared ahead of himself. The dark altar was coming into form, with black linen, and golden chalices. Behind the altar was the broken cross.

The black priest reached for the golden chalice. "Come here," said Kensington.

Oh God, pleaded Alex within. His side ached, and his breathing caught. Obey him? Obey?

He moved forward to stand before his father.

"Kneel," said Kensington.

Shit! Alex felt. *Shit!* He knelt.

"Now, drink," said Kensington, and again the chalice was before him. Alex stared into it. Blood. The chalice was filled with blood.

Nausea filled him. He closed his eyes tightly, but could not escape the smell. To willingly drink it was impossible.

"No," he whispered. His father struck him across the face, and pain seized his chest, and now, instinctively, he grasped the arm that had struck him.

"Stop!" he said. "Stop!"

"I will not stop!" said his father's voice. "I will not stop until you drink every last drop!"

He was being dragged again across the floor, again up against the wall, but this time he resisted.

"No!" he said, fighting the arms, twisting his own wound. "You can't do this!"

He fought him, but his father was taller; his father's rage was stronger.

"I will do it," he said, and now he began to punch him in the wound in his side.

Excruciating pain took Alex. In agony he stared at the broken cross.

"God!" he cried out. "God!" Might he die? Might his father break his ribs?

"Don't try crying out to God for help," said his father. "Why would God bother with a worthless piece of shit like you?"

Alex sagged against the wall to the ground, and the priest thrust the golden chalice into his hands.

"Drink," he said. "There is only one god, and he is me."

Alex caught his breath, staring into the chalice. Play? Play along with the tyrant?

"What do you want me to do?" he whispered.

"I want you to stop the enemy," said Kensington.

"Which enemy?" asked Alex, staring at the blood.

"The Joshua Movement," said Kensington. "I want you to kill Rau Petera."

Confused, Alex looked up into his father's white intense face, still gripping onto the chalice with both of his hands.

"What?" he asked. His father was afraid of a few singing people on a beach?

"Stop their lies," said the black priest.

"What lies?" asked Alex.

"The deception is all through Parliament," said Kensington. "Rumours that Joshua is alive again. Propaganda that Rau Petera miraculously healed those the army shot, that Rau has the power of Joshua."

Alex stared into his face. "Rau Petera?" he asked. "The Maori priest?"

"The leader of the movement."

"But he ran away, didn't he?" asked Alex, for a moment taken out of himself. "He wasn't there when Joshua was shot."

"And after Petera," said Kensington, "I want you to kill John Robertson."

"John…" Alex closed his eyes tightly, feeling his hands trembling on the chalice of blood.

"Kill Petera and Robertson, and there will be no witnesses."

"Witnesses?" breathed Alex, looking back up at him.

"To the false resurrection, imbecile!" spat Kensington. "A false resurrection for a false god, all over again! Stop the lies, Alex! Kill them at their source."

His father moved the chalice to his left hand, and put a gun into his right hand.

Alex jerked, looking down at it. The gun felt cold and awkward. His fingers curled around it, and into the trigger.

"Kill the two apostates," said Kensington. "They are not part of the plan."

Alex felt dizzy. His chest was still stabbing with pain. The chalice of blood was in his left hand, and the gun was in his right.

"Wake up," said Kensington, and his father lifted the chalice to his lips.

121

"God!" he cried, shoving it away, and he staggered to his feet, gripping onto the gun.

"Kill them," said Kensington, "and reap my reward."

Alex stared at him, trembling. A reward? A reward, from his father? He ached. Kensington was grasping his shoulders, and now he shoved him out of the Shrine.

Alex stood outside of the Shrine. A few drops of rain fell around him. A few people were walking the streets of central Wellington. He hurriedly hid the gun in his jacket pocket, pressed his arm into his side, and walked down the road.

Oriental Bay was where the Joshua Movement had met. Would they be there again? He remembered in the news, the army had shot three people there. And then they had spread the fable of the resurrections.

Why would his father be so afraid of a children's story?

Alex reached the retaining wall, and climbed over it onto the beach. He remembered seeing the blood before, but now it was gone.

The ocean lapped gently on the sand. Alex stared down at it. Then he turned.

Rau Petera was standing before him, his face breaking into a warm smile.

"Kia ora," he said, reaching out a hand. Alex released the gun in his pocket to shake his hand.

"Kia ora," whispered Alex.

"Have you come for the meeting?" asked Rau, and Alex swallowed.

"What meeting?" he asked.

Rau's brown eyes looked a little cautious. He glanced over the beach, and Alex followed his gaze. There were only a handful of others, and no army. Then Rau suddenly grabbed a stick, and drew a symbol on the ground.

Alex gazed down at it. He tilted his head thoughtfully. Then he gasped.

Five dots within a koru, the Maori spiral symbol of the fern. Five bullet holes and new life.

Now Rau handed Alex the stick, gesturing to the sand, questioning with his eyes.

Alex closed his eyes. Pain, in his chest! This priest had no idea! No idea how much danger he was in. And yet, maybe he did know. And yet, maybe he was searching for people anyway.

Alex felt his throat constrict, and tears prick his eyes. He looked down again at the sand. He grasped the stick, and poked it into the sand. Bullet holes! His side hurt with each jab. Five! Five holes, for each bullet he had been responsible for – each bullet that had landed in Joshua's chest.

He stopped with the bullets. No koru! No new life. He looked back at Rau. But Rau was taking the stick from him, and now was gently caressing the sand, drawing the gentle spiral from the centre of the bullets progressively out.

New life.

Alex stared at his care with the symbol, at his offering and the risk he was taking. He fell to his knees in the sand.

Pain! Pain! He grasped his side, and began to weep.

Rau's hand came to his shoulder. He was silent and present. Alex knew he would not be able to kill this man. He pulled out his gun, and laid it on the sand.

Now another man was standing before him. Alex looked up the blue jeans to the young face. Tristan Blake! This was Selena's brother, the one Alex had used to kill Joshua! His forehead was creasing, as he held Alex's eyes.

"Who are you?" asked Tristan.

"I'm Alex Kensington," he whispered.

Tristan's eyebrows went up, and his face hardened. "You're the bastard who led my sister into the Shrine?"

Alex felt his own face contorting. "Yes!" he confessed. "Yes."

Tristan's hand moved, and he pulled out his own rifle. Alex stiffened, and gasped, and grasped his own side, and Tristan's eyes moved over him. Then he laid the rifle down in the sand barrel to barrel with Alex's gun.

Alex stared down at his gesture, and covered his face with his hands.

"I'm a worthless piece of shit," he said. "I don't deserve your grace."

"That's the beauty of it," said another voice. "That's the whole point of grace."

Now Alex looked up, into the face of John Robertson.

There was a light about the man, about his face. Alex tilted his head. Green eyes, and depth – Alex remembered him, even from before Saint Peter's. This was the one! The one who had wept with his entire being, at Joshua's dead side.

"I killed your beloved friend," said Alex, and John's eyes misted.

"I know," he whispered. "I know."

"You know?"

And now, a sudden rage seized Alex – a rage he had never felt unleashed before. He rose to his feet before this man, and braced his side in preparation.

"Then do you know the rest?" he cried. "Do you know why I had to do it?"

John's eyes intensified with a sudden hidden awareness.

"Yes," he whispered. "Yes, I'm starting to see why."

Alex stared at him. "Do you still believe in Love?" he cried. "With seeing my hell?"

John's face contorted. "I do," he whispered, and the eyes moved over Alex's face, searching. "I do still believe in Love."

"Do you still believe in a resurrection?" asked Alex, fixing his eyes on him.

"Yes," said John, holding his eyes. "I do."

"And what about Joshua Davidson?" asked Alex. "Do you have the nerve to say to me right here, right now, that you saw him alive after I arranged his death?"

John swallowed. Alex watched him glance down at the guns in the sand and then look up into Alex's eyes. He set his jaw.

"I saw him," he said quietly. "He was standing next to the open coffin, alive again, even after he had been killed. He drew my fingers in to touch his wounds, to show me that he was real."

"No," whispered Alex. "No."

"I was sure he was dead," continued John. "Rachel was certain. We both watched him killed. I was at his funeral, I watched his burial. But then he was alive again. Then he was showing me these."

And John reached into his pocket, and pulled out five deformed bullets.

Alex stared at them. He stared back at John's face. Then, suddenly, as if driven by another, he struck John across the face.

"No!" he cried. "No, you can't say that!"

And he found himself hitting him again and again, and John was standing and taking it, without resisting, until his face was bleeding.

Alex's chest was in agony, but he could not stop. He stooped to grab Tristan's rifle from the sand, the more powerful weapon – the weapon he had used to kill Joshua.

"You can't claim a resurrection," commanded Alex, and he lifted the rifle to point it at John's chest. "Deny it," he said. "Deny it, and you will live."

John's eyes were on him, wide, without fault. His breathing was quickening. Alex watched his fear, intrigued, almost as though he was outside of himself, watching the scene unfold between two different people.

"Deny it," said Alex, and he felt power, and it frightened him, and it whispered intoxication.

"I can't deny it," said John, his body starting to shake, and Alex stared at him again.

"Can't?" he said. "Can't?"

"No," whispered John, and Alex frowned at him, but now Tristan was moving.

"Stop!" cried Alex, pointing the rifle at Tristan. He had been stooping down toward Kensington's gun, lying on the sand. Tristan put his hands up and straightened, staring at him.

"Put the gun down, Alex," he said quietly.

"No," whispered Alex. "I can't."

"Can't?" murmured John, and Alex glanced back at him. Kill him? Kill the one who could not deny his own witness?

"I can't," whispered Alex, and he pointed the gun to his own head.

John's eyes widened further, and horror filled his gaze. "No!" he cried. "Don't!"

Alex stared at him. This man cared about his life? This stranger?

"Why would you give a shit about me?" cried Alex. "Why would any of you? Why would I trust in any semblance of humanity, when my own father is going to trample me to death?"

John's face contorted. "If you die, I die!"

"Why?" cried Alex. "I killed your beloved friend! I killed the very offering of faith, and hope, and love...I did it on purpose, John! I did it because..." And now tears welled up in his eyes. "...because I couldn't bear to see anyone else claim that they can see Light!"

He began to weep again, bridging his side.

"Don't you understand?" he cried. "Don't you understand the hell I am living?"

"I'm starting to understand it," whispered John. "I'm starting to."

"No you're not!" cried Alex. "You have no idea!" And he hit him again, this time with Tristan's rifle.

John gasped, turning his face away. Alex regretted! He felt his pain, the pain he had inflicted, as his own pain. He was becoming like his father! He was turning into his father.

"You don't understand," he cried. "Your light heightens my darkness! Your goodness makes me writhe in my own shit! I can't stand you, because you are everything I can never be!"

John's face turned back to him, contorting with Alex's pain. "And what about you?" he cried. "Why don't you understand, even you, with all of your profound insight? The light has come for the darkness! That's the whole point! It is for you, Alex – the Light has come for you!"

His voice was rising with a passion that transcended Alex's father's wrath, and Alex trembled, staring at the man.

"Let the light come!" cried John. "Let the goodness in! Writhe, Alex! Writhe, and wrestle, and shout, but let it in, and be changed, and be loved, and do away with fear!"

Alex stared at him. He trembled. He looked at Tristan's frown, and at his own gun still lying on the sand. He looked at Rau's gentle patience. And he looked back at John.

"I can't sustain love," he whispered. "I am too broken."

"I know," said John quietly. "That's why you must face death first."

"But why?" asked Alex. "Why must I face death?"

"Because that is the necessary price," said John, his eyes holding him. "Joshua knew that: you also know it."

Alex swallowed. Pain, and death, again and again and again...

"There's a connection," he whispered to John. "A kind of fellowship in the suffering."

"Yes," murmured John. "Yes."

"There's a commonality."

"Yes."

"Is it possible?" breathed Alex. "Somehow to reach for it, somehow to grasp for a resurrection after death?"

"It is possible," said John, and his face broke into a radiant smile. Alex gazed at him. He looked at Rau, and down at the symbol at his feet – five bullets, and the koru. New life! New life out of death...

He dared to hope...but then he saw his father's gun lying in the sand.

His father! He had failed him! He would be punished.

"Oh, God," he whispered. Beatings! More beatings! Pain!

"No!" he cried. "Where is God, in our agony? He is locked away in the sanctuary! Any hope of life, or love, is bound up with the saints, far away from the wretches lost in hell!"

And now a breeze off the ocean lifted his curls from his face, and he grasped Tristan's rifle to himself and ran.

Saint Peter's! He ran, and struggled for breath, and contorted in agony, and thrust himself somehow up the steps and through the glass doors.

The windows! He stared up at the windows. The images were stuck there! Stuck in the sanctuary! Peter, and John, and James, and Jesus himself, stuck with the saved.

"No!" he cried, "No!"

And he lifted Tristan's rifle from his side, and fired up at the windows. Glass shattered and fell. The images were shattered, the martyrs were gone! Alex stared at the wide open spaces, high up in the Cathedral – and now, suddenly, a vast powerful gust of wind filled the Church.

Alex gasped as the wind surrounded him, as it lifted up his hair from his face. His eyes filled with tears, looking up at the vast spaces where the martyrs had been.

"It's open now!" he cried. "The Church is open!"

And he fell down to his knees, wrapped his arms around his chest, and cried.

"Selena!" cried out Mark's voice, muffled by the wind. "Stop! The glass!"

Alex looked up to see Selena hesitating at a side aisle, wincing with the sounds of dropping glass, looking at him, wanting to reach him. There was no congregation, the service had ended. But Mark Blake was in the centre aisle, straight in front of him.

Alex rose shakily to his feet. He lifted Tristan's rifle to point at Mark's chest.

"Are you a martyr too?" he whispered. "Father?"

Mark's blue eyes were on him, deep, intense.

"Dad!" cried Tristan's voice, and Alex saw Tristan out of the corner of his eye, to his right, pointing Kensington's gun to his head.

"I'm so sorry, Dad," said Tristan. "He's got my gun! I put it down! I thought he could be reached, but he's gone mad!"

"No," said John, and Alex glanced to his left to see John standing there, his eyes lit. "No – everything he is doing is for a reason."

The Price of Redemption

"Yes," said Selena, and she appeared alongside her father, her black curls lifting with the wind, her eyes shining. "A breath of fresh air for the Church."

Alex swallowed, and held Mark Blake's eyes.

"Are you a martyr, Father?" he repeated.

Mark frowned at him. He looked to his right, to his daughter, and to his left, to his son. Then he stepped forward, knelt before Alex, and stretched his arms out, bowing his head and closing his eyes.

"I am a martyr if you are a murderer," he said.

"Dad!" cried Tristan, and Alex searched his white face and the aim of the gun, trembling but secure.

"Do you think I care about dying?" he muttered to him. "Physical death would be a relief."

Tristan stared at him, looking confused and dismayed.

Alex turned away from him to look down at Mark's bowed head under his gun – at the offering before him, his own power over this Father.

"Oh, shit," he breathed. The power terrified him. He stepped back away from the bowed man, and reached to lift him up. He laid Tristan's rifle in his arms, and then knelt before him, closed his eyes, and stretched out his own arms.

"Kill me," he said. "I am a threat to your very way of life."

But the sound of weeping filled his ears. Surprised, Alex looked up to see Mark crying, hugging the gun to his own chest.

"What is it?" breathed Alex instinctively.

"This was the gun!" said Mark. "The gun we all used to murder Joshua Davidson."

Mark reached down to grasp his hand, and now led him, amidst the wind and the shattered glass, up the aisle to the altar.

Alex stared at the white linen, and watched as Mark laid the rifle on top. Then Mark went to his knees before the altar.

Alex gagged. He stepped back. He watched as Selena knelt alongside Mark. He glanced at Tristan, to find him looking bewildered; he had lowered Kensington's gun.

John was alongside him. Alex swayed on his feet, and John's hand came to his shoulder.

"I don't understand," whispered Alex, and he searched John's smile.

"Which part?" asked John. "Why Mark would not want to kill you?"

"I just blew your church to pieces," said Alex. "My father would have killed me for that."

"Maybe so," said John, "but are all fathers the same?"

Astonished, Alex heard him, and he lifted his eyes above Mark's bowed form to Jesus on the cross.

"They're not all the same?" he murmured.

"What do you think?" asked John. "Is God a tyrant?"

"Oh, yes!" said Alex. "Of course! The ultimate Mastermind, in control of all the chess pieces, moving the parts into pain at his bidding."

"Would your father have done that?" asked John, and he gestured to the cross.

Tears blurred Alex's vision. "No!" he whispered. "No."

The man, suffering! Suffering, out of his own choice, to save others.

"A tyrannical Father then," whispered Alex. "A good Son of a tyrannical Father."

"Jesus never spoke of his own Father as a tyrant," said John.

"It was God's will," said Alex. "God's will that he should die."

"But not God's desire," said John, and Alex stared at him.

"Not his desire?" he whispered. "Is his desire different from the outcome?"

Now John's eyes captured him; now John had all of his attention.

"God's desire is goodness, Alex," said John. "Goodness, and love, and light, and freedom."

"Freedom..." pleaded Alex.

"But how will we use our freedom?" asked John. "What will we choose? The pawn has his own choice, within the moves he can make. The bishop has his own choice, within the moves he can make. The queen has her own choice. And..."

"...the king," whispered Alex. "The king has choice."

"The king hasn't chosen to be king," said John. "He has been made the king by the Chess-player – he has been given his own limited power. The other pieces are there to support the king, so the king can live – so the White King can outlive the Black King, if he so chooses."

Alex lifted his eyes again to the King on the cross. Was he the Chess-player? Could it be possible?

"A White King doesn't live just for himself," said John. "He lives for the entire side. All the white pieces do."

Alex glanced at Mark's back, the bishop, and at Selena's back: the queen.

"If the White King attacks the Black King on his own," said John, "he may well lose the game for his entire side."

Tears pricked at Alex's eyes. "You mean I need support?" he said, and John nodded.

"You need support," he said.

"But...I've never had support before..."

And now Mark and Selena lifted to their feet, and turned to face him.

Alex looked from one to the other, at the warmth of Mark's face, and the beauty of Selena's face. A family? Could they possibly be a family?

He swallowed, his chest ached, and now Tristan was shifting backwards and forwards on his feet. Alex glanced at his face. He had used this man – how could Tristan possibly receive him as a brother? Tristan had laid down his gun, only to have Alex steal it off him, shoot out the windows of the church, and threaten his father.

"Stay," said Mark, and Tristan frowned, and Alex stiffened.

"No," he whispered. "I must be getting back."

"Back there?" cried Selena.

"It's either there or prison," muttered Alex.

Tristan pulled out Kensington's gun, and fingered it. Should Alex take it back? Alex frowned. Should he take it back unused to his father? Worse still, should he leave it?

Tristan looked at him.

Michelle Warren

"If you don't take this back to him, you're dead?" he asked, and Alex flushed.

"If you report him, I'm also dead," he said.

"And if we report you for this?" said Mark, gesturing around the broken windows of the church.

"It's just delaying the inevitable," said Alex, sighing. "He'll get me in the end."

Tristan was gazing at him, his face changing. What was that? Compassion?

"You need a body guard," he muttered, and Alex suddenly grinned at him.

"Applying for the job?" he asked, and Tristan also grinned.

"Can't get my head around that one," he muttered. "Too many shifts and changes for my liking."

Alex found himself starting to like the man.

"I have committed a lifetime of crimes against you and your family," he said. "May my death, when it comes, be a relief to you."

Now Tristan was frowning at him, shaking his head, tears filling his eyes.

"No," he whispered. "May someone else's death never be a relief again."

Alex gazed at him. This man had been to war – they had a lot in common. They were both pawns! Both pawns in another person's battle.

"Goodbye," said Alex, and he glanced over the faces, of Tristan, Mark, Selena and John, and set them to memory as he walked out of the broken Cathedral.

Chapter 16

REGROUPING

Tristan stood in Saint Peter's Cathedral. The wind was still sweeping through the church, through the broken stained glass windows above. He looked across the seats and down the central aisle, at the broken shards of glass. He looked at the gun in his hand, and then started.

"Oh!" he said. "Alex didn't take it!"

It was Kensington's gun. Tristan swallowed. What would happen to Alex? Would they even see him again? Would they ever find out his fate? Tristan fingered the gun. Should he give it to the police? Tristan was certain Alex would not testify against his father: to do so would mean a death sentence.

He frowned, tucked Alex's gun into his right pocket and wandered up the aisle, stopping at the altar. His own rifle was lying on top of white linen. Tristan hesitated, and then reached to pick it up, tucking it into his left inner pocket.

"Still holding onto that?" said Rau from behind him. Tristan turned to see him panting and lifting his face to look at the shattered windows.

"You missed all the action again, old man," said Tristan. "Knees slow you down?"

"Not my heart this time," said Rau wryly. "Was this Alex?" He gestured to the windows.

"Yeah," said Tristan. "The man's a lunatic, but, hey, I can't exactly judge."

He pulled out his rifle, and remembered Joshua. At least Alex had only shot images in the end. Tristan had been in full blown war.

"No, I guess not," murmured Rau gently, and Tristan watched him smile as his black curls were blown over his face. Tristan replaced the gun again.

"Okay, so cut me some slack here," he said. "Why are you smiling?"

"Oh," said Rau, eying the windows. "The boy has talent."

"Yeah," said Tristan, "I'll say! He has a steady aim. Or at least a vigorous aim."

"Passion," said Rau. "He has passion."

"Passion?" said Tristan. "Harm to property..."

"No, no," said Rau quickly. "You're missing the point."

"Wouldn't surprise me," said Tristan. "I'm guessing it's not the thousands of dollars' worth of repairs that will be needed?"

"Ae," said Rau, "quite right: it's not that."

"Then what?"

Rau grinned up at the windows. "He'd take things further," he said. "Much further than we would ever think to go."

"Further?" asked Tristan.

"Windows can be replaced, Tristan," said Rau. "It will take some time, but they will be replaced. A life, though: a life is precious – a life is worth more than a thousand windows.

"He knows it. He dares to show us it. He dares..."

"...to face prison, and beatings, and...and..."

"Death?" asked Rau. "That remains to be seen, whether he can dare face a death of the soul."

Tristan watched him. A death of the soul? What did that even mean? He shook his head, and wandered up to his father.

The Price of Redemption

"Well?" said Tristan, and Mark's eyes came to him. "Alex totally munted your Cathedral."

"So he did," said Mark quietly.

"Going to do anything about it?" asked Tristan. "If I had done that, you would have had my guts for garters. You would have handed me to the police yourself!"

Mark smiled at him. "The prodigal son," he said.

"What?" asked Tristan.

"You are the older brother, and he is the prodigal son."

Tristan frowned at the analogy. "I don't think so," he said. "I don't believe in God as Father, and Alex never had an inheritance..."

"I'm not talking about God, Tristan."

Tristan stared at him. "What?" he said.

"The boy..." Mark gazed at him, and Tristan shifted uncomfortably. "You know I love you, whatever happens."

"Whatever happens?" said Tristan. "You mean, if he kills you?"

Mark frowned. "If that was to happen..."

"What?" said Tristan.

"If something happens to me, look after Selena."

Tristan held his eyes. "Dad," he said, "you can't put your life on the line for him."

"Can I not?" asked Mark. "Should I not?"

Tristan frowned again. And then he looked at John.

"What about you?" asked Tristan. "What do you make of everything that just happened here?"

"Ordained," said John, smiling quietly.

"Ordained?" asked Tristan.

"From God," said John, and Tristan looked to his sister.

"Okay," he said, "so am I the only one thinking that this was just an out of control abused adolescent who was acting out, and who is still in danger and needs an intervention?"

Selena smiled at him. "All true," she said, "but there is so much more."

"I don't see it," said Tristan. "You people perplex me."

"So be it," said Selena, and she wandered back up to their father.

Tristan frowned, and returned to Rau.

"So," he muttered to him, "I'm confused. You're still saying you want me to get rid of my gun?"

Rau smiled quietly. "There's something about guns," he said. "They tend to shoot people."

"The idea is that one can match the threat of another," said Tristan.

"Eye for an eye?" said Rau.

"Not necessarily," said Tristan. "Defence. I'm not into punitive executions, not since…"

Joshua was suddenly again before him, in his mind's eye, and he was shooting him again.

He closed his eyes. "Joshua was a pacifist," he said. "He would never have carried a gun."

"No," replied Rau.

"But do you just stand by and watch someone kill your family?" asked Tristan. "Because I can't do that."

"I know," murmured Rau.

"I…" Now Tristan frowned, confused. "Alex was about to shoot Dad, Rau. Would you have had me let him?"

Rau's eyes were on him. "Did he shoot?"

"No," muttered Tristan.

"And if you had shot him?"

Tristan swallowed. "I would have transcended his father's abuse," he said.

Rau grimaced. "A pre-emptive attack is a dangerous strategy," he said. "It assumes a certainty which may not necessarily apply at all."

Tristan fingered the gun in his right pocket. "On the other hand," he said, "some forms of certainty are wholly legitimate."

And he pulled out Alex's gun.

Rau looked down at it. "I know what you're thinking," he said.

"Why was Alex carrying a gun, Rau?" asked Tristan. "Why did he bring this to Oriental Bay?"

"For self-defence?" offered Rau.

"Perhaps," said Tristan, "but it wasn't self-defence against us."

Tristan fingered the trigger. "He pulled it on John," he said. "As if he was experimenting. As if he was testing himself."

"He couldn't do it," said Rau. "That is my point."

"Took the gun to his own head instead," explored Tristan, "as if…"

Now he stiffened, and stared at Rau. "He was sent."

"Sent?" asked Rau.

"His father," said Tristan. "His father sent him, to kill John."

Tristan returned Alex's gun to his right pocket, and wandered back up to John.

John was standing at the altar with his back to Tristan, silently touching the wood as the wind swept around him.

"I think Alex was sent to kill you," said Tristan, and he watched the back of John's head as he looked up at the cross.

"I know," answered John, his voice lifted by the breeze. "His father wants me dead."

"We should hide now," said Tristan. "All of Joshua's friends should hide."

He glanced to his right, to his father, the Bishop, still clad in his purple tunic, and to his sister, standing at their father's side. Rau had joined him again on the left.

All seemed to look up at John in that moment. His hand was lying on the white linen of the altar, next to the silver chalice and plate.

"The movement will adapt," he said. "Wherever Joshua's friends find themselves, they will find a way. They will meet in hiding, they will develop their own codes, they will share what they know, and…"

"And some of them will die for it," finished Tristan for him.

John turned and looked him straight in the eye.

"Yes," he said quietly. "Some of them will die for it."

Tristan stared at him, at the quiet sorrow.

"You would still spread this message?" he asked. "Even knowing it will kill some of those who choose to follow it?"

"I would," said John, without hesitation.

"Why?" asked Tristan.

"Because it is the truth, Tristan," said John. "Because this kind of Light must never be hidden."

Tristan gazed at him – at his girded idealism, almost romantic in intensity.

"And what if I had the chance to save some of them, John?" asked Tristan. "Would you have me surrender my gun? Would you have me stand back and let our nation's freedom and safety be overridden, in the name of martyrdom?"

John's eyes held him. "I would have you do what you must do," he said quietly, and Tristan felt his eyebrows rise in astonishment.

"But I killed Joshua…"

"Yes, yes," said John, almost impatient in his affection. "That's old news now."

Tristan almost laughed at him. "You're saying you trust me?" he asked.

John's head tilted slightly, looking at him. "You were in the army for five years, Tristan," he said. "The army is looking the other way. There must be a reason."

Astonished, Tristan stared at him. Redemption? A chance for redemption?

"A use for my past?" he whispered.

"To protect our nation's freedom and safety?" said John. "That would be true national defence."

"Sometimes there is a time," said Tristan. "A time when one must shoot."

"Yes," muttered John. "I don't doubt it. But I do know that that person will never be me."

His eyes smiled. "As to whether that person is you, Tristan?" he continued. "Only you can decide."

The Price of Redemption

Now Tristan pulled out his own rifle. He turned it over twice, and looked up at the altar, where his father had laid it. He reached out with his other hand to touch the white linen of the altar.

His father's eyes were on him – he could feel them, on the back of his neck.

"Well, Dad?" he asked. "Use this same weapon for good?"

He turned, and saw tears in his father's eyes. "Just get it right this time," whispered Mark, "for both of our sakes."

Tristan reached out to grasp his arm. "I will," he whispered. "I promise you that."

"A weapon is dangerous, Tristan," continued his father. "What if it should fall into the wrong hands? What if your hands turn out to be the wrong hands? But, no, I trust you."

Tears pricked Tristan's eyes. "Thank you," he whispered.

"Get it right," said Mark. "Make it right with the army. Sort it out with Connor. Start again, but this time without the trauma."

Tristan nodded vigorously. "Okay," he said. "I'll make it right! I'll sort it out with the army."

And with renewed purpose he drew his rifle back into his pocket, and strode out of the fractured Cathedral.

Chapter 17

PREPARATION

John stood in the Cathedral. He looked up at the shattered windows. He breathed in the gentle wind swirling around the altar and chairs. He lifted his eyes to the blue sky peeking through the clouds, seen through the jagged remains of the stained glass. Then he turned and looked back at Jesus on the cross, standing amongst the sharp fragments in the inner sanctuary.

"Poignant," murmured Mark's voice in his ear.

"Yes," whispered John, and he fleetingly closed his eyes.

"Our lives are in danger," said Mark.

"I know," said John, and he looked at Mark's face.

The Bishop was calm. His Cathedral had been assaulted, yet he seemed untroubled by the reality. John was intrigued by the man.

"What would you have us do now, Bishop?" he murmured, and Mark frowned, looking up at the cross.

"Well," he sighed, now looking at the windows. "Plastic covers, I guess."

John grinned. "Plastic covers?" he asked.

"Not exactly living up to the glory of the original windows," said

Mark, "but beggars can't be choosers."

"Beggars?" asked John.

"Well," said Mark, "the Church isn't exactly owned by us, John. Having the windows shot out wasn't exactly what I had in mind, but if God deems it necessary…"

John looked at him in wonder. "You're not just talking about glass, are you," he whispered.

Mark's eyes intensified. "The original believers went underground, John," he said. "When they began to be killed, when their religion was deemed illegal, they dispersed and went underground. Is that what you would have me do?"

Now Mark's face became troubled as he looked around his church, at the damage and the shards of glass lying on the seats.

"Would you have me, as Bishop, instruct all of the Anglican churches in Wellington to close shop? To disappear? Or would you just have me close the Cathedral in Wellington, the governing church, and expect all the others to continue despite the example of their leader?"

"The followers of Joshua have been dispersed," said Rau, and John glanced at his peaceful face. "They will spread word of everything that has happened everywhere they go, I am sure of it."

"They will," said Mark. "The army instructed them to disperse, it was not their choice. That's not so with us. For us, it is our choice."

And Mark wandered down the aisle, crushing glass under his feet.

Selena followed him, close behind. John found himself following Selena, looking at the back of her head, fascinated by her. Something had happened to her, something had changed. She was united with her father. She had somehow found her peace.

Mark pushed the glass doors of the Cathedral open, and walked outside. John followed and moved to Mark's left side, perching himself on the steps, while Selena stood on Mark's right, and Rau stood just behind.

"Look," said Mark, and John followed his point across the street to the Beehive. The army was standing alert within the iron gates, rifles poised, as Tristan spoke to a Major.

"Do they have Alex?" asked Selena, but John shook his head.

"I don't think so," he said. "They're not the police."

"They don't see him as a threat to national security?" asked Selena.

"No," replied Rau. "They see us as the threat to national security."

John frowned sadly, looking at the rigid faces of the officers.

"They heard crashing noises from the Cathedral," he murmured. "They keep rifles up, in case the threat should advance. But what is their response to the fate of the Cathedral itself? Indifference."

"We are an appendage to them," murmured Mark. "Only an appendage."

"We are New Zealand citizens too!" said Selena.

"We are," said Rau. "Ae. But much more than that: we are all Aotearoa."

Mark stood silently, listening to the Maori priest.

"Aotearoa," he murmured. "One Iwi. One tribe. They haven't realised yet: if one part dies, the entire body suffers."

And he turned, and moved back into the Cathedral.

Mark's long legs strode purposefully back through the shards of glass to the altar. John moved alongside him as Mark knelt, amongst glass, and leaned his head forward against the wood, closing his eyes.

"If you keep this place open," said John, "people will die here."

"I know," whispered Mark. "I know."

"Will you close up shop?" asked John. "Will you close the doors of the church, and keep the congregation safe?"

"I will not," whispered Mark. And now he covered his face with his hands, and began to rock on his knees, amongst glass.

"We are the neighbours of Parliament," he said, his voice strangely clear in his hands. "Our nation is in turmoil. I won't hand them over! I won't hand them over to a random fate. I won't hand them over to corruption."

"The cost…"

"The Church will remain open!" Mark said, uncovering his face, lifting his eyes again to the gaping holes overhead. "She will remain as open as she can be! The light must not be hidden: true Light cannot hide."

"Then you have heard him," murmured John, looking up. "You have heard his message."

"Each one must decide," said Mark. "I will inform all of the congregations…"

"Each one," said Selena, moving alongside him. "Each individual."

Mark rose to his feet and took her hand. "Each individual," he said, "must decide for themselves what risk they are willing to take."

"There is a responsibility," murmured Selena. "A responsibility that matches the opportunity each one is given."

"Ae," said Rau, from behind. "There is responsibility, when we have light, to bring that light into the darkness. The light given is not only for us, it is for the darkness."

"It is for the darkness," repeated John, and he reached down to pick up a shard of glass, and remembered Alex.

The glass pricked him. A few drops of blood flowed. John frowned, feeling the sharpness of the pain. He stopped his instinct to drop the glass.

"I still choose you," he whispered, and he closed his eyes, and prayed, and the wind blew around him.

The Cathedral doors opened. Who was it, someone new? John looked up to find Rachel walking down the aisle.

Rachel! Why had he forgotten about her? He had been swept up in the events of the Cathedral!

Now her face was contorted. John frowned. She stared up at the broken windows, as she walked; she stumbled on the broken glass on the ground. Then she reached him.

"What the hell happened here?" she asked.

John shrugged slightly. "Alex shot out the windows."

"Alex Kensington?" asked Rachel, her eyes widening.

"You know him?" asked John.

Rachel looked at him. "I…" she began. And then she shut her mouth. "Confidentiality," she said.

John looked over her face, drawn, tense, looking up again at the jagged windows. She had also been away for a while, in her own headspace, busy and focussed on work.

"What is it?" asked John. "What's going on?"

Rachel looked at him again, and her eyes suddenly filled with tears. John instinctively reached out to take her hand, but she pulled it away.

"Can't," she whispered. "I can't."

"Why?" whispered John.

"Because…" Her face contorted again. "Because…"

Her hands were tightening into fists.

John moved closer to her. "It's okay," he murmured. "This place may be broken, but it's still a church."

Rachel looked at him, hesitated, and then began. "I'm facing something I've never faced before," she whispered to him. "A situation I can't bear to be in."

"What kind of situation?"

"A situation at work."

"With the patients?"

"No." Now Rachel tightly closed her eyes. "No."

"Then the staff?"

Rachel's face contorted again, with tears. "Yes," she whispered, "with the staff."

John wanted to touch her, but he held himself back.

"How much can you tell me?" he asked.

"Not much," Rachel whispered.

"'Confidentiality.'"

"Yeah."

John searched her face. She was distraught! Something was going on, something big. Her eyes lifted over his head to Christ on the cross, and then they returned to him.

"What do you do?" she whispered with tears. "When the entire foundation of your trust is collapsing away? When everything you ever believed in is evaporating before your eyes?"

John held her eyes.

"Is that what's happening?" he whispered, and she wrapped her arms around herself and turned her back to him, staring up at the broken windows.

"The Cathedral is shattered!" she said, and her voice lifted in sudden rage. "You bastard, you shot out the Cathedral!"

And she strode off to the left, between the seats, to the inner wall, and started to beat her fists against the stone.

Shocked, John strode after her, and now Mark was also by her side.

"Rachel," said Mark, and Rachel shook her head, still beating her fists, closing her eyes tightly.

"Don't talk to me!" she said. "You shouldn't even be here! You're a murderer!"

"Rachel!" said Mark, and he grasped her arms and turned her to himself, and she sank down to her knees before him.

"I can't work!" she said. "I can't do it!"

"It's okay," said John, "if you need time off."

"You don't understand," said Rachel, "it's so much more than that!"

Her eyes were on Mark and Mark held her gaze, supporting her, on her knees.

"It's the same thing," murmured Mark, gently and intuitively. "You're hitting the same thing all over again. Corruption! Corruption."

"Damned humanity," whispered Rachel, writhing in his arms. "I hate us! I hate all of us! Humanity destroys everything that is good and precious, everything that is pure and right."

"There is still hope for humanity," whispered Mark, and Rachel shook her head.

"No," she said. "No."

"Joshua still saw hope," said John.

"Don't talk to me about Joshua!" said Rachel. "Joshua's dead! He's dead!"

And now Rachel began to beat her fists against Mark's chest.

"Rachel!" cried John, but Mark was sustaining her assault, supporting her, while tears filled his eyes.

"I understand," he whispered. "It's devastating to be so caught between death and life."

And now she suddenly sank against the chest she had beaten.

Mark went down to his knees with her. "How do I offer you hope, Rachel?" he asked. "How do I offer you strength?"

"Bring Joshua back," she whispered, and her voice lifted into a cry, and she lifted herself to her feet and jabbed her finger pointing to the ground in front of her. "Bring him back, and have him stand right here where I can see him, and prove to me that he's stronger than all of your bullshit!"

John stared at her. How? How could he cause Joshua to appear? He could not. But Rachel was looking at Mark, and Mark was smiling slightly at her.

"There are other kinds of proof, Rachel," he said.

"Like what?" asked Rachel.

Mark shifted slightly on his feet before her. "Lives changed," he said.

"Like hell," replied Rachel.

"What happened?" asked Mark. "At the hospital?"

Rachel stared at him then turned away, staring up again at the broken windows.

"My heart was swept away," she whispered. "In one foul sweep."

John gazed at her, and then closed his eyes. Pain! Her pain! Why had he not seen it before? She had locked herself away.

He opened his eyes to step toward her, but she stepped further back away.

"The healer brought pain," she said. "The life-giver brought death. The light…"

"…was swallowed up by darkness," murmured Mark.

"Another tsunami," whispered John. "More devastation."

"And you still believe there is a God?" asked Rachel, her face contorting. "What kind of God would do this? There is no God! There is only humanity, and humanity is lost."

"No," whispered John, and tears pricked at his eyes, and he strode toward her. "No, Rachel, it isn't true!" he said. "Sometimes we have to walk through death to find the life on the other side! Sometimes we have to face the darkness in order to see the light…"

He was reaching for her now – reaching! Almost finding her shoulder, almost passing on the comfort he longed to share – but she was withdrawing! She was throwing off his hand.

"No, John!" she said. "There is no life after death! There is no eternal future! There is no light! There is only now! There is only here! And, right now, there is only me."

With pain he listened to her: his wife! His wife!

"There's only me!" repeated Rachel, with tears, and pain. Was she separating? No! Only trapped! Only entrapped in a situation she could not share.

"There's only me, and I can't bear this. I have to act! I have to act, and…and…"

Now John straightened: danger! He felt danger.

"What will happen?" he asked.

Her eyes set on him. "I don't know," she whispered. "I don't know. But I can't live this way, John. I can't work like this. I must try to make it right."

And she glanced back at Mark, who was smiling and frowning at the same time, and then she turned and walked out of the church.

Chapter 18

ANTICIPATION

Rachel strode out of the Cathedral. The army was before her in front of the Beehive, their rifles by their sides. She wrapped her arms around herself and quickly walked down the steps, tucking her head down.

"Rachel?" It was Tristan's voice.

She shook her head. "I have to go to work," she said.

"I'm sorry, Rachel," he said.

"Bullshit," she whispered, and she brushed past him to leave, but now he was grasping her arm.

She looked at him – at the concern in his eyes, and the gentle sad grimace of his mouth.

"What do I need to do to make it up to you?" he asked.

"Make it up?" she cried. "Do you want to try to bring him back from the dead?"

Now Tristan's face contorted. "I can't!" he said. "But I've seen some weird shit…"

"I don't care about your weird shit!" said Rachel. "I only care about your shooting!"

He flinched, and then grasped for her hand.

"Rachel!" he pleaded. "You're killing me! You're executing me! Is that what you want?"

Rachel stared at the distraught lines across his face. Was this man a tyrant? No! No! He was...only human...

She reached up fingers now to the distraught face.

"I'm not the judge," she said. "If you can find some kind of peace in this hell-hole, Tristan, then find it! Don't bother yourself with what I think, leave me! Just leave me, and live."

But now his fingers were finding her hand.

"No," he said. "You've copped it hardest of all of us. I'm not going to leave you – you are innocent."

She stared at the kindness in his eyes, and at the guns in his pockets.

"I'm not innocent," she whispered. "I'm a judgemental bitch, executing everyone in my path."

"No," whispered Tristan.

"That's what you would say!" cried Rachel. "That's what everyone would say!"

"No," said Tristan, holding her gaze, moving his hand into his pocket. "There is a time to shoot."

Rachel stared at him. "A time to shoot?" she whispered. "Don't you understand? I desperately, desperately do not want to have to shoot."

Tristan's eyes misted over. "Then we are the same," he whispered.

Rachel gazed at him. "You didn't want to have to shoot Joshua?" she asked.

"No," whispered Tristan. "I love him."

Rachel stared at him. "Love?" she whispered.

"He was my friend," said Tristan.

Rachel held his eyes, and her own vision blurred.

"I'm sorry," she whispered. "I'm sorry, Tristan."

Weeping suddenly seized her, but she had to drag herself away from him. She turned, and launched herself toward work.

At Hardwater Hospital, Rachel strode into Ward Eight, and into the office.

Her white coat was hanging on a hook, her stethoscope in her pocket. She stared at them for a moment. She swallowed. Then she reached to put on the coat, and placed her stethoscope around her shoulders.

She turned, and James was in front of her. Rachel started, and quickly turned her gaze away.

"Where have you been?" asked James.

"It's Sunday," said Rachel.

"Church?" asked James, and Rachel knew he was smirking.

"It doesn't matter," said Rachel, and she turned away from him.

"It's time for a ward round," said James. "Business as usual, Doctor Connor."

"Like hell," whispered Rachel, and she grasped the tablet, and followed him into the first room.

James walked up to the first patient, an Indian man in his thirties. Rachel cast her eyes over him, over his nice warm face.

"Pulse eight-four, irregular," said James, and Rachel fixed her gaze down at the tablet and entered in the information. "Now you examine the chest."

Rachel stared at him. Examine the patient? Follow James? As if nothing had happened?

"You do it," she said.

His eyes were on her. "I'm the consultant, and…"

"…and I'm just your dogsbody," said Rachel, "covering for Fatima, taking notes. I'll keep taking notes."

James's face flushed. He turned back to the patient and listened to his chest.

"Heart sounds dual and a pan systolic murmur at the apex," he said woodenly, and Rachel typed his findings into the tablet. Then James rose to his feet, and left the room.

Rachel swallowed, looking after him. Where was he going? She hesitated, and then followed after him. There he was, in Room Two, with Margaret.

The Price of Redemption

"No," whispered Rachel, and she followed him in.

James sat on the bed next to Margaret, and reached for her pulse. Now Rachel felt physically sick.

"Ninety-six," said James.

Rachel recorded the number, and James reached to examine her left thigh. Rachel looked at her face, contorting with the examination.

You bastard, thought Rachel. *You're doing this on purpose!*

"The mets are growing," said James. "She needs more morphine."

Now Rachel stared at him as he continued. "Chart ten milligrams three times a day," he said.

"I'll sort it out later," she said.

"She's in pain now, doctor," said James.

"Then I'll go and get the dose straight away," said Rachel, and she laid down the tablet to leave, but he was shaking his head.

"No need for that, Doctor Connor," he said, "Kate will give the dose."

Kate was standing at the bed with a syringe, her face white, and her eyes distraught.

Oh, shit, thought Rachel. *She's back! He's made her come back.*

"Chart the morphine, doctor," said James. "Your patient is in pain."

Kate was poised, ready to give the dose.

"Not yet," said Rachel to Kate. "We'll sort it out later."

"I am the consultant," said James. "You will chart the morphine."

"Here," said Rachel, handing him the tablet. "Feel free to chart it for her."

A record...a written record.

James stared at her. "I'll sort it out later," he said, and he rose to his feet away from Margaret's side, stooping next to Rachel's ear.

"You will follow me now," he said, and Rachel followed him into the office.

James shut the door. His face was red.

"You will not humiliate me in front of the patients!" he said, and Rachel glared at him.

"Humiliation?" she said. "We both know who that morphine is

Michelle Warren

intended for!"

"You know no such thing!" said James curtly. "The patient is in pain."

"Yes!" said Rachel. "You are in pain!"

"That's enough!" said James. "Keep this up, and you're out of here!"

Rachel flushed, reaching to finger her stethoscope lying on her chest.

"And don't think it'll be easy to continue to specialise, Rachel Connor," continued James. "You need a reference for your next job!"

"I have references," muttered Rachel, before she could stop herself.

"Yes," said James, "but I'm on the training committee."

Rachel stared at him, at his sense of control. "I'm not prescribing morphine for you," she said.

"The morphine is for the patient, Doctor Connor," said James.

"Then you'll be happy to prescribe it for yourself," said Rachel.

"I am asking you to prescribe it," said James.

"Then I will prescribe it," said Rachel. "I'll prescribe a morphine pump."

She reached for the tablet.

"No," said James, and he snatched the tablet from her. "You will not."

Rachel stared at him. Pain! Margaret's pain, and James's addiction.

"I can't do this," whispered Rachel, and she laid her stethoscope on the table.

James was staring at her, and his body seemed to stiffen.

"Don't leave," he whispered. "Don't leave."

"I'm not leaving," she said. "But I can't work like this."

She grasped her stethoscope to her pocket, opened the office door and walked down the corridor.

"Where are you going?" James's voice rang out behind her, but she kept her eyes forward, and did not reply.

Rachel strode out of the ward and moved quickly forward to the administrative rooms, just next to the lift.

The manager's door was in front of her.

Swallowing, Rachel stared at the name: Martha Harrison. She knocked on the door.

"Come in," a voice answered, and Rachel entered.

The manager was sitting behind her cluttered desk, a slim European in her thirties. Rachel had never spoken to her before, despite having worked on the ward for four months.

"How can I help you?" asked Harrison.

Tell her? Or just ask for a transfer? Take the easy approach, and let the situation continue...?

"I..." Rachel felt her throat constricting, but made herself continue. "I've come across a situation on the ward."

"Oh, yes?" said Harrison, her eyes flicking over the document sitting on her desk before they lifted again to Rachel.

"Yes," said Rachel. "A situation with Dr Lester."

"James?" said Harrison, her eyes smiling. "What's he up to now?"

Rachel shifted in discomfort at her apparent sense of familiarity. Were they friends?

"Something has happened," said Rachel. "Something I so profoundly disagree with that I don't think I can keep working."

"Are you going through some troubles?" asked Harrison.

"Well, yes," said Rachel, a little surprised, "but that's not the point."

"James mentioned you had some mental health issues."

Rachel stared at her, and frowned. "Mental health issues?"

"And that you were eying the morphine."

Now Rachel laughed, before she could stop herself.

"He said that, did he?" she asked.

Harrison's eyes were on her. "But what did you come here to say?"

Rachel set her eyes firmly back on Harrison.

"I came to inform you that James is using morphine on the job."

There, she had said it. She felt herself flushing a little, in exposure.

Harrison was quiet. Her eyes floated back down to the papers on her desk then returned to her again.

"Will you be taking this further?"

"Excuse me?" asked Rachel.

"Will you be taking this any further?" asked Harrison. "You clearly have a chip on your shoulder, and you want to use this opportunity to further your career: maybe advance earlier to the consultant position."

Rachel stared at her. "That's complete bullshit!" she cried, launching herself to her feet, and now dismay took her as the words poured out. "You already know! How can that be possible? You already know, and you don't give a shit!"

"Don't talk to me like that," said Harrison, also rising to her feet. "You have a warning now, Doctor Connor: any further inappropriate behaviour and you will be dismissed."

Rachel stared at her. Dismissed? By the manager indifferent to morphine use in the consultant?

"You're partially responsible!" she said to Harrison. "You are partially responsible for allowing this to continue!"

"I implore you not to take this further," said Harrison. "Unless you want his suicide on your conscience."

Rachel shook her head. Manipulation! Yet she knew the words were true. Somehow she had already known.

She left the office and stopped at a window, leaning heavily against the frame, staring out. It was raining outside. Big drops rolled down the windows, while a grey haze masked the streets below.

Harrison already knew?

"Dear God," she breathed. How many others knew? How many others were allowing this, even endorsing it?

He would be suicidal if pushed? Yes…or…or homicidal.

Rachel closed her eyes. Too much! It was all getting too much. Then her cell-phone rang. She reached for it – it was her father! She answered it quickly.

"Rachel!" said Connor's voice.

"Yes, Dad," whispered Rachel. "Thank goodness it's you."

"I…" He hesitated, and then continued. "Rachel, something's going on."

"Yes," said Rachel, closing her eyes tightly again. "Something is going on."

"Parliament," whispered Connor's voice. "Rachel, something's not right in Parliament."

"No," whispered Rachel. "No."

"I need to act, Rachel," whispered Connor, "but I'm afraid to act."

"Why?" asked Rachel.

"Because…" Rachel frowned, in anticipation, and listened hard. "Because," said her father, "if I do, it might be at high cost."

"What kind of cost?" asked Rachel, staring out of the window, reaching out her fingers to touch the window while the rain dripped down the other side.

"I'm not afraid to lose my own life, Rachel," whispered her father, "but I am afraid to lose yours."

Now Rachel stiffened, and tears filled her eyes. "My life?" she whispered.

"There's a man," said Connor. "An evil man. Do you know him, Rachel? You would know him if you had seen him."

Rachel tilted her head, and looked toward the door of the ward; through the little window in the door, down the corridor.

Was it James Lester? The evil man?

"You would know, Rachel, if you had seen the face of pure evil."

Rachel shook her head. No, it wasn't James. He wasn't pure evil. There was still humanity in him, still some sense of struggle for the soul. There was still…love.

Pain took her, deep in her chest. She shook her head, and tried to draw her attention back to her father.

Pure evil? Unadulterated by goodness? Had she seen it? Something resonated…

Alex Kensington's face appeared before her, struggling to breathe.

"At least this way no one else need die…"

Rachel turned in her mind's eye to his father, demanding his discharge. His face was cold, emotionless and calculating. The injury inflicted on his son had been calculated; the injury inflicted on James calculated...

"Yes," whispered Rachel to her father. "I have seen the face of pure evil."

"He is the enemy, Rachel," said her father, "not any of us. He is the true enemy of the state."

Tears filled her eyes again. "I understand," she whispered.

"How do we contain evil, Rachel?" asked her father. "How do we contain it without getting ourselves burnt?"

Now Rachel saw Joshua again before her eyes, getting shot: willingly taking Tristan's bullets.

Tristan...he had a soul! A soul still battling for what was right. She felt love! In that moment, she felt love for him. As Joshua had felt love.

"We can't," whispered Rachel. "We have to accept getting burnt."

"For love, Rachel?" asked her father. "For love?"

Rachel frowned, looking at the figures in her mind: Joshua and Tristan. Joshua's love for Tristan; Tristan's love for Joshua.

"For love," she whispered.

"Love for New Zealand?" asked Connor. "Is that why? Is that why I must do what I must do?"

Rachel laughed quietly into the phone. "Redemption," she said. "Redemption."

"We're Anglican," said Connor's voice wryly, "not Catholic. We don't believe in Purgatory, remember?"

"Not punishment," said Rachel, "but a change, within – a change that costs."

"A change that costs," said Connor. "But what if it costs my own daughter?"

Now Rachel caught her breath. The price of her own life? "Are you asking me?" she whispered. "Are you asking for me to consent?"

Connor's voice fell silent. Rachel stared at the rain, and then closed her eyes.

"I loved him," she whispered to her father. "I loved Joshua."

"I know," her father whispered back. "I know."

"I wanted to be just like him," said Rachel, and now her body shook with weeping. "Do you understand, Dad?"

"Yes," whispered Connor. "Yes, I understand."

"Then I consent," said Rachel. "I consent to whatever cost is necessary."

"Rachel..." breathed her father's voice, but Rachel straightened in readiness.

"I have to go now," she said to him. "I have to continue."

"Okay," said Connor. "I love you, always remember that! Always know it!"

"I will!" said Rachel with tears. "I do. I love you too."

And she closed her cell-phone, and strode back onto the ward.

Chapter 19

CONFRONTATION

Alex stood in the Shrine. His father towered over him in his tall black robes. The black altar was behind him, with the golden chalices sitting on the black linen, waiting. The priest was carrying another gun.

Alex swallowed. Kensington began to pace backwards and forwards in front of the altar.

"Tell me what happened again," he said.

Alex shifted on his feet. "I went down to the beach," he said. "No one was there."

"No one?" asked Kensington, fingering the gun.

"No one," said Alex. "The army had dispersed them."

"And then what did you do?"

Alex hesitated. "I went to Saint Peter's," he said.

"Why?" asked Kensington.

"Because…" Alex felt himself choking, but made himself continue. "Because I knew they would be there."

Now Kensington's eyes were on him. "Who was there?" he asked.

"Rau Petera," said Alex. "Mark Blake."

"Was Selena there?" asked Kensington, and Alex stiffened.

"Yes," he whispered. "She was there."

Kensington's hand tightened on the gun. "Betrayal," he said coldly. "She has changed sides."

Alex watched him, as he paced.

"Rau Petera was there," said Kensington, "and yet you didn't kill him."

"In front of the others?" asked Alex.

"You shot the windows out instead," said Kensington, "with Tristan Blake's gun."

The pacing stopped, and his father was before him again.

"Why did you do that, Alex?"

Alex stared up at the penetrating gaze. "I don't know," he whispered.

"You don't know?" The voice was getting louder and higher.

"Something came over me," said Alex. "It was stupid! A crazy thing to do…"

"All of Parliament is talking about it," said Kensington. "The army could have shot you down. My son! Fraternising with the enemy!"

"'Fraternising,'" protested Alex. "I shot out their windows!"

"And spared their lives!" roared Kensington suddenly, and he hit Alex across the face with his gun.

Pain took Alex, and he gasped.

"I can't kill them, all right?" he cried out. "I don't know why! I just can't do it!"

"Can't?" said Kensington. "Can't?"

And now his father was hitting him, again and again with the gun, backwards and forwards.

"Can't!" gasped Alex. "Can't!"

"Won't!" roared Kensington, and he shoved Alex back against the wall, and applied the gun to his throat.

Alex stared up into the darkness. His body was shuddering, beyond his control. Death! Death.

"If you don't align yourself with me," said Kensington, "I will kill you."

"I know," whispered Alex, his body now breaking out into a sweat. "I know."

"You don't care about your own life?" asked Kensington.

Alex shook. "I don't know," he whispered.

"Why spare them and put yourself at risk?" asked Kensington. "Foolishness! Sentiment! Don't dare to love, Alex – don't you dare. Love will kill you."

And now the door to the Shrine opened, and blinding light poured in.

Alex gasped, closing his eyes tightly. Who had entered? He could hear a struggle. He opened his eyes, and struggled to see again in the darkness. A shorter figure was there, dumped on the floor. His father had lowered the gun from his neck, and Alex breathed more easily. But who…?

His eyes adapted, and then he saw Selena.

She was lifting herself from the ground, her face white, her wide blue eyes shifting from Kensington to the black altar.

Alex stared at her. "What are you doing?" he whispered, and now her eyes found him, filling with determined tears.

"I had to come," she said.

Kensington grasped her by the throat, and pushed her up against the wall.

"Did you," he said sardonically, and his hand began to squeeze.

Selena clutched at the hand around her throat. She began to choke.

"Stop," said Alex, and Kensington's hand tightened. Selena's face began to turn purple.

"She's not the one you want," said Alex, and Kensington laughed.

"She betrayed us," he said. "She knows the cost."

And he threw her back down to the floor.

Selena sucked in breath, coughing, reaching both hands to her own throat. Kensington reached for a chalice, and reached to grasp Selena's shirt.

"Drink," he said. "Drink, as you drank before!"

Selena stared straight into his eyes, and exposed her wrists. The tattoo

160

- 666, and the eye – they were gone! A scar was in their place.

She took the chalice into her own hands, and suddenly flicked the blood up into Kensington's face. He roared in fury, but now Selena was on her feet – now she was rushing to the black altar, tearing off the black linen, sweeping aside the golden chalices.

"Go to hell!" she cried at the top of her lungs. "I'm never drinking from your cup again!"

Alex stared at her in horror. "Suicide!" he cried. "Suicide!"

"No!" she cried out to him. "Salvation! Salvation!"

"There is no salvation," whispered Alex. "You have sacrificed your life for nothing."

His father grasped her arms, and pinned her back on the altar she had disrupted.

Alex stared at his face – at his eyes, as they passed over her body. And then the dark eyes were on him.

"Tell me," asked Kensington, his gaze penetrating. "What does she mean to you?"

Alex stared at him. "What do you mean?" he whispered.

Selena's head was tilting back, her eyes, wide with terror, set on him.

"What does she mean to you?" repeated Kensington, and he reached under the altar and pulled out the cursed crown.

"Don't!" said Alex instinctively, and Kensington shrugged.

"She used it on Joshua," he said. "It is only just."

"It killed him," said Alex, "and he was much more powerful than she is."

"She betrayed us," said Kensington, "after using our weapon."

"She was foolish," said Alex. "She doesn't deserve to die."

Kensington's eyes returned to him. "Answer me," he said. "What does she mean to you?"

Alex swallowed, looking at her terrified eyes. Foolish! She was foolish to enter! Foolish to provoke one ten times her strength!

"Let me take the crown," said Alex. "Let me keep it safe."

"The crown is your inheritance," said Kensington. "You have not yet claimed it."

Alex stared at him. "Death," he whispered. "The crown is death to everything that I am."

"Everything that sets itself up in opposition to me," said Kensington.

"Joshua died," breathed Alex. "His entire being was in opposition to you."

"Only one who submits to the crown will live," said Kensington.

"You have submitted," said Alex. "You have borne it."

"I bear it daily," said Kensington, smiling darkly. "The question is, can you?"

His dark eyes were searching Alex. "One who 'cannot kill': you are weak – you are insipid. But she…"

His eyes moved over Selena's body and returned to her face.

"She was glorious," he said. "Wielding our power with ease! I would have her back! I would have her take your place!"

He was fingering her shirt, and Selena began to writhe, but now Kensington's stare was back on Alex.

"What is she to you?" he asked. "Lover?"

"No," whispered Alex, feeling himself writhing in union with Selena. "No."

"Girlfriend?" asked Kensington, and he stroked a finger down Selena's face, and Alex stepped instinctively forward.

"No!" he said. "No."

"Whore?" asked Kensington, and he suddenly gripped her shirt in his fist.

Alex stepped closer, next to the altar. He reached out to take his father's hand off Selena's shirt.

"No," he said. "She is not a whore."

"Then what is she?" asked Kensington. "To lead you to defend her honour?"

Alex held Selena's eyes. He wrestled, and then confessed.

"Sister," he whispered. "She is a sister."

"Sister!" roared Kensington. "Then she can share in your inheritance after all!'"

And, suddenly, he seized the crown, grasped Selena up to his own chest, and thrust the crown on her head.

She screamed. Alex watched as her body stiffened – as she reached up to claw at the ancient metal spikes on her head, while his father held the crown firmly down on her head.

"No!" cried Alex. "It's not her choice!"

He reached to grasp the crown off her head, and clutched it to his own chest.

Selena collapsed off the altar, onto the floor. Was she dead? Alex peered after her, and then lifted his eyes to the knowing smile of his father.

"How far will you go?" he asked. "To protect her?"

Alex held the crown tightly to himself, with both arms wrapped around it.

"It's mine," he whispered, "no one else's."

And Kensington nodded. "Yes," he said. "It always has been yours, but now you finally acknowledge it."

Alex laid the crown on the naked altar, and reached down to draw Selena up into his arms. She was swaying on her knees, reaching to cling to his shirt.

Her face was covered with blood, as Joshua's face had sweated blood.

"Leave this place," said Alex, leaning into her. "Leave it and never come back."

"But you!" whispered Selena. "What will happen to you?"

"The crown belongs to me, Selena," whispered Alex. "It always did. I killed Joshua Davidson with it; I must carry it myself now."

"It will kill you too, Alex," whispered Selena.

"Never come back," said Alex. "Never talk to me again. If you do, you will not know me."

Tears filled her eyes, spilling over, mixing with blood on her face.

"Don't you get it?" she asked. "I came here to save you! I came to save you!"

163

Michelle Warren

"No one can save me, Selena," whispered Alex. "Haven't you figured that out yet?"

"No," whispered Selena. "No, I haven't!"

And Alex lifted her to her feet in his arms, and led her to the door.

"Leave," he said with tears. "Forget about me. Forget you ever knew me. Forget about this place."

And he opened the door, and thrust her into the blinding light and the rain, and shut the door behind her.

"No!" Selena's voice sounded from outside, and her fists began to pound on the door. "No! I won't leave you! I won't leave you to die!"

But soon Alex heard her being dragged away, and he was alone again, in the Shrine, with his father.

Kensington's eyes were on him. "Take the crown," he said, "and conquer Parliament."

Alex straightened, on his feet. "You have the Socialist Party primed," he said.

"Yes," replied Kensington. "But we need your skills; we need your mind. Fix the election, deceive the crowd, manipulate the funds..."

"Food," said Alex, "power, oil, the army..."

"We already own the army," said Kensington.

"Weapons..."

"Use the Sydney Naval Base," said Kensington, and Alex swallowed. Nukes.

"Connor," said Kensington. "I am silencing him. He is worth more alive than dead."

"Clarkson plays right into our hands," said Alex.

"Take on my empowerment," said Kensington, "and transcend me."

Alex held his eyes, and reached toward the altar to take up the crown in his hands.

"Give me two weeks," he said to his father.

"Prepare," said Kensington. "Prepare all the pathways."

The Computer...live! Make the entire programme live.

"Two weeks," whispered Alex, and he placed the crown again under the altar, stooped to pick up the black linen and lay it back over the wood, and reached to replace the golden chalices.

Blood. He swallowed. Blood. He must drink – and then there would be no going back.

Chapter 20

DECISIONS

Rachel sat next to James. He was at the computer; always, always looking at the computer.

Her body felt rigid. She stared down at her tablet.

"Carrington," said James, and Rachel looked up.

"What?" she said.

"Look at his renal function."

Rachel stared at the rising blood test level: his kidney function was failing.

"What did you give to him?" asked James.

"I don't know," said Rachel, and she rapidly flicked through her notes on the tablet, until she reached Carrington's notes.

"Anti-inflammatories?" asked James.

"Yes," said Rachel, frowning. He had spinal pain, and they thought it might even be osteomyelitis…

"Did you see he was on an ACE inhibitor?"

"Yes," said Rachel, "but he wasn't on a diuretic as well, and isn't yet sixty-five…"

"Do you see his creatinine?" snapped James at her. "Why didn't you give him morphine?"

Rachel stared at his hard gaze and thrust herself to her feet, squeezing away the tears from her eyes.

"I don't want to talk about this," she whispered. "If you want to use morphine, you prescribe it."

And she walked away toward Room One.

"Don't walk away when I'm talking to you," said James, and Rachel swallowed, stopping in the corridor, staring ahead. "You have set the patient's renal function off. How are you going to fix it?"

"I'll monitor," said Rachel, staring at the sign to Room One. "It might just be a fluctuation."

"We've already been monitoring it for three days," snapped James. "You must change your management now, or I'll deem you incompetent."

Rachel shifted her gaze through the room to the window on the other side, the driving rain of winter.

"I am not incompetent," she said quietly.

"What is your strategy?" asked James.

"I'll stop the anti-inflammatory and monitor his renal function."

"And his pain?"

"I'll consider tramadol and codeine," said Rachel. "You already know this. You know how we prescribe."

James's voice fell into silence. He brushed past her, and walked into Room One.

"Examine the patient," he snapped, pointing to a young Korean woman. Rachel grimaced, and moved forward. Obey him? Comply? Keep the peace? She gritted her teeth, and took the woman's pulse: eighty, regular.

"What brought you in?" she asked the woman, glancing up to her name: Eun Ae Choo! The Dean of the Cathedral!

Eun Ae smiled. "I think the Lord is giving me some rest," she said, and Rachel gazed at her.

"Some rest?" she asked, reaching for her stethoscope. "From being priest?"

Rachel listened to her heart: the sounds were normal. She listened to her chest: her breathing was normal. Rachel reached to check her abdomen.

"A chance for a different kind of life," said Eun Ae, her face radiant, and Rachel noticed a bulge in the lower part of her abdomen.

"Pregnant!" said Rachel, and Eun Ae beamed at her.

"An answer to prayer!" she said.

Rachel reached for her chart. "What brought you in?" she asked.

"A cough," said Eun Ae. "But it's gone now."

IV Augmentin…

"That must have been quite a cough," said Rachel, reaching to scan her charts. The chest x-ray result showed pneumonia. But her chest was clear.

"And did you hear about the Cathedral?" asked Rachel, as she reached to cross off the IV medication and chart oral antibiotics instead.

"What about it?" asked Eun Ae. "I've been on leave."

"Someone blew out the windows!" said Rachel. Alex Kensington, mention his name? No…

"Really?" said Eun Ae, her face breaking into a frown. "Why would they do that?"

"Get on with it!" James's voice interjected. "You're taking too much time!"

Rachel turned to look at his rigid face, feeling her fists clenching. Hold back? No! No, speak!

"If I'm taking too much time," she said, rising to her feet before him, "maybe you can start seeing some of the other patients!"

James's face flushed before her. Rachel held her breath.

"Get out," he whispered, and Rachel stared at his rigidity.

"What?" she asked.

"To the office," said James, "now."

He turned on his heel, and left the room.

Rachel stared after him, and looked back to Eun Ae's widened eyes.

"Easy," said Eun Ae gently. "Take it easy."

Rachel looked at her kind face. "Trouble is," she whispered, "it's not easy, for either one of us. It's not easy at all."

And she followed James out of the room, and into the office.

James reached around her to shut the door, and he locked it. Then he straightened before her.

"You will not humiliate me in front of the patients," he said. "One more time and you're fired."

Rachel stared at him. Quit? Was she ready? She wasn't ready.

"I didn't mean to humiliate you," she said. "It's just, if you were worried about time we could have shared the ward round. That's all I meant."

"I was commenting on you wasting time."

"I wasn't wasting time," said Rachel. "I was just using it differently."

"The Cathedral isn't relevant," said James.

"Not for you," said Rachel, "but it is Eun Ae's spiritual home."

"Spirituality is bullshit," said James. "Just a walk with the fairies, pure fantasy. Stick with reality."

Rachel grimaced at him, even as she felt the same familiar affection arising.

"Whatever you say," she muttered, and she reached to unlock the door, but then he physically moved to block her.

"No," he said.

Rachel shifted uncomfortably before him. "What are you doing?" she asked.

"I hear you've been talking to Harrison," said James.

She held his hard eyes, and swallowed. "Well, yes," she said.

"You have no right to share my personal business with the manager," he said.

"It's not just your personal business," said Rachel. "Not when it has a direct bearing on your job."

"It doesn't affect my job," said James. "It's under control."

"Like shit," said Rachel, before she could stop herself, and his face contorted.

"Don't talk to me like that!" he said.

"You're using morphine on the job!" said Rachel directly into his face. "You are not fit to practice medicine!"

And now, suddenly, he hit her across the face.

Rachel gasped. Hit! She had never been hit before. She reached to finger her jaw, and stared up at his face.

"You are mentally deranged," said James coldly, his eyes wide, his face flushed. "Delusional! Tempted to use morphine yourself, projecting yourself onto me."

"Listen," whispered Rachel, still fingering the growing bruise. "I know this is hard for you. I know medicine is your life."

"You're a bitch," whispered James. "It's just more 'holier than thou' crap. You have no idea! No idea what I've been through."

"I do know," whispered Rachel, looking at him. "I think I have some idea."

"No!" said James. "No idea!"

"Then tell me," said Rachel.

"Go to hell," said James.

"Your father..."

"Shut up..."

"Your sister..."

"Shut up!" cried James, as he hit her across the other cheek.

Rachel gasped. The pain! She shrank away from him, against the wall, and hid her head in her arms.

"You don't know me!" cried James. "Don't pretend that you do!"

"I can feel you," said Rachel into her arms. "You feel like a brother."

"I'm not your brother!" said James. "Get that into your thick skull! Stop trying to intervene! Stop trying to save me!"

Rachel felt weeping threaten to erupt from within her. Her brother was gone! Lost, at five! And this one had the same name! The same idiosyncrasies! The same connection...

"Love," she whispered into her arms. "It's just the way that it is! I choose it! I choose to continue with it."

"That's bullshit!" he cried. "You're a mess! Just a mess!"

"Loss," whispered Rachel. "I can feel your loss. Your abusive family."

"Don't," whispered James. "Don't."

"A lost sister," whispered Rachel. "A sister you loved – a sister abused, who died, like my brother died."

"Don't!" he cried, and Rachel looked up at him, with tears.

"Don't you see it?" she cried. "Surely you see it, as I see it? Surely you feel it too? Brother and sister? We are like brother and sister?"

"No!" cried James. "I don't want you! I don't want you, and I never have!"

"I know," whispered Rachel. "I know that, and I accept it."

"You're enough to drive anyone to morphine!" said James, and he suddenly reached out, opened the door, and left.

Rachel stared at the open door. Where had he gone? She knew where. And now he returned, slamming the door closed, locking it again.

He sank down against the wall in front of her. He gathered the needle and syringe together, drew up the morphine in front of her, changed the needle, and injected it into himself.

Rachel stared at the puncture wound in his arm. She felt sick. She closed her eyes, and swayed slightly.

"I can't do this any more," she whispered. "I quit."

"Don't leave," said James, his voice starting to slur. "I need you."

"You don't need me," said Rachel. "You're a better doctor than I am."

"I can't do the job," said James. "You said it yourself."

Rachel buried her face in her hands. "Neither can I," she whispered. "Not any more."

"I..." His voice caught, and she lifted her head. He was under the influence of a narcotic now; he had less defence. "I..."

She gazed at his naked vulnerability. She understood him. She loved him – a kind of love that gripped her, and would not let her go.

"Don't leave," he whispered. And then his head fell back against the desk, and he was sleeping.

Rachel sat quietly opposite him. The door was locked. She wanted to reach out, and lay a hand over his hand. She could not. She knew he would not bear it, in his normal self – he would push her away.

She gazed at his dozing form. He had hit her – her cheeks were swelling. She had reason to report him, and yet she knew, his damage was worse than hers – his family tragedy had been worse than hers.

Was he her long lost brother? Back from the dead?

She watched his chest lifting and falling, and in that moment, to her, he was as a brother – old or new, a brother, almost a twin. They were so similar! And yet so opposite. Simultaneously! Simultaneously the same and different.

She understood him as she understood herself. And yet she knew he would never understand what she had to do.

With deep pain, she rose to her feet. The patients were waiting in the ward, unattended, uncared for. He was dozing, in the office.

"Forgive me," she whispered. "Forgive me for what I must do."

She lifted herself to her feet, opened the door to the office, and locked it closed behind her.

The general manager's office was on the top floor of the Hospital. Rachel stood outside of the door. What was she doing? This move would end his career! This move might end his life.

She stood, hesitating, and lifted her hand to knock on the door.

"Enter," a male voice said, and she walked inside.

The general manager was a Maori man, sitting behind a large rimu desk, with tall windows behind him showing a view of the choppy harbour. He rose to his feet and stretched out his hand.

"Doctor Connor," said Jones, and he gestured for her to sit.

Rachel hesitated, and then sat in front of him.

"How can I help you?" he asked, his face attentive.

"Well," said Rachel, reaching for her stethoscope around her neck and placing it now in her pocket. "I need to tell you that I am resigning."

"I'm sorry to hear that," said Jones. "Moving on?"

"Not exactly," said Rachel. "There is a situation I must inform you about."

"Yes?" said Jones.

"Doctor James Lester is using morphine on the job."

The brown eyes stayed with her. Then he smiled.

"I see," he said, then he turned in his seat to look out of the window. "And how long have you observed this for?"

"About a week," said Rachel. "I informed the manager, Harrison, but…"

"Yes," said Jones, "I was informed."

"What?" Rachel frowned, looking at him. Then she made herself continue.

"Anyhow," she said. "I have told you what you need to know."

"And what will you be doing now?" asked Jones, still looking out of the window.

"I don't know," said Rachel.

"We can place you in a different ward," said Jones.

Rachel cast her eyes over the papers on his desk. Should she continue?

"What will you do about Doctor Lester?" she asked.

Now Jones turned back to her. "What do you want me to do about him?" he asked.

"He needs to be removed!" said Rachel. "He is a danger to patients! He is overriding patient rights! Virtually the entire profession would agree!"

"Do you want to replace him?" asked Jones, and Rachel shot up to her feet.

"I resign!" she said. "You have the information you need: my duty is fulfilled."

And she turned away from the desk and launched herself out of the office.

Flushing, Rachel jabbed at the button at the lift. Replace him? Was the general manager serious? Couldn't he see what was blatantly obvious? What was before his eyes?

Flustered, she stepped through the opening doors into the lift, and turned around, watching the lift doors close. The general manager knew? He already knew?

"Oh, dear God," she whispered, and darkness threatened her. Was the entire organisation corrupt? The leadership of the entire hospital? Did even the Medical Council already know?

She couldn't work, not like this! She couldn't work. And yet the patients! The patients!

She stopped at Ward Eight, on the eighth floor. She exited the lift, and turned to the manager's office.

"I quit!" she said to Harrison. "I'll use my sick leave and annual leave for the next three weeks. I'll get a doctor's certificate."

"Fine," said Harrison, "but don't expect to ever work in this hospital again."

"Will you be able to replace me?" asked Rachel.

"Undoubtedly," said Harrison.

"Immediately?" asked Rachel. "Will you be able to replace me immediately?"

"I've already been advertising the position."

Rachel stared at her, and flushed. "Today?" she asked. "Can you bring someone in urgently today?"

"Don't you worry about that," said Harrison. "We'll do fine without you."

Rachel shifted on her feet. "All right," she said. "I'll get my things."

"Good luck with that mental illness," said Harrison, and Rachel grimaced.

"I don't have a mental illness," she said. "The consultant should not be practising medicine, and I have lost faith in the leadership of…of…"

"Of the entire universe, no doubt," said Harrison smugly, and Rachel gritted her teeth.

"Goodbye," she said, and Harrison didn't answer, and Rachel turned, walked out of her office, and turned to the entrance of the ward.

Ward Eight…Rachel swallowed. Tears! Tears were taking her. She blinked them rapidly away. How could she do this? Just walk in there, get her things, walk out again…was this it? Was this the end?

"Courage," she whispered to herself. "Courage."

And she drew in a deep breath, and walked down the corridor.

Kate's eyes met her, from Room Two. Rachel swallowed, nodded quickly to her, and walked straight into the office.

James had gone. Rachel reached quickly for her bag. She took off her white coat, and draped her stethoscope around her shirt on her shoulders. She must be quick! She gathered her medical books off the shelves of the office, into her bag. Morphine on the job: it was illegal! Illegal to use morphine: illegal to use it practising medicine.

"The police…" she whispered, and then she turned, and James was in front of her.

His eyes were intense, penetrating, searching her.

"Where are you going?" he asked.

"I've resigned," she said.

"You spoke to the general manager," he said. "How dare you?"

"I did what I had to do," she said.

"You can't take it further," he said, and now his face was as flint. "You can't take it any further."

Rachel held his stare, and swallowed. "You make the decision," she said. "You know this is wrong."

He laughed, now. He laughed at her.

"The manager is behind me," he said. "The general manager is behind me. It's you who is wrong! Stirring up trouble, looking to do me in."

"They don't understand," said Rachel.

"They understand enough!"

"No!" said Rachel. "They don't understand what they are doing! They don't understand the harm they are causing!"

James's eyes narrowed. "And you do, do you?" he asked. "You

understand more than any of the establishment what is right and what is wrong?"

"I understand what the vast majority believe," said Rachel. "I understand what the vast majority would choose, if they knew."

James shook his head. "Don't you dare take this further," he said. "I'll have you for harassment!"

Rachel flushed. "Harassment?" she said, and she reached to finger her swelling cheeks. "You have no idea, James Lester! How can you? It is we who are at fault! We, who stood by and let you continue!"

And she reached into her trouser pocket, and pulled out her cell-phone.

"What are you doing?" whispered James, and Rachel frowned down at the phone.

"I'm not sure," she whispered back.

"You can't put me away!" he said. "I won't let you put me away!"

"I have to go," said Rachel, and quickly she pocketed her cell-phone, grasped her bag, and rushed down the corridor of the ward and away, into the lift.

The numbers…She scrolled through the numbers. Who could she talk to? Who? Her father's name was there. James's name was there…

The police. What was the local police station number? She searched for it, on the hospital wireless, and found it: Wellington Central Station.

The lift opened. She walked out, into the main foyer area, and out of the main doors of the hospital. She stood in the rain, holding her cell-phone. The police number was entered, but she hadn't yet called.

Pain took her chest. She was standing alone, in the public eye, outside of the hospital. Where could she go? Where?

"Saint Peter's," she whispered, and she thrust herself forward in the rain, toward the broken Cathedral.

Chapter 21

ESCALATION

James stared at Rachel striding down the corridor, leaving the ward.

"Where are you going?" he whispered. "What are you doing?"

He followed after her, and saw her disappearing into a lift. He jabbed a button. Where was the next lift? Furiously he tapped his foot – it was taking too long! He thrust himself away from the lift, through doors, into the stairwell and down the steps, two at a time.

His heart was pounding. The morphine – why wasn't it working? Why had it worn off so quickly?

She was leaving. His chest ached, and he struggled for breath. Six floors were gone, and there were two more to go. His cell-phone rang, and he ignored it. He must stop her! He must silence her! He reached the ground floor, and forced himself not to run out into the main foyer.

His stethoscope was around his neck. Strange, he never usually put it there – that was her thing. He fingered it, frowning, and strode through the foyer.

Was that her, standing in the rain outside? James hesitated for a moment. Her body was shaking. Was she crying? He frowned. Then, suddenly, she moved away, clutching on to her cell-phone.

"Who are you calling?" he whispered. "Who?"

And he rushed after her.

His own cell-phone was sounding. He fumbled at it inside his right trouser pocket, and answered it as he moved out of the main sliding doors and stood in the rain.

"Go to Oriental Bay," said a young man's voice.

"Who is this?" asked James. He could vaguely recognise the voice.

"Do you care about your career?"

Chills went up his spine. "Yes," he whispered.

"Then do what I say."

The voice was gone.

James shifted on his feet. Go after Rachel? Follow her to the right? The voice was telling him to go in the opposite direction, left! Left, to protect his career. Was it a threat? A more sinister threat? He swallowed, and launched himself left down the street, in the direction of Oriental Bay.

The rain was falling, and the sky was grey. James barely noticed it as he strode toward the harbour. The wind was picking up, a strong sea breeze off the water. He climbed over the retaining wall and stepped onto the sand.

A few random people were there. Who was he supposed to meet? Who was the voice, holding him to ransom?

A young man was pacing up and down the beach, also frowning. Who was it? James thought he recognised the gait, almost marching. The man's hands were both inside his jacket pockets, and his right hand was clutching onto something.

The green eyes found him, framed with blonde curls.

"Tristan Blake," murmured James. The lieutenant! They had fought together in the army, in the Middle East.

"James?" asked Tristan. "James Lester? Is that you?" He broke into a grin. "I didn't recognise you, with the stethoscope!"

178

James grimaced at him, fingering the bell sitting on his chest. "Maybe it was a mistake leaving the army," he muttered.

"A mistake?" said Tristan. "Leaving war?"

"At least it made sense," said James. "The objectives made sense."

"Not to me," said Tristan. "Not there; not then."

And he pulled out a rifle, from his left inner pocket.

James stared at him as he fingered the weapon between his hands.

"You still have that?" asked James.

"It's..." Tristan hesitated, and then continued. "It's the weapon I used to kill Joshua Davidson."

"I know," said James, and he reached out his hand. "Can I have a look?"

Tristan looked at him, and shrugged. "Once army always army, right?" he said, and he handed over the weapon.

James looked down at the gun in his hands.

"I remember," he muttered. Connor, Tristan, Davidson... "It was a tidy execution."

"Tidy?" Tristan choked. "He was innocent!"

"Who is really innocent?" asked James. He lifted the weapon, smiling, and pointed it at Tristan.

Tristan stared at him. "What are you doing?" he asked.

"Playing," said James, shrugging. "Just playing."

"Did you call me just now?" asked Tristan, and James scowled.

"What?" he asked.

"Did you call me?" repeated Tristan.

"No," answered James.

"Because someone called me," said Tristan, "and told me to come down to Oriental Bay."

James looked at him. Tristan had been summoned as well?

"Someone called me too," he said.

"Then..." Tristan was thinking as he spoke. "Then this has been set up."

James felt his heart suddenly pounding hard again. "Don't say that," he said. "Don't say anything."

His fingers stiffened on the gun, still pointed playfully at Tristan.

"We're being used," said Tristan. "Do you see it, James? We're being used."

James shook his head, and lowered the gun.

"It's all just a game," he muttered. "All of life, just one big game."

Suddenly he felt very tired. He fleetingly closed his eyes, and wanted to sleep.

"The voice," said Tristan. "I think I know it! I think I recognise it."

Now James's cell-phone rang again.

James stirred. He moved the rifle to his left hand, and reached down into his right trouser pocket for the cell-phone.

"Don't answer it," said Tristan. "It will be him, a set up."

"I have to answer it," said James. "He has information."

He opened the phone.

"She's arrived at Saint Peter's Cathedral," said the voice.

"Who?" asked James.

"You know who," said the voice. "She hasn't yet made the call."

James shifted on his feet. "What call?" he whispered.

"The call to inform the police of your morphine habit."

Chills went up James's spine. The voice, again, was gone. He stared at Tristan's trusting face.

"Rachel," he whispered, and Tristan straightened with another frown.

"Rachel Connor?" he asked.

Then, instinctively, James grasped Tristan's rifle to his side and ran.

Saint Peter's Cathedral! A Cathedral! That would be the height of irony, to return, after all these years! To...to confront Rachel there.

"James!" Tristan's worried voice called out from behind him. "What are you doing? James!"

But James blocked him out, and set his sights ahead.

The Cathedral...James felt sick. Suddenly a memory was before him: his father. He shook his head, he pushed the memory away, but this time it would not stay put.

"Stop, you little bastard!" said his father, and now he was beating him.

Communion...vessels! Vessels with blood – literal blood, Catholic blood, the body and blood of Christ. He gagged on the alcohol; he choked on the wafer.

"Can't," he whispered. It was literal! Literal! "Can't!"

And now, his sister.

"Oh, God!" he pleaded, and desperately he pushed the memory away. His father! His father and his sister...Morphine! He needed morphine! He couldn't get morphine, but he had the gun....

And now, her body...her life, gone. Gone, taken from her...the bottle of pills, next to her – antidepressants! The overdose, after...after...

He closed his eyes tightly. Medicine. He would take up medicine, and the army. He would fix the shit in the world: he would cure it.

And now...and now Rachel was about to take the cure away from him.

"No," he whispered. "I won't let you rob me. I won't let you strip me bare."

And he thrust himself toward the Cathedral.

Chapter 22

THE CHOICE

Alex stood in the Shrine.

The cursed crown was before him, sitting on the black altar. His father was standing next to the altar in his black robes, waiting, holding the golden chalice in his hands.

It was time. It was his fate! He must now embrace his fate.

"Who did I just kill?" asked Alex, slipping his cell-phone back into his trouser pocket.

"You know who," answered his father. "At least now you are paving the way."

He had just tracked her, it was so easy! Tracked her cell-phone out of the hospital, through the streets, into Saint Peter's Cathedral.

"Rachel Connor," he whispered, and Kensington nodded.

"She is the necessary cost," he said.

Rachel...Alex frowned, remembering her face in the hospital; remembering her kindness.

"Connor resisted," said Kensington. "That bastard went ahead and informed Clarkson of our little domestic, even knowing the price."

"Clarkson knows?" asked Alex, shifting on his feet.

"Not yet," said Kensington. "I will discredit Connor's testimony: I will crush him. Clarkson will trust you more than Connor – you are the one Connor said he saw. You will move into Parliament. You will take my place."

Alex swallowed, looking at the crown. Yes, he would take up his inheritance.

"It's time," said his father, and Alex nodded.

"Yes," he whispered. "It is time."

And now he went to his knees.

Black robes were appearing – his father was laying the robes over his shoulders. The golden chalice was in Alex's hands. He gazed down at the blood. Murder. He was to embrace murder. The crown...his father was reaching for the crown.

Alex closed his eyes. This was the moment. Submit, or die. He had chosen to submit – he had chosen to lose himself.

Why...? His last fleeting thought was of Selena. She was beautiful. A sister...like a long lost sister. She would remain beautiful now. She would remain alive.

The crown was descending onto his head. But then, suddenly, blinding light filled the Shrine.

Kensington gasped. Alex shifted, on his knees. The crown faltered – it fell to the ground with a crash.

Alex looked up to see fury fill his father's face. He strode forward – he slammed the door shut. He dragged the one responsible to the altar, and pulled out a knife.

It was Selena.

Her face was rigid now, not rebellious but somehow fixed – somehow set, ready.

Alex stared at her. He was dressed in black, in the black robes of the priest. Her eyes passed over him, on his knees. Her blue gaze set on him.

"I am the White Queen," she whispered to him. "The White Queen is the most powerful piece, and is willing to die to defend the White King."

Alex felt his jaw dropping. "I am not white," he choked. "I am covered with darkness."

"But why?" asked Selena. "Why remain covered in darkness, when you could be drinking from the opposite chalice?"

"Communion," whispered Alex. "Communion."

And now Kensington tore away her shirt.

Alex rose to his feet, staring down at her on the altar. Her face was rigid, in anticipation. She was ready. She was girded for hell.

"See it," she whispered to him. "See what you will become if you fall to him."

Alex kept his eyes on her face, and would not allow himself to look at her body. She was trusting him, even now! She was speaking beyond their bodies.

"See it," she whispered. "A purity greater than depravity. A life greater than death."

She grasped the knife from Kensington and gave it to Alex.

"Choose," she said, and Kensington straightened behind her, at the altar.

"Choose," his father said.

Alex looked down at the knife in his hands. He looked at Selena's face, at her nobility in the Shrine of Hell. He looked at his father's face, at his quiet darkness.

Death was before him: Selena's death; the death of his own soul. Or Selena's life, and his own physical death. Which could it be? Which should it be?

He gazed at the light in her eyes, at the light in the midst of death. Nobility.

The White Queen.

He preserved her clothes; he shed off his own black robes. He laid the knife on top of the robes. Suicide! It was suicide, to turn away from his father on the very verge of his father's actualisation in himself! Suicide!

He grasped Selena's hand and pulled her off the altar.

"The White King defends the Queen," he said.

"No!" she said, shoving him away. "You're playing for the entire side!"

"The entire side?" breathed Alex.

"Go!" cried Selena. "Go! Without you, we all lose!"

Alex stared at her, and watched the iron rigidity cross over his father's face.

"Do not betray me," he whispered, "or I will make you suffer a thousand deaths."

Alex held his eyes, as Kensington pulled out his gun.

"Go!" pleaded Selena. "You know where you must go! You know what you must do!"

Alex cast his eyes over her drawn face and over his father still behind the altar, blocked by her half naked body.

With agony he understood. "Oh, Selena," he breathed. "I'll never stop grieving for you…"

"Live!" she whispered, and tears spilt down her face. "Live, Alex! And let others live!"

She suddenly reached for the crown sitting next to her, on the altar, and thrust it into his arms.

The crown! He stared down at it. White! A White King, not Black! Suddenly he could see. Suddenly he understood.

"Go!" cried Selena, and he turned on his feet, shoved the door open, and ran into the light.

Chapter 23

CRISIS

R achel stood in Saint Peter's Cathedral.
The church was quiet. Rachel looked up at the window frames above, at the gaping holes, now covered with plastic. A wind was blowing around the church, a howl that sounded like a gale. It beat at the plastic covers, but for now they were not giving in.

The glass shards had been cleared from the floor and chairs. Rachel walked down the aisle, lifting her eyes to the tiled figure of Jesus stretched out on the cross.

"If you're out there," she whispered, "please tell me what the hell I do now."

She stopped at the steps leading up to the altar, and sank down to her knees.

Her cell-phone was still in her right hand. She lifted it now, and stared at the number – Wellington Police Station.

"Do I call?" she whispered, looking up again at Jesus on the cross. "It might kill him!"

Tears filled her eyes. "I don't want that! I don't want him to die!"

Suddenly her cell-phone rang. Startled, she stared at it and then answered it.

"Rachel?" said her father, and she gripped her phone more tightly.

"Dad," she said.

"Is everything okay?" asked Connor.

"Ah…" Weeping threatened to override her. "No," she whispered. "It's not okay."

"What's going on?" he asked, and his tone sounded urgent.

"Well," said Rachel, "I…I resigned."

"Resigned?" he asked.

"I…I found out something at work."

"What kind of thing?"

"Something bad."

Her father's voice paused. Then he continued.

"Where are you now?" he asked.

"At Saint Peter's," she said.

"Don't leave there," said Connor. "I'm coming across, right now."

And his voice had gone.

Astonished, she looked at the phone. Then she jabbed in the previous number, the Wellington Central Police Station.

Do it? Push call? She swallowed. She was still on her knees, before the altar. She gazed at the silver chalice, sitting on the white linen – at the bread wafers, sitting on the silver plate.

Communion…

She looked up at the face of Jesus, at the blood dripping from the crown of thorns. She remembered Joshua, blood on his face, kneeling before Tristan.

"Father!" he had prayed. *"Don't hold it against them! They really have no idea what they are doing!"*

Pain filled her. She wished for Joshua's presence – she wished for his wisdom, beyond her own, but he was dead.

"What do I do?" she asked, and John suddenly appeared, walking past her, standing next to the altar.

"What do you want to do?" he asked.

187

"I want to save him," said Rachel, "but I can't. I want to protect him, but I can't. I want to make him right, but I can't."

John smiled sadly at her. "Can you bring him here?" he asked, and she grimaced.

"I wish," she whispered, and John turned to finger the silver chalice. But then, suddenly, his fingers stiffened on the wine.

Now Rachel felt it: a gun, to her temple.

She stiffened, and stared up at John at the altar – at his back.

"Would you kill your colleague?" asked James's voice. "Just to get your own way?"

Rachel felt her throat tightening with sudden fear.

"I don't want to kill you," she whispered, staring at John's stiffening spine.

"Like hell," said James. "You want to do away with me."

"I don't," whispered Rachel, closing her eyes tightly. "I just want things to be right."

Someone else had entered into the church. Who was it? She could hear the doors opening and closing.

"James!" called Tristan's voice, with alarm. "That's my friend! You're holding up my friend with my rifle!"

His footsteps sounded down the aisle. Rachel opened her eyes. John's head was tilted up in the direction of Jesus on the cross. His knuckles were white, gripping hard onto the communion chalice of wine.

Rachel could see, out of the corner of her eye: Tristan standing alongside her, a few feet away, his arm outstretched, pointing a gun at James's head.

"Where'd you get that one from?" asked James, his tone annoyed, the rifle not shifting from Rachel's temple.

"Alex Kensington," said Tristan, and Rachel glanced sideways at him.

"Alex Kensington?" she asked.

Tristan's face looked white for her, his eyes wide. "He laid it down," said Tristan quickly. "Next to mine in the sand."

The Price of Redemption

"Never mind Alex Kensington, Rachel," said James curtly. "I'm here to stop you making that call."

Rachel looked forward, and felt her fingers tightening around her cell-phone as he continued.

"I trust your word," he said. "Tell me that you'll do nothing, and we'll all go home and pretend none of this happened. Business as usual! You can even have another interview for your job, and…"

"I can't," whispered Rachel, staring up at John's tension; at his hands on the communion vessels, and the back of his head looking at Christ. "I can't pretend this is just business as usual."

James reached for the trigger, and Rachel noticed Tristan shifting on his feet, keeping his aim steady.

"James," he murmured. "Don't make me do this. This is stupid, we're on the same side."

Rachel glanced again at Tristan's face: PTSD! He still had some degree of trauma, from the war – from the shooting of Joshua.

"Poetic, don't you think, Tristan?" said James. "If I should use this gun against her? Connor's defence?"

The doors opened again, and a voice cried out. "Rachel!"

Rachel gasped. It was her father! Distress suddenly engulfed her. She longed to turn to him, but she could not.

James pressed the gun more firmly into her temple.

"Your father is here," he said. "He was the most powerful man in the land, the General of the army. I'm a dead man now. Any way this pans out, I am dead."

"No," whispered Rachel, staring up at the chalice in John's hand – at the cost of Christ for the salvation of others. "I don't want you to die. Call the police yourself. Tell them the truth."

And she handed her phone back over her head to James.

He laughed over her – she felt him move to pocket her cell-phone.

"Is this a trick?" he said. "Of course, you will call them the moment you leave this place."

"Not if you call them first," said Rachel.

"Suicide!" said James. "Don't you know I have nothing else but my career?"

"You have something else," said Rachel, and the gun started to shake on her temple.

"Shut up," he said. "Shut up, Rachel. You are no family of mine."

Now Rachel could see her father standing to her left, reaching out a hand toward James.

"Soldier," he said. "Whatever she's done, I can help."

"How?" asked James over her. "You're a back bench loser: posing as the General, posing as the Prime Minister."

She glanced at her father's face, at his middle aged lines drawn with regret.

"I should never have arranged for the assassination of Davidson," he whispered. "I will pay for it now for the rest of my life."

Tristan shifted again on his feet, to her right, and then there was another voice.

"No," said the Bishop. "No, Prime Minister, you have forgotten about redemption."

Connor's face contorted. Rachel couldn't quite turn her head to him, but now Mark Blake was standing alongside him, reaching out a hand to his shoulder.

"Redemption?" scoffed James over her head. "Like hell! It's all bullshit! It's all lies! Fairy tale wishes of the mentally ill!"

And the gun was beating against her temple with his vigour.

"There is no resurrection," he said, behind the gun. "Say it, Rachel! Say it in this bullshit place! Joshua Davidson is dead! There is nothing else."

Rachel stared back up at John, at his stiff back and his white knuckles, clutching onto the communion chalice. Joshua was before her, in her mind's eye: bullets, to his chest! Five bullets, killing him! His face was smiling in his pain, his hand was reaching out to her.

"It's finished!" he said. *"It's sorted!"*

Rachel stared at him, and then back at John. He was turning now to her, releasing the chalice, turning his back to Christ. His face was white, his green eyes distraught, passing over her face, and over James and his gun.

"Say it," said James to him. "Say it's all bullshit."

Rachel stared up at John, on her knees before the altar.

"I don't want you to die," whispered John, and tense tears filled his green eyes. "I would have died, but I don't want you to die."

Rachel felt her body ready to erupt with weeping.

"My life doesn't matter," she whispered. "Joshua is all that matters. The truth is all that matters."

"Damned right," said James. "Tell her the truth, and set her free of all this bullshit."

John's eyes were on her. He stepped forward toward her, and went to his knees on the top step. He reached into his pocket.

"Easy..." said James, and the gun became firm on her temple, ready.

John pulled out the deformed bullets. His whole body was shaking as he stretched out his hand to Rachel and to James, with the five bullets on top.

"Joshua gave these to me," said John firmly, his eyes set on Rachel with agony. "He is alive. He is alive."

And now he laid the bullets down on the step between them, took a deep breath, and prepared for death.

Rachel stared at him. John was readying himself for her death? She knew! She knew his watching would be more agonizing for him than his own departure, just as Joshua's death had been for her! She knew this for him was the greatest cost.

She stared down at the bullets on the ground: she saw in her mind, again, Joshua. Tristan's shots into his chest! His smile.

"It's finished," he said. "It's sorted."

"Oh my God," she breathed, staring at Joshua's face, at his smile of certainty; staring up at John, on his knees, preparing for her death in his testimony. "Oh my God, it's real."

Joshua's smile...alive! He was alive!

"Oh my God!" cried Rachel, and she slapped a hand over her mouth, and found herself suddenly weeping for joy. "He's alive! He's alive!"

John was weeping now before her, watching her. His body was shaking, his eyes lit through his tears.

"He's alive," he whispered, "and now all of us can live too, even if we must first die."

"No!" said James. "No, you bastard! You have corrupted her! You have tainted her mind!"

"The truth is the truth," whispered Rachel, joy filling her chest in the midst of her own imminent death, suddenly one with John's tearful joy. "Even if you kill me, the truth remains."

"Truth?" scoffed James. "I'll tell you truth! My father was a bastard, despite all your bullshit! Rape is real! Murder is real! Abuse is real! I don't care any more! I don't care if I have to rot in prison, I have to show you my reality! I have to prove it to you!"

And Rachel felt him beginning to pull the trigger.

John's eyes widened before her.

"Don't look," she whispered to him. "It will kill you. Don't look."

"I have to look," he whispered back, with tears. "This is your cost: this is your sacrifice."

"James!" cried Tristan. "James, don't make me kill you!"

"Soldier," choked Connor to Tristan. "Stand down. I am your commander."

"There is no commander," whispered James. "There is only us."

Rachel stared into John's horror; she felt James ready to kill. She closed her eyes, and waited to receive his bullet.

The Cathedral doors sounded again. As if in a dream, Rachel opened her eyes again.

"No!" cried a young voice. "Stop! We don't have to be cogs in his wheel! She's not the enemy!"

His urgency snapped her to attention. Who? Who was crying out? The voice, it was familiar.

"Stop!" he said, much closer, maybe half way down the aisle.

"Alex!" breathed Mark. "Where have you been?"

Rachel heard wind, a gust of wind, suddenly surrounding the Cathedral. And then the doors opened again.

"Stop!" Another low voice sounded. "This is not part of the plan!"

And loud heavy footsteps were sounding up the aisle.

Alex brushed past Rachel, on her knees – he rushed past John. Rachel stared up at the young figure: it was Alex Kensington! He was clutching something to his chest – the crown! The same crown Selena had put onto Joshua's head! The crown of poison.

"It's all my fault!" cried Alex. "I killed Joshua Davidson! But I can fix it! I can fix it!"

And he laid the crown on the altar and went to his knees, pressing his head into the white linen.

"I'm your slave now!" he said. "I'm your slave! Take me! Have your way!"

Rachel stared at the young man on his knees, weeping at the altar. What was happening, repentance? But now another large form brushed past her: Kensington! His father!

"No!" he roared. "You little bastard, you are overriding my plan!"

And now he was dragging Alex around, thrusting him back onto the white altar.

Kensington's face was cruel, his eyes calculating. He was reaching for the silver chalice.

"I'll expose you!" cried Alex, staring into his father's face. "I'll reveal your agenda! I'll set Parliament free!"

Kensington pressed a large hand over his nose and mouth, and Alex's smaller form wrestled beneath him, choking.

"James!" cried Tristan. "The real enemy! James!"

"Shoot," ordered Connor. "You must shoot, Lieutenant Blake: democracy is under threat."

Rachel glanced up at Tristan's face, at his conflict as he still aimed his gun at James. Shoot Kensington? That would expose Rachel to

James's bullet.

"Do it," breathed Rachel. "Save the boy."

Tristan shook his head. "What about you?" he breathed with tears. "Who will save you?"

Tears filled her eyes – she blinked them away.

"My life doesn't matter," she whispered. "Save the nation. That is your job."

Tristan's eyes were wide, staring at her. She looked back, to see Kensington shifting his hand to unblock Alex's mouth. The young man thirstily sucked in a breath, and Kensington swiftly poured the communion wine down his throat, making him choke.

"That's what you get for choosing their chalice, you bastard," said Kensington. Alex clutched erratically at the linen on the altar, struggling to breathe, and Kensington reached into his pocket and pulled out a gun.

Rachel stared as he set it against Alex's temple.

"Stop," said John, and he rose from his knees to stand next to Alex on the altar, away from Rachel; away from her protection. "This boy doesn't belong to you any more."

"If he doesn't belong to me," said Kensington, "he will belong to no one."

And Kensington reached to grasp the crown, and thrust it on Alex's head.

The young boy stared up at him, gasping for breath. He was wearing the crown. Kensington stared down at him.

"The curse is broken," said John. "He has handed it on to one more powerful."

"Joshua…" whispered Rachel, and now she understood. Alex had deliberately given Selena the crown, to put on Joshua's head! And Joshua had carried it, willingly! Willingly carried the darkness, to take it into the grave: to undo it, and overcome it – to outlive it.

Kensington stared at Alex's choking face. Struggling! He was struggling to live! Kensington hit him across the face. Then he broke into an evil smile.

"Stalemate," he whispered, and he pressed his body over Alex, laid his mouth over his, and went to pull the trigger.

"Shoot!" cried Rachel, watching Alex writhe with horror under his father's invasion. "Shoot!"

I don't care about my life any more! She thought. *Shoot me if you must, James, just save the boy! Save the boy!*

"Shoot!" cried Tristan, and her father's voice was aligned.

"Shoot!" cried Connor.

John was shifting, next to Alex, reaching out his hand to his contorted body...

Suddenly Kensington's body was thrust off Alex. A reverberating shot sounded as his body fell dead behind the altar, between communion and the cross.

Rachel stared through the empty space of the altar's wooden frame, under the white linen. A shot to the head! Fatal! But who? Whose bullet?

She looked up to Tristan. His arm was pointing Alex's gun straight and steady toward Kensington. His face was rigid. He had fired! He was back, true army! With tears, Rachel saw it: redemption! Redemption! She glanced to her left, to see her father collapsed on his knees, profound relief crossing his face. His eyes were for her, filled with happiness! Happiness, for the first time in months! Rachel gazed at him, and instinctively smiled, and he smiled back at her.

"Democracy!" he cried. "Now we can be free again!"

She looked at Mark Blake still on his feet, staring at Alex on the altar, his eyes filling with tears.

And now, from her knees, she looked up.

James was pointing Tristan's rifle over her head at Kensington. His arm was straight, unflinching, his jaw set.

"He fired!" cried Tristan. "One shot! He fired, and so I could fire!"

"Two bullets?" breathed Rachel, and she peered under the altar. There had been two bullets! One to Kensington's head, and one sideways through his chest.

"You aimed for his heart, and I for his brain," muttered James to

Tristan. "Fitting."

Rachel looked back up at James's face. Shock was starting to penetrate his rigidity. He was beginning to sway on his feet.

"Oh my God," he whispered. "I've just killed him."

"Defence!" said Tristan. "It was national defence!"

"You don't understand," whispered James. "There's so much more."

And he staggered back, and lifted the rifle to his own head.

Rachel thrust herself to her feet and reached out her hand.

"James," she whispered. "Don't."

"Oh my God," he whispered, staring at her. "I was going to shoot you!"

His body trembled, and she shook her head.

"I don't matter," she said. "I don't matter."

"Why shouldn't you matter?" he whispered, frowning in confusion.

"I'm just the dogsbody, remember?" said Rachel. "Just the dogsbody."

"No," whispered James. "No."

"I clean up after everyone else's mess," she said. "I work to save everyone else."

"No," he whispered. "You're key."

The rifle was dropping from his temple.

Rachel shrugged, and reached for her stethoscope in her pocket.

"Here," she said with tears, laying it against his chest. "You needed this. You needed me gone."

James stared at her. He crouched, laid the gun at his feet, rose again, and reached for the stethoscope around his own neck.

"Cardiology grade," he murmured, laying it around her neck. "You need the right tools, Doctor Connor, to be the best doctor you can be."

Rachel gazed at his face. Weeping took her as she fingered his quality stethoscope around her neck.

"No," she whispered. "No."

He reached for her cell-phone out of his own pocket, and dialled 111.

"Ambulance, police or fire?" asked the voice at the other end of the phone.

The Price of Redemption

"Police," whispered James. "I've just shot a man."

"Where are you?" asked the voice.

"I'm in confession," whispered James, and he collapsed.

Shocked, Rachel rushed forward to catch him in her arms. She awkwardly lowered him to the ground, and reached for his pulse. It was weak, and erratic, and fast! And now, behind her, Alex screamed.

Rachel twisted around to look at the young man, still stretched back out on the altar. He was staring up at the broken windows, his arms clutching erratically at white linen.

"I can't see!" he cried out. "Darkness! Darkness!"

And his voice lifted into a wail that chilled her to the bone.

John rushed to him, leaning over his contorting body, guiding his hands to grasp onto his own shirt.

"Death," murmured John. "It's death! But hold on, Alex; hold onto me! Hold on through the death, and you will live!"

Alex's eyes blindly stared up in the direction of John's face. His right hand reached to try to find John's cheek.

"Help me!" he cried out. "Save me!"

"Light," murmured John over him. "Let there be light." And now a sudden gust of wind shook the church, and the plastic covers were ripped off the broken windows, and a cold gale blew through the Cathedral, and Rachel shivered, and Alex gasped, and sucked in a deep breath, and reached to finger John's eyes.

"I can see," he whispered. "I can see!"

John lifted Alex in his arms off the altar.

"Time for life to begin," he said, and he carried him down the steps, past Rachel, to Mark Blake.

Tears filled Mark's eyes. Rachel gazed at the Bishop, in purple and white, standing next to her father, as John placed Alex into Mark's arms, and Mark received him.

"Come," murmured Mark over him, and he lowered him to the ground, kneeling beneath him. Alex was curling up like a child against him, moving his arms over his head.

"Peace," murmured Mark, arranging him on his own chest. "Peace, Alex."

Alex began to sob. Mark's arms tightened around him, and wonder fleetingly crossed his face as he reached out a hand to cover and protect Alex's face.

Rachel drew her eyes back to James. He had laid himself on his side, and was hiding his head in his arms. She reached again for his pulse, it was gaining strength.

Tristan had reached for her cell-phone, and now he started informing the police.

"Defence," he said down the phone. "National defence, at Saint Peter's Cathedral."

"No," whispered James into his arms. "No."

Rachel knelt with her knees supporting his back, keeping him in recovery position. Had he fainted? He had almost fainted.

"There was no choice," murmured Rachel. "The boy was going to die."

"That doesn't matter," whispered James back, his eyes closed. "A boy still can't kill his own father."

Rachel's gut churned, and she reached to feel his head. Was it a fever? Was he delirious?

"Alex never wanted to kill his father," she said.

"No," whispered James. "No."

"Then…" She cast her eyes over his brown hair. "Then why…?"

"It's metaphorical," whispered James. "Doesn't anyone understand metaphor any more?"

Rachel frowned, and reached out tentatively to touch his hair. He was talking about his own father, the one who had abused – the one who had overridden and driven his sister to suicide.

Now James wasn't resisting her touch.

"It was an impossible situation," whispered Rachel, with tears. "There was no solution."

"There was," said James, his eyes still tightly closed. "I just didn't have the courage to do it."

"What?" murmured Rachel, and James opened his eyes, staring out ahead of himself.

"A change," he whispered. "Redemption." And now his body shuddered. "But a new life means facing death."

"What is redemption?" murmured Rachel, looking down at him. "What would it look like for you?"

James grimaced. "Like nothing I have ever known," he said.

"I don't want you to go to prison," said Rachel with tears. "I never wanted that."

"I know," said James. "I know."

"I wish..." said Rachel. "I wish we could just go back to work together, and help the patients, and that it could be..."

"Business as usual?" asked James, and he smiled wryly, and Rachel noticed he was looking at Alex in Mark's arms.

"It's not possible!" said Rachel, also looking at Alex. "It's not possible."

"Some boundaries must never be crossed," said James, staring at the good Father. "Some crimes can never be reversed."

"I would wish for your career to continue," said Rachel, "and yet I know it must not."

"No," choked James, and he wrapped his arms around himself. "My refuge is gone. There is no home any more, not for me!"

Tears filled Rachel's eyes. "I care about you," she said, and she tentatively reached out a hand to his shoulder. "If you must go to prison, I will visit you there."

"Don't visit me," said James. "It will only make it feel worse."

"I will visit you," said Rachel, "and I'll ask for your advice, and I'll leave my stethoscope with you in prison, and I'll bring yours when I visit, and..."

James stiffened. He reached for her hand on his shoulder, and suddenly gripped it hard.

"I'm scared!" he said to her. "I'm scared, Rachel! No one has ever given a shit about me, and now…now I'll be ostracised…"

"Don't be afraid," murmured Rachel. "It's only a gateway, James: death is only a gateway into a better life."

"I don't have faith," whispered James.

"Then use mine," said Rachel.

"I…" He twisted himself, and his face contorted as he found her eyes. "I don't know how to say I'm sorry."

Now the tears flooded her eyes.

"That's okay," she said. "That's okay."

"I should never have…"

"Don't," Rachel interrupted him, blinking the tears away. "You don't have to."

"I love you."

Now Rachel stared at him, and threw a hand over her mouth, and felt her face contorting.

"There," said James, glancing away again to Alex in Mark's arms. "I said it."

He pushed himself off the floor, and sat up in front of her.

"Love," he muttered, almost to himself. "Why does it have to be so damned difficult? Especially family love, that's just the pits."

And he pushed himself to his feet.

Rachel rose to her feet before him, and reached again to finger his stethoscope on her chest.

"My career is over," he said. "You keep it. I couldn't let it go, I didn't have the guts."

"You can come back," said Rachel. "You can recover. I'll keep it for you."

"No," said James, looking at her. "A doctor cannot kill. A doctor must never kill."

"You were army too," said Tristan. "We needed army too."

"No," said James, holding Rachel's eyes. "I'm not talking about Kensington." And Rachel shook her head.

"I don't matter," she whispered. "Don't hold up your career on account of me."

"You do matter," said James. "And what I did matters too."

"It's the patients," said Rachel. "If it was only me, I would never have…"

"I know it's the patients," said James. "I know, Rachel. I know how you think, I'm a doctor too."

Relief filled her at the words. She grasped a hold of his stethoscope, and held his eyes.

"You won't come back?" she asked, and he shrugged.

"I guess there's life after medicine," he said.

"What will you do?" she asked, and he smiled wryly.

"I'll have plenty of time to think about it in my cell," he said, and Rachel could hear sirens outside of the Cathedral.

James straightened, his face stiffening in fear. She reached out a hand to his hand. He automatically pulled his away. Then he hesitated, looking at her; looking at her hand.

"Are you my brother?" asked Rachel, and James gazed at her. Then he smirked.

"You don't need a brother like me," he whispered. "That kind of love will kill you."

Rachel smiled, and James seemed captured by her eyes. He smiled in return, and then he was taken away.

Tears filled Rachel's eyes again. She turned back to the altar and looked at Jesus on the cross.

"That kind of love will kill you," she murmured. "So be it."

She went to her knees, and took in a deep breath, and the wind, once again, blew through the Cathedral, and she was lifted up to her feet.

Chapter 24

OFFERINGS

Alex stared up into Mark's face. Agony! Agony! His father had just been shot! Over Alex's body, while kissing...

"Oh my God," pleaded Alex, and he reached out to grasp Mark's robes. "Don't leave me! Don't let me go..."

He shook, and Mark's embrace tightened around him. Mark's face was contorting with Alex's pain, his blue eyes penetrating, but not to control – to connect, to feel, to love, to give him life...

"Hold on," whispered Mark over him. "Hold on to me, and live."

He was bending closer to him, his face hovering above.

"Hold on," he repeated. "You have to get through this."

Alex felt Mark's large hand grasping his own, and a wave of nausea flooded over him – his body contorted, and now it was jerking.

"Help me," he pleaded. "Help me."

"Stay with me," said Mark. "Stay with me."

Alex stayed, and pain consumed him, and violation tainted him. He hid his face in Mark's shoulder while his body jerked out of control, but Mark was murmuring over him, and the horror was lifting slightly.

"You're safe now," said Mark. "You're safe."

"Safe?" whispered Alex. "Is anywhere safe?"

"Yes," murmured Mark. "Yes, Alex, there is safety here. There will always be safety here."

Alex covered his face with his hands, and leaned against Mark's chest, and clung to his robe, and cried. Who was this man? Who was this man, who was rescuing him? The Bishop? The Bishop he had corrupted to his father's side?

"I'm sorry," whispered Alex. "I'm sorry, I'm sorry, I'm sorry…"

Weeping erupted from within him, weeping that would not let him go.

Mark's arms wrapped fully around him now, rocking him on his knees.

"It's all right," he whispered. "I understand now. I'm so sorry, I understand."

"Hell," pleaded Alex into his chest. "Hell."

"A living death," murmured Mark. "Sometimes the cure is as bad as the disease."

Alex gritted his teeth, and rocked in pain. Mark rocked with him, and soon Alex found himself dozing on his chest. Escape! Escape for a while into sleep.

"Will you stay with him?" asked John's voice.

"Yes," replied Mark's voice. "I will stay with him."

"Adoption?" asked John.

"I will," said Mark. "If he will have me."

"I will," whispered Alex into his chest. "Please, please…"

Then darkness took him.

When he awoke he was still in the Cathedral, lying on top of the steps leading to the altar. Mark had taken off the white covering of his Bishop's robe, and lain it over him. Mark was standing with John, in his purple tunic, at the altar.

His father…Alex shuddered, looking quickly beyond the altar and looking away again. His body was gone. Relief consumed him, almost collapsing him into a faint. The police must have come – they must have taken him away.

Alex wrapped his arms around himself, and then looked up into Rachel's face. The doctor…she looked quiet, her eyes passing over him thoughtfully.

"Are you okay?" she asked, and he felt his face contort.

"No," he whispered, and she nodded.

"Fair enough," she murmured. "That was some serious shit."

Astonished, Alex gazed at her. "Thank you," he whispered. "It was."

He found himself shaking, and she smiled gently at him.

"I guess you would recommend antidepressants…" began Alex.

"No," said Rachel quietly.

"…or counsellors," said Alex.

"Maybe," replied Rachel.

"Some kind of psychotherapy," Alex said, "or…"

"Give it a rest," interrupted Rachel, with another gentle smile. "This was terrible trauma."

Alex gazed at her as she continued.

"You need a little light," she said quietly. "A little bit of light, growing steadily, day by day; some goodness, to offset the bad, over time. Some light to offset the terrible darkness."

"Light," whispered Alex, looking at her. "What kind of light?"

"Humanity," said Rachel gently to him, and her eyes lifted to Jesus on the cross. "Some goodness of humanity, to offset the bad, and when humanity fails so profoundly as this, something deeper. Something stronger."

"There is still hope for humanity?" asked Alex, and Rachel gazed at him, her eyes filling with tears, and Alex noticed she was pretty.

"Yes, Alex," she whispered. "There is still hope for humanity."

"And the deeper?" asked Alex. "The stronger?"

Rachel looked up again at the altar, and then moved to sit alongside him.

"I didn't grasp it," she said to him. "I saw Joshua die with my own eyes, and I never grasped why."

The Price of Redemption

Alex followed her gaze to the altar, and saw his own crown sitting there.

"He died to save me," he whispered, and then, choking, he thrust himself to his feet. "He died to save me!"

Joshua had known all along! The crown He had chosen to take the crown onto himself!

John's eyes came to him, from the altar.

"See what Joshua has offered," he said. "Goodness, to transcend our bad. Light, to transcend our darkness."

"Life to transcend our death," said Rachel, rising to her feet.

Alex lifted his eyes now to the jagged open windows, the windows he had shot out; the saints he had blown away.

"He has saved my life," breathed Alex, "when I shot him to pieces."

"Salvation is the beginning," said John, "while redemption is the end."

"Redemption," murmured Alex, and he lowered his eyes to Tristan.

Tristan held his gaze: the soldier, the one who had shot Alex's father.

"You saved my life too," said Alex, and Tristan shrugged.

"I wasn't about to let that bastard take out my brother," he said.

"Brother?" whispered Alex with tears. "You would take me as your brother?"

Then, suddenly, he looked up again at the shot martyrs.

"Where's Selena?" he breathed.

Urgently he looked around the church, down the central aisle, across the chairs, down the side aisles, before the altar, beside Mark's side...

She was missing.

In horror, Alex stared into Mark's eyes. "Oh, no," he breathed. "Please God, no..."

Mark's eyes widened with a reciprocal horror. "Where did she go?" he whispered.

"Into the darkness!" pleaded Alex with new agony. "Into my darkness, to save me!"

And now he ran, and he knew Mark was at his heels, with Tristan,

John and Rachel close behind.

The Shrine was before him. Alex slapped a hand over his mouth, staring at the locked doors.

"Oh, dear God," he pleaded, and his body shook with dread. "I can't do this. I can't go in there."

Mark's hand was on his shoulder. Alex looked up at his face, to see another kind of private hell, but also a strange purpose.

"She knew," choked Mark. "She knew what she was doing."

"The White Queen!" pleaded Alex. "I can't bear to look!"

"The White Queen fights for the White King," Selena had said. *"She is the most powerful piece, and is willing to die to defend the White King."*

Weeping took Alex, and John's hand moved to his other shoulder.

"If she has saved your life, Alex," he whispered, "you must have the courage to look at what she offered for you."

"It wasn't just for me," whispered Alex, trembling. "It was for the entire white side. It was to secure freedom for us all."

He reached into his right trouser pocket, pulled out the key to the Shrine, unlocked the door, and thrust it wide open.

Light poured into the darkness.

Alex stared at the black walls, now flooded with light. He stared at the black pile on the ground, where he had shed his black priestly robes. His father's knife was sitting on top, where he had left it, but now it was stained red. He could smell blood. He closed his eyes, and then opened them again, making himself look.

Selena's body was lying on the black altar.

"Oh my God," breathed Mark, and the tall man swayed on his feet, looking ready to faint. Tristan's voice rose behind Alex's back into a scream.

"You bastard!" he cried. "I'll kill you! I'll kill you!"

"You already did," whispered John. "But before the threat of corruption."

Alex couldn't move – he felt himself frozen. But Rachel was slowly approaching the altar. Alex watched as she moved silently to Selena's head – as she looked down to her chest, and reached mechanically to take the pulse at her neck.

Now Alex could move.

He stepped up to the altar. He took off his jacket, and laid it around her half naked body. And now he lifted her in his arms, and lowered her to the ground.

Her head of long dark curls fell against his chest; her blood smothered his shirt. He held her white cheek in his hand; he held her beauty in his arms. He saw the golden chalice sitting on the altar – it was her blood! Her blood. He threw his head back, let down the floodgates, and grief drowned him.

"Selena!" he cried, and his voice rose to a wail, and Mark was choking in agony at his side, and Tristan was prostrate on the floor. "Why?" cried Alex. "Why?"

Her beauty was before him, in his mind's eye: the light, conquering the darkness in her soul – her wilful offering, to confront his father's malice.

Blood was dripping down her face, as it had dripped down Joshua's face. Mark reached now for her face – he reached with both hands to his daughter, and bowed down to kiss her forehead.

"My precious girl," he whispered over her. "Oh dear God, what did he do to you?"

Weeping took Alex. He saw her again, sitting on the altar, imploring him to leave – blocking his father with her own body.

"Oh my God," whispered Alex. "You delayed him just long enough! Just long enough to let me reach the Cathedral…"

"Just long enough to undo the Curse," whispered John, and Alex looked into his intense gaze, and now John handed him back the crown.

Alex stared down at it. Mark reached to lift Selena away from his arms. He gently enfolded his arms around her, rocking with her, weeping over her.

"You understood!" he cried over her. "You understood it all, in the end!"

The crown was light in Alex's hands, now devoid of power. Alex fingered its ancient spikes.

"Sovereignty," he murmured. "The crown represents sovereignty."

"Return the sovereignty to the rightful owner," said John.

"The right owner?" asked Alex, frowning thoughtfully. Democracy had been overridden. Restore the system? Undo the corruption?

"Redemption," whispered Mark, with light in his eyes, even as he was doubled over in pain over his daughter's body.

"Redemption," whispered Alex, and he looked up, and saw Connor at the entrance to the Shrine.

His eyes were wide with horror, his gaze quickly moving from Selena to his daughter.

"It might have been you!" he whispered. "So easily, Rachel! So easily, my choices might have killed you!"

"You killed Joshua instead," said Tristan woodenly from the ground, his face covered in tears. "We killed him instead."

"I targeted the wrong enemy," whispered Connor, and Tristan lifted himself onto his knees.

"What about the Governor General?" he muttered. "Did she target the wrong enemy too?"

John was standing alongside Alex again. "Undo the harm," he said. "Change the course of history."

"Change the course of history," whispered Alex, and he rose to his feet with the crown, and walked over to Connor.

"Take me into Parliament," he said. "Take me in there, and I will testify to the entire truth."

"Your father has allies," said Connor. "If you do this, your life will be in danger."

Alex looked down to the blood stained face of Selena, to her pain, and her peace.

"This was always her game," he whispered. "Her strategy, from beginning to end."

"The White Queen is dead," murmured John. "But if the King acts alone, he may lose the entire game for everyone."

"The Black King is still alive," said Alex. "His spirit is still outworking its influence in Parliament."

"You will need a body guard," said Tristan, rising to his feet. He reached into his jacket pocket with his right hand, wiping the tears from his face with his left hand.

"You will need a Bishop," murmured Mark, rising to his feet, standing next to his dead daughter lying on the ground.

"You will need a political leader," said Connor, smiling sadly, his eyes back on Rachel.

"You will need a doctor," she murmured, and she wandered over to Selena's body, knelt next to her, and reached for her cell-phone.

Alex looked at each in turn. He swallowed, and then nodded.

"Come," he said, and he led Connor, Tristan and Mark out of the Shrine.

Chapter 25

REVELATION

A lex walked up to the black iron gates of the Beehive. The sky was overcast, grey, with the threat of rain. Alex grimaced.

In front of him was the army, stationed outside of Parliament House, on guard. Behind him were Mark, Tristan, John and James Connor. Alex took a deep breath and stepped forward.

"Halt," said a Major, fingering his rifle.

"It's all right," said Connor behind him. "He's with me."

"No," said the Major. "It's not all right. You are blocked from Parliament, James Connor: you are a threat to the security of New Zealand."

Alex glanced back at Connor's face, white and shocked.

"No," muttered Alex. "It's all a set up."

Tristan Blake stepped forward.

"Major," he began, "The Right Honourable Prime Minister…"

"He's not the Prime Minister any more, Blake," interjected the Major.

"Nonetheless," said Tristan, "he is a political servant…"

"I have my orders, Lieutenant," said the Major. "As of today, Connor is blocked."

Alex watched Tristan frown. "May I ask where the orders originated?"

"You may ask," said the Major, "and I need not answer. I am your superior: you will answer to me."

Tristan swallowed, and Mark Blake stepped forward.

"Mr Connor has information vital to the security of New Zealand," he said.

"You are also blocked from Parliament, Right Reverend Blake," said the Major. "You are associated with Connor."

Alex watched Mark's controlled face, and then looked beyond him to John. The green eyes were on him.

"The balance of power has shifted," said John quietly. "The pieces have changed."

Alex straightened, and turned back to the Major.

"Please escort me to the Debating Chamber," he said. "I am Alex Kensington."

The Major frowned. "Kensington's son?" he asked. "Of the Socialist Party?"

"I am here to take up his position in Parliament."

And Alex extended to him the crown.

The Major stared down at it. "The weapon," he said. "The force that subdued Joshua Davidson."

"I have evidence to present to the Governor General," said Alex. "Please let me pass."

The Major frowned at him. "This isn't standard procedure," he said.

"Nothing about this situation is standard," replied Alex.

"Let the Governor General decide," said Tristan. "Let the evidence be presented."

"Socialist and Conservative," said Connor. "If Anita Mayes still considers me a traitor after we have both reported to her, you may escort me permanently out of Parliament yourself."

Alex looked at Connor, at the resignation in his eyes. The Major shifted on his feet, and looked to Tristan.

"If you have advised me to escort enemies of our state into the heart of Parliament," he said, "both of our futures will be over."

"I know," said Tristan. "But if you don't do it, our entire purpose as army will be over. Democracy will disappear, to be replaced by a veneer, a manipulation, an empty shell of everything we believe in: a hidden agenda – a thrust for insidious control."

The Major stared into Tristan's eyes. Alex watched him. Trust? Would the Major trust the Lieutenant? Is that what the fate of New Zealand depended upon?

"More forces I don't understand," muttered the Major, and Tristan nodded.

"Yes," he said. "Forces we do not understand."

"My authority is on the line," said the Major. "Very well: do what you must, Lieutenant."

He stepped aside, and let Tristan pass.

Alex followed Tristan through the ranks of the army, across the grass of the courtyard, and in through the glass doors to security.

There Tristan surrendered two guns. Alex stared down at Tristan's rifle, and at his father's own gun. They were gone now, in the hands of the other officers. All that was left were words.

A guard gestured to the crown in his arms. Alex hesitated, and then handed it over. The officer inspected it, and then handed it back.

"Move on," he said, and Alex followed Tristan through security and into the foyer.

The Beehive was to the left, and Parliament was to the right.

"Which way?" asked Alex, and Connor again moved forward.

"Follow me," he said. "Come quickly."

And he moved forward, toward Parliament.

Alex knew where he was taking them. He hesitated, and held back, and felt Mark stumble against him.

"What is it?" asked Mark, and Alex shuddered.

"He stabbed me there," he whispered, staring ahead at Connor's disappearing form. "He stabbed me in the Debating Chamber."

Mark's hand grasped his. Alex stared down at the large fingers, confused.

"You will live," said Mark. "You will live to see the light of day."

Fear took him, but Mark's hand was strong, forging him, somehow! Forging him.

"Courage," said John from behind. "You are doing the right thing."

"Even if I should die?" whispered Alex. The stab! He could feel it now, as though it had just happened! He could see his father's eyes, hard, and calculating...

"Even if you should die," murmured John, and Alex straightened and set his shoulders.

"Even if I should die," he said, and he launched himself after Connor.

The doors to the Debating Chamber were before him.

Connor stood facing the doors, clenching his fists at his sides.

"Don't be afraid," said Mark. "You carry the truth. You carry the true mantle of leadership for our nation."

"Even if my career should die," said Connor, and he thrust open the doors.

The Chamber was full. Gasping, Alex clutched the crown to his chest. Here? In front of all of these, expose his father? Expose his own inheritance; his own corruption?

"Courage," said John. "Courage."

"Courage," whispered Alex, and he followed Connor into the Chamber.

Faces were all around, muttering and gesturing toward him. Alex felt giddy. He took a deep breath and marched forward, with Tristan by his side.

Connor was approaching the Throne. Alex stiffened, and suddenly felt sick. The Throne! Here his father had done the deed! Here his father had pierced his side!

"Oh God," he pleaded. "Oh my God..."

John's hand was suddenly tight on his shoulder.

"Peace," murmured John. "Peace."

"Peace," whispered Alex, and now, swallowing, he lifted his eyes.

Anita Mayes, the Governor General, was sitting on the Throne. Her eyes fixed on Connor as he approached. The golden mace of the Queen's authority sat on the table in front of her.

Alex instinctively reached over and lifted the golden staff from the table. The muttering in the room suddenly subsided. Who was this? Who dared to break with etiquette? Who dared to lift the mace?

Alex looked to his left, to the members of the New Conservative Party. Scott, the new leader, was sitting in the fourth chair forward, staring at Connor in bemusement. Alex looked to his right, at Clarkson. He was also sitting in the fourth chair along, in the position of the Leader of the Opposition, opposite Scott.

With fear, Alex looked across the rest of the Socialist Party. There was an empty seat next to Clarkson. Across the rows, some faces looked bewildered, but others, Alex recognised, were associates of his father, gathering dark frowns.

"It's an emergency session," whispered Alex. "The Governor General has called for a crisis session."

Anita Mayes rose to her feet.

"Honourable James Connor," she said. "You will cease approaching the Throne."

Connor stopped, and stood rigidly before her.

"Sit in your designated position," she said. "The back row of the New Conservative Party."

"I cannot," said Connor. "From the back row I will not be able to voice my concerns."

"Then leave the Chamber," said Mayes. "Your concerns are no concern of mine. We will have order."

And she gestured to a Whip, responsible for discipline in the House.

Connor glanced up at the solidly built man, and then looked at Clarkson. "Patrick," he whispered. "Please."

Clarkson's face creased into a frown. "Right honourable Governor General," said Clarkson.

"Right Honourable Patrick Clarkson," said Mayes.

"The Right Honourable James Connor made a statement…"

"Not 'Right Honourable,'" said Mayes. "I have stripped him of his title for disgraceful conduct."

Alex lifted the golden mace high into the air with his left hand, and the Chamber fell silent.

Now Anita Mayes's eyes were on him.

"Young man," she said, "put the mace down or you will be imprisoned."

Alex clutched onto the crown with his right hand.

"Hear me," he said, "or the gold of this pretty looking mace will become more worthless than scrap metal."

Muttering spread around the Chamber.

"An enemy of the State," said Anita Mayes.

"Yes," replied Alex, and he walked across to his right, handed the mace to Clarkson, and stepped into his father's empty seat at Clarkson's right hand.

Muttering lifted in the House, and Clarkson stared at him.

"Alex?" he said. "Alex Kensington?"

"Yes," said Alex. "My father is dead, and upheld me as his replacement."

"Dead?" asked Clarkson. "I know his intentions were for you to replace him…"

Alex took the crown, and laid it on the desk in front of Clarkson.

People shifted around him, Alex could sense them. Behind him sat two of his father's closest associates.

Clarkson stared down at the crown.

"Why are you here?" he asked.

"The Right Honourable James Connor made a statement about my father Kensington."

"Yes," said Clarkson, "but Kensington disputed it."

A firm hand was on Alex's shoulder, squeezing his neck slightly.

"Order," said the Governor General.

"Democracy is under siege," said Alex. "I have come to testify."

"The boy is mad," said a voice from behind him. "Mad with grief, at the passing of his father."

"No," said Alex, "the Prime Minister is innocent. We made a mistake."

"What mistake?" asked Anita Mayes.

"We slayed the scapegoat," said Alex. "We attacked the wrong enemy."

"Who was the right enemy?" asked Mayes. "If not the corrupt Prime Minister?"

"Me," whispered Alex, and he swayed on his feet. His vision was blurring. The crown! The crown in front of him was turning hazy…He vaguely felt a prick to his shoulder. Poison! Surely it was more poison…and now he collapsed.

Hands reached for him; hands were lowering him to the ground.

"No!" called Tristan. "An attack on National Security!"

And he stood between Alex and his aggressor.

"Corruption!" cried Connor. "Corruption in the Socialist Party!"

"My father," pleaded Alex, staring up toward Mayes. "He attacked me in this place. He stabbed me."

His father's face was above him, his eyes hard, penetrating and calculating – and now the knife was twisting in his side.

Alex gasped. John's face was over him, and Mark's hands were on his shoulders.

"Don't you see?" Alex breathed to John, reaching out to grasp his shirt. "I deserve it! It hurts so badly: it's all my fault."

"No," replied John. "I won't let you become another scapegoat. You are not the sacrifice."

"No," said Mark, and his hands tightened on his shoulders. "No more death. No more darkness."

And Alex found himself suddenly lifted up to his feet.

The Price of Redemption

"I saw him!" cried Connor. "I saw Kensington almost murder him!"

Alex stiffened again with pain, grasping his side on his feet, but his vision was clearing. The truth! The truth.

"His poison is spreading throughout the Socialist Party!" said Connor. "His grip is tight around the heart of the next election!"

"I have proof!" said Alex, turning back to Clarkson. "I have access to his records."

"My own party?" asked Clarkson, casting his eyes over his own.

"Corruption can take us all," said Mark. "It is like a crouching tiger, waiting to devour us."

"But there is still hope," said John, "if we keep pursuing what is right, no matter what the cost."

"No matter what the cost," whispered Alex, and he grasped the mace from Clarkson, and marched it up to Anita Mayes.

"Governor General," he said. "My father planned for the death of Davidson, and the dismissal of Connor. He then infiltrated the Socialist Party, and fixed the next election, to gain control over New Zealand."

"How do you know this?" asked Mayes.

Alex laid the crown on the table before Mayes.

"I know it," he said, "because I was his Mastermind."

Tears blurred his vision. He handed the mace to Mayes. He turned to his right, and pointed to his father's associates.

"These are the pawns," he said, "each and every one. But I was the Queen."

Shame filled him. He had played the part of the Black Queen! No more! No more. He turned back to Mayes, but another tight grip was on his shoulder.

"Stalemate," whispered a harsh voice in his ear. "The White King is dead."

Dizziness took him. He swayed again, and sank to his knees. Behind him, Tristan was knocking his assailant back, pinning him down to the floor.

"Wait!" cried out a voice. "Let me in! He's being poisoned!"

"Rachel," whispered Alex, and her steps sounded in the Chamber.

"Governor General!" called Clarkson. "I withdraw my party from the coming election! Corruption! I believe Connor."

"You believe your opponent?" asked Mayes.

"Yes," said Clarkson. "I didn't see what was in front of me, but I see it now. Isn't that the purpose of the Debating Chamber? To find each other's blind spots?"

Rachel was in front of Alex, reaching for his arms. He sank against her, toward the ground. Her face, hovering over him, was beginning to fade.

"Can you hear me?" she asked, reaching for the stethoscope around her shoulders. Vaguely he felt her fingers on his wrist, searching for his pulse.

"Get these infiltrators out!" commanded Mark's strong voice, and Clarkson's voice joined him.

"Whips!" he cried. "Traitors! My party will start again! For now, we are stepping out of the election."

Rachel's fingers were reaching for his neck. "A puncture wound!" she said. "The entry point for poison!" And she reached for her cell-phone to call 111.

Vaguely Alex heard her asking for an ambulance.

"The Socialist Party has withdrawn from the coming election," said Mayes. "I declare this election null and void."

Voices rose in the Chamber.

"Will we stay under the Queen's direct rule?" asked Clarkson. "Do we not all want a true democracy? Have we not toiled under direct rule too long?"

Alex turned his head to gaze up past Rachel's shoulder to the figure of Anita Mayes, standing holding the golden mace tightly in her right hand.

Her eyes moved down to him, lingering.

"Our land is like a struggling youth," she said, "beset with oppressors, also surrounded by friends rich with all kinds of advice."

The Price of Redemption

"What do the people want?" whispered Alex, grasping his side. "An ongoing dictatorship, an enforced form of Socialism, or a truly elected Prime Minister who is truly repentant of his flaws?"

"Right or left," said Mayes, "the people had always spoken."

And she walked forward with the mace, and handed it to James Connor.

"Right Honourable Prime Minister," she said. "The Queen has endowed her authority to me: I now endow it to you. The Constitution bows down to the good of New Zealand.

"The Debating Chamber is yours."

Mayes signalled to her left, took the mace from Connor, and placed it in its right position on the table before the Throne.

A man stepped forward: the Speaker of the House. He looked astonished. He took up his position on the Throne. The Governor General lingered, watching, waiting, ready to leave – wanting to leave.

Connor moved to the Speaker's right side of the Chamber. Scott, the new leader of the New Conservative Party, looked bewildered.

"Matthew," muttered Connor to him, "I'm sorry, but…"

"No," said Scott, hastily stepping aside. "We've all been a mess for months. Put it right, Connor! Put it right, and I'll gladly follow you."

Connor stepped into his right position, and lifted himself straight.

"Mr Speaker," he said.

"Right Honourable Prime Minister James Connor," said the Speaker.

"I ask that we return to a general debate over the nature of the National Lawful Use of Force Bill."

"Mr Speaker," said Clarkson. "My friend over there still needs to give an account for his actions."

Connor's eyes misted again. Alex gazed at him The Prime Minister looked down at him, and then he smiled gently.

"I was lost," he said, "but now I am found. I was blind, but now I see.⁴"

"Plain English," said Clarkson, "I beg you!"

Connor grinned, and Alex found himself grinning – and now, through a deepening haze, he reached out to Rachel's shoulder and took up her gaze.

"I've fixed it," he whispered. "Now I can die! Now I can die in peace."

Tears filled his eyes, and Rachel's pretty face hovered again over him.

"Not this time, my friend," she whispered. "This time the patient will live."

And he trusted her, and grasped onto her shirt, and surrendered himself to darkness.

Chapter 26

THE BROKEN LAMPSHADE

The darkness was lifting…

Alex opened his eyes. He was lying in a hospital bed, covered by a sheet. Rachel Connor's face was hovering over him again.

He reached out to grasp a hold of the sheet, gazing up at her face. She looked radiant.

"Are you a spirit?" he whispered, and she broke into a grin.

"Certainly not," she said, and a stethoscope was draped over her shoulders.

"Then I'm not dead?" asked Alex.

"No, my friend," said Rachel. "You were poisoned, but we've seen you through."

"The Socialist Party…"

"Sorted," said Rachel. "The Whips and Tristan had some support from the Major."

She reached for his pulse and then pulled herself back.

"Sorry," she said, "habit. I came with you in the ambulance, but now you're in the care of others."

Alex glanced to the other beds in the room. An Indian doctor was sitting next to a Maori woman in bed.

"Where am I?" he asked.

"The Hutt," said Rachel.

"A different hospital?" muttered Alex.

"Yes," said Rachel. "I had you transferred."

"You'd get a job here easily enough," he said.

Rachel's head tilted slightly, looking at him. "Here?" she asked.

"Well," he muttered, "with all the mess that passed before, time for a new beginning, I should think."

Rachel gazed at him, and broke into a gentle smile.

"Life after death," she murmured.

Alex smiled back at her. "There's no need for belief," he said, "when you have already experienced the reality directly."

"No," murmured Rachel. "I guess not. Reality is reality."

She sat back, and Mark moved to sit next to him on the bed.

Alex gazed at his tall form, and his insightful eyes.

"I'm not sure how well you'll sleep here," muttered Mark. "We should get you out of this place as soon as possible."

Alex smiled sadly at him. "Where would I go?" he asked. "Get a flat?"

"No," said Mark. "Not yet." His face clouded over, and he glanced back at Tristan, standing behind him. "Selena's room," he said. "Maybe…"

"No," said Alex. "The couch. I'll just lie on the couch in the lounge."

"The couch?" said Mark. "It's not that comfy."

Alex shrugged. "I'll adapt," he said.

"No," said Tristan. "My room. You can use my room for a while."

"Your room?" asked Alex.

"Two beds," Tristan said. "I'm used to dorms with the army."

Alex gazed at his face. "How…?" he muttered, and then he shook his head. "You're not worried I might kill you?"

"That depends," said Tristan, "are you worried I might kill you?"

Alex broke into a grin, despite himself. "After what I've lived with?"

he said. "No."

"Well, then," said Tristan. "My room it is."

Alex noticed his hands reaching into his pockets, but the pockets were empty.

"My father's associates…" whispered Alex. "They might come for me."

"No," said Tristan. "That's not going to happen. With your help, we'll find them all."

"He's clever," said Alex. "He'll get me. Even after his own death, he'll get me."

"No," said Mark. "We'll see to it you are safe."

"The poison…"

"We stopped it," said Rachel.

"He got to me before you could stop him," said Alex to Tristan, but the soldier shrugged.

"I'll ask for army protection."

"The army's on my side?" asked Alex, bewildered, and Tristan smiled.

"Of course," he said. "You are now on the side of New Zealand."

Astonished, Alex gazed between Tristan and Mark. The Blakes lifted themselves away, and John sat next to him.

Alex swallowed and then reached out to grasp a hold of John's sleeve.

"All this talk of confrontation," he whispered. "I never understood how terrible it would be."

"I know," murmured John gently. "It will take you some time to recover."

"Death!" whispered Alex. "Like my soul was being crushed!"

"Yes," whispered John, and his face contorted. "I felt it too."

"My chest," said Alex. "It was penetrated. I don't know how to breathe again. I don't know how to live again."

"We will help you," murmured John. "With every faltering breath into new life, we will help you."

Alex gazed at him, and nodded. He took a deep breath, and gasped with stabbing pains in his chest.

"Do it again," said John, and Alex grasped more tightly onto his shirt, and took another deep breath, and again was racked with pain.

"God," he whispered, and tears filled his eyes, and John's hands grasped both of his arms.

"Again," said John, and Alex clung to him, and breathed deeply, and was taken by agony, and his voice lifted into a sustained pressured wail as he kept breathing, and now John was breathing in unison with him, and somehow, with John's contorted face with each breath, the pain was easing.

"I don't understand," whispered Alex, and John smiled sadly.

"You will," he said.

Alex searched his green eyes. "Death," he whispered. "Death is the channel into a fuller life."

"Sometimes it is the necessary cost," said John.

"The pain is the pathway into resolution?" asked Alex.

"Pain is our friend," said John. "It alerts us to our harm and need, but sometimes is our necessary companion on the road toward healing."

"Suffering," whispered Alex.

"We can manage the suffering," said John, "if we can find the right kind of fellowship in the suffering."

Alex smiled sadly back at him. "Yes," he said. "I understand."

John pulled out the five deformed bullets, and put them into Alex's hand. Alex looked down at them.

"Joshua," he murmured, and John closed Alex's hand firmly over the bullets.

"These are yours now," he said.

"Mine?" asked Alex.

"Yours to share."

Alex looked at him, frowning. "Why mine?" he asked.

"Because you understand," said John, "more than me. Because you have tasted hell and returned. Because you have shared in the suffering in ways I have not. Because..." And now John hesitated and continued.

The Price of Redemption

"Because you sent these bullets into Joshua's chest and then willed for them to be removed. You have what is necessary, Alex."

"What is necessary?" whispered Alex.

"What it takes to bring light to the darkness."

Now tears welled up in Alex's eyes, and he stared at John through them.

"You must be joking," he said, but John shook his head.

"I'm not joking," he said.

"I was steeped in darkness," said Alex.

"And so how much more effectively can you offer the light?" replied John.

Alex looked quickly away from him, and closed his eyes tightly. Light, in the darkness? Selena! Selena, in the Shrine! Dead, at his father's bidding! Lying on the altar…

"Oh, God!" he whispered, wrapping his arms around himself. "I'm just a broken vessel! Just a cracked lampshade!"

"Exactly," murmured John. "That's why they'll be able to see the real light: through the cracks."

"Hope," whispered Alex.

"And faith," murmured John.

"And…" The pain twisted again in his side. He winced, and opened his eyes, and, grasped tightly onto the bullets, and grasped tightly onto John's shirt. "And…and…"

"Say it," John said, and Alex fixed onto his green eyes with agony.

"Love," he whispered. "There must be Love."

He trembled, and John's grip was strong on his arms.

"Love?" asked John, smiling.

"Without Love," gasped Alex, "it's all a waste of time. Meaningless! It's all meaningless."

And he thrust his legs over the side of the bed, and rose to his feet.

Joshua's bullets were still in his hand. He gazed down at them; he fingered their deformity.

"The right kind of fellowship in the suffering…" he murmured, and he grasped his own side, and put the bullets into his pocket.

He swayed on his feet.

"Hey," said Rachel. "Take it easy." And her hand came to his arm.

"I don't want you at risk again," she said, and Alex shrugged.

"I'll be all right," he said.

"Are you planning to self-discharge?" asked Mark. "Against medical advice?"

Alex smiled, and looked to Rachel.

"What do you think, doctor?" he asked. "Do you believe in a resurrection after death?"

"I do," said Rachel, smiling.

"You have seen it for yourself," said Alex, "but what of those who have not?"

"The Light must shine in the Darkness," said John, and Alex felt himself breaking into a wide smile.

"Yes," he said. "The broken lampshade must be lifted up for all to see."

And he reached for the drip in his hand, drew it out, grasped a cotton ball to his wound, and walked straight out of the room.

Chapter 27

RESTORATION

Rachel stood in the wardroom. Alex had just disappeared, out of the door and down the corridor. Rachel stared after him and smiled. Alex Kensington: he was nothing ordinary, nothing usual. Rather he was quirky, outside of the box, balancing on the wall between death and life, unafraid...

"There's no containing him," muttered Rachel, and Mark stood alongside her.

"There's no container big enough," he said. "And why would we want there to be?"

"Scary," muttered Tristan, on her other side. "He's a scary little bastard sometimes. I'm sure he already knows where we live."

"Does that bother you?" asked Rachel, smiling wryly at Tristan.

"Not at all," replied Tristan.

"A 'scary little bastard' is okay by you?" asked Rachel.

"Now that he's on our side," said Tristan, "scary is good. Scary is strength."

Rachel studied his face, warm and firm. "You've changed, Tristan Blake," she said.

"Have I?" asked Tristan, looking a little startled.

"Yeah," said Rachel. "You're not afraid any more."

Tristan's face blushed, looking at her, and tears suddenly filled his eyes.

"I guess not," he whispered, and he looked to his father, and Mark smiled.

Instinctively Rachel reached for her stethoscope around her shoulders. The drum felt unfamiliar. She grasped it in her hand, and looked at it.

James…Pain seized her. He was lost, wasn't he? His career, lost…

"You miss him," murmured John from behind her.

"I do," she whispered. "I love him."

John moved around her, and stood before her.

Rachel lifted her eyes to his green gaze. His face was suddenly handsome, suddenly alluring…

"Come with me," whispered John, and his fingers were reaching, touching hers…slipping between hers…

"Wait," whispered Rachel, and she drew away and turned to the Indian doctor.

He looked up at her; his brown eyes smiled at her. "I see my patient's self-discharged," he said. "And I hear you are looking for work?"

"Yes," said Rachel, swallowing, holding his gaze. "I am looking for work."

"Send us your CV," he said. "We need a medical registrar. We can have you working here in two weeks."

"Okay," she said. "I'll do that."

And now John's hand pulled her away.

He drew her down the corridor of the ward and away, down the lift and outside of the hospital.

"Where are you taking me?" she whispered, and his hand tightened on her.

"Home," he said, and he drew her into the valley of Lower Hutt.

The Price of Redemption

Rachel stood in a wide field, looking up. Pohutukawa trees, pines and rimu surrounded the park. She looked up at the hills, to the houses poking out from between the trees. The sun was shining; the air was cool and crisp.

"Come," murmured John into her ear, and he drew her across the field, between the trees.

Rachel's heart pounded...was he...was he going to lay her down? He was leading her beyond the park now, over the streets, between the shops of Lower Hutt, and alongside the Hutt River.

Rachel panted, following him, gazing down at the gentle running water.

"No flooding, you see?" murmured John to her. "Just a gentle stream."

She squeezed his hand, tugging him closer – but he was drawing her away, now toward the train station.

Rachel stood on the platform. The train was already waiting. John drew her into the train and sat down next to her, holding her hand in his lap. Rachel gazed out of the window as the train began, and soon the wide breadth of the Harbour was before her, the sun sparkling off the water.

"I lost my brother," she whispered, and tears blurred her eyes, and John's hand tightened on hers.

"I know," he murmured into her ear, "but the officers didn't stop us getting onto the train."

His breath was on her cheek, his lips brushing her.

"How did you know?" she whispered, closing her eyes, turning into his cheek. "How did you know I wasn't betraying you?"

"I know you," he whispered. "I know us." And now she turned into his lips, and received his kiss.

She pulled him closer to her own body.

"I want you," she whispered into his lips. "I've only ever wanted you."

"I know," he whispered back. "And I've only ever wanted you."

His fingers were reaching, twisting her greenstone wedding ring.

"We're on a train," she whispered. "A train trip that goes on and on and on…"

"Not for long," whispered John, and the train stopped.

John pulled her up to her feet. He led her, aching, off the train. He led her through the station, in front of many faces, drew her under the road, and up the steps, before…before…

Rachel stiffened. It was the Beehive! With the green courtyard in front, and the black iron gates now open.

"Look," John murmured to her. "Where is the army?"

Rachel stared at the wide open courtyard. "Gone!" she cried. "Gone!"

"Joshua's death worked, you see?" said John. "Alex's confession worked!"

He was turning her, and now he drew her across the road – the road on which Joshua had died.

Saint Peter's Cathedral was before her. Rachel swallowed, and tugged back on his hand.

"Come," said John, and, heart pounding, she let him draw her up the steps and into the Cathedral.

The plastic covers were off the broken windows. A gentle breeze freely blew through the church. Rachel trembled, as John drew her down the aisle and stood alongside her, in front of the altar.

Here she had almost died. Here James had almost killed her.

Rachel stiffened, and John reached for her face.

"Come," he whispered, his fingers shaking on her cheeks. "Come."

She sank against his body, and he drew her into his arms. His whole body was shaking as he lowered his lips over hers – as he entered her mouth.

Rachel clung to his arms, and wrapped her arms tightly around his head.

"Would you make love to me here?" she whispered into his face. "In a church?"

"Why not?" whispered John. "Love is the most profound of gifts!"

But now he lifted her in his arms, and carried her back down the aisle.

The streets were deserted. John shifted slightly at the top of the steps outside of the Cathedral, moving her in his arms.

"I can walk, you know," said Rachel, grinning, and he shook his head, sweating slightly.

"No," he said. "Not this time."

And he shakily lifted her down the steps.

"Honestly," said Rachel, grinning, as he reached the bottom, "you'll give us both a head injury at this rate!"

"More like a heart attack," puffed John. "You've put on a bit of weight."

And he carried her forward.

Rachel gazed at his face, as he struggled on through downtown Wellington.

"You'll kill yourself!" she protested. "Honestly, let me look after myself."

"No," said John. "Not now."

"It's not your fault," said Rachel, and tears filled his eyes.

"Just let me do this," he said. "I should never have...have..."

She stopped him, and lowered herself onto her feet, pressing into his panting body.

"I had to do it," she said. "I had to do all of it."

"He might have killed you," choked John. "I...I almost let it happen..."

"I had to do it," said Rachel.

"I should have stopped you."

"I..." Now Rachel reached to slip her fingers into both of his hands. "I love you."

And now, suddenly, she kissed him.

His arms were wrapping around her. She closed her eyes, leaning into his kiss, into his body, and then, suddenly, he lifted her again.

"Hah!" he said. "You don't call all the shots!"

231

He was carrying her again, and she laughed, and they approached their home…

John's flat was before her.

Rachel reached out a hand to his door, but John had already pulled out his key.

"Over the threshold," he whispered. "I've got to get you over the threshold."

And he turned the key, opened the door, lifted her inside, and slammed the door shut.

They were alone. Rachel gazed at him, trembling. John was gazing at her.

"Think I can make a few more metres?" he whispered, and now, suddenly, he was moving quickly down the corridor. Now she was in their bedroom, and he was laying her on top of their bed.

His face was over her, his green eyes gazing at her.

"I'm a bit sweaty," he whispered, grinning. "Stupid, really…"

She grasped his body to her own, and he grasped her body to himself.

They made love. Rachel gasped. Love! Love! Ecstasy…She lay in his arms, in peace. She slept, in his arms. She stirred.

He had pulled the sheet over her; he had pulled their duvet over her.

He was dressed in his pyjamas. He was sleeping.

Tears filled Rachel's eyes. She reached over to touch his arm, and touched his hair.

There had been no nightmare of Joshua's shooting, only rest! Only peace. The gentle joy of lovemaking. The gentle security of home.

"Told you he was alive," whispered John, his eyes still closed, and he broke into a gentle smile. Rachel grinned at him, and slapped on his arm, and he opened his eyes.

"What?" he asked, and now he had pulled her back into his arms, and was lying over her again.

"I had what you needed," said John, hovering over her face, smiling. "You do see that, don't you? All this time, I had what you needed."

"Yes," whispered Rachel up to him. "All this time, you had what I needed."

She uncovered herself, and uncovered him, and he sighed, and she received him.

He gasped. She held him. Bliss! He sank down into her arm; his face was buried in her neck.

"Love," he whispered to her. "It's all meaningless without love."

"Yes," said Rachel with tears, stroking his back. "It's all meaningless without love."

Now John was asleep over her, and was at peace. Now she was holding him, and was whole.

Love...she gazed up to the ceiling of his flat. Love. It was stronger than death! It was more powerful than the grave.

Dangerous, was this kind of love! The source of life! The enemy of death.

"I love," whispered Rachel, and she stretched her arms out on the pillow, and she was naked, and she breathed in, and she was free.

Chapter 28

DEATH

Tristan stood in the graveyard. Selena's gravestone rose up before him; Tristan gritted his teeth. He looked away from the stone, and then looked back at it. Death! His sister's death! How could it be possible?

Mark stood next to him. Tristan looked his face, as he read the name on the stone – as his eyes moved over the details of his daughter's life.

"Dad?" whispered Tristan. Mark was silent. He fleetingly closed his eyes then moved forward and reached out to touch the stone.

Tristan swallowed. He looked down into his own hand, and found a white orchid there. With tears he stared at it: purity? Had his Dad chosen white for purity? He felt rigid.

"Come," said Mark. Tristan looked up at him. His eyes! Tristan had never seen him like this before. His blue gaze was intense, and wet – harrowed, and yet simultaneously somehow accepting of Selena's fate.

"Come," repeated Mark, and Tristan obeyed him and moved forward.

He reached out tentatively to the grey stone, and touched the letters of Selena's name. He laid the white orchid on top of the stone. Then, suddenly, pain gripped him.

"Oh my God," he whispered. "Oh my God." And he sank down to his knees.

The stone was in front of his face. He closed his eyes, and his father's hand came to his shoulder.

"I'm sorry," whispered Mark, and Tristan looked up into his contorting face. "I failed."

"No," whispered Tristan, and he looked again at Selena's name. "You were right, she knew what she was doing."

"She went in there," whispered Mark. "She went into hell to save her brother."

Tristan turned his head away as tears overpowered him.

"All my training," he whispered. "The frickin' army, Dad! All my training to protect my home, and…and I couldn't even protect my own sister."

Now pain consumed him. Mark sank down beside him – Tristan felt his father's arm around his shoulders.

"You were trying to protect your mother," he whispered, and now Tristan swayed. He felt his vision dim, but his father's grip tightened on his shoulder.

"Death," whispered Tristan. "How can there be so much death?"

He felt himself fading away. But now Mark's arms were both around him, holding him up!

"There is also life," said Mark. "There is also hope, and light, and joy."

"Oh, God," pleaded Tristan. Selena! Selena, dead on the black altar.

"She did it to save her brother," repeated Mark, and Tristan covered his face with his hands and wept, and his father held him.

In time Tristan lifted his head. The tombstone was still there. His father was still there. The numbing sense of obliteration was still there. He staggered to his feet and turned.

Alex was in the distance, sitting on a hill well away from the tombstone. His back was to them.

"What is he doing, Dad?" whispered Tristan, and Mark rose alongside him.

"I don't know," whispered Mark, and he moved forward, and Tristan followed him.

Alex was staring out across the view, to an estuary, and wide sweeping hills beyond. His face looked rigid. Tristan watched Mark sit alongside Alex, leaning slightly into him.

"Look," whispered Alex. "There are yachts, and the sun is shining, and the water is sparkling…"

Mark was reaching for his hand, and now Alex's face contorted.

"Oh my God," he whispered. "Oh my God, oh my God, oh my God…"

He reached out to grasp blades of grass in his clenching hands, as if to hold on – as if to desperately hold onto something. Mark's arms moved around him, and Alex's body stiffened.

His voice lifted into a wail. Tristan shivered – it was the same wail he had cried, when his father had been snatched from him! When Tristan had snatched him away…

"No way to live," whispered Tristan. "To stay is to die; to leave is to die."

Alex's body began to jerk in Mark's arms. "She's dead!" he cried. "She's dead!"

He clutched at Mark's shirt, and Mark rocked with him, and Alex wrestled with distress and grief, and writhed, and clung to Mark's arms, and sank, utterly spent, against his chest.

Tristan stared at him, and then willed himself forward.

He reached for him, drawing him out of his father's arms and into his own arms. What was he doing? He'd never handled a man like this before. He lifted him to his feet and stood with him, upright, a pillar, holding him up.

"Can't," whispered Alex, his legs shaking, his body threatening collapse. "I can't stand."

"You will," murmured Tristan over him. "You will."

"How long?" whispered Alex. "How long must I be plagued?"

"The wounding will forge you," said Mark. "Your weakness will be God's medium."

Alex sank down Tristan's body, inadequately supported, and now he was on his face in the grass.

Astonished, Tristan gazed down at him. His arms were stretched out, and his body was limp. He seemed to have stopped breathing. But then he pushed himself to his knees, lifted himself to his feet, and turned to Mark.

"Please," he whispered. "Take me to Saint Peter's again."

Mark swallowed. "Are you sure you're ready?"

Alex's face was flint. "Take me," he whispered. "I have to do this."

Mark nodded, and turned, and Tristan followed after his father and brother.

Chapter 29

COMMUNION

A lex stood before the steps of Saint Peter's.
The glass doors were at the top of the steps. The Cathedral was beyond.

Alex glanced to Mark's worried face, and to Tristan's frown behind him. Family! These were his family. He smiled sadly at them, and then turned away and launched himself up the steps.

He was in the sanctuary, alone.

Taking a deep breath, he slowly walked down the aisle. The windows were gaping above him, jagged and sharp, the sky easily seen, blue and grey. The Cathedral was his, now! In this moment, it was his.

He reached out to touch the wooden chairs of the nave as he passed them by, and walked up to the steps leading up to the altar. Here he had lain, decimated! Here Mark had covered him with his white robe.

He walked up the steps, and stood before the altar. White linen...It was white...

He reached out his fingers to touch the linen, and reached beneath to touch the wood. Here his father had lain him! Here his father had choked him.

The Price of Redemption

Communion...The silver chalice was still there, sitting on the white linen. The silver plate was still there. He reached out to take the bread wafer; he reached to hold the silver chalice.

"'This is my body, given for you,'" he whispered, and he took the wafer onto his tongue.

He gazed into the silver chalice. Blood! The blood of his father...the blood of his Father...

Wine. With relief he gazed into it.

"'This is my blood, shed for you,'" he whispered, and he drank the wine.

Warmth...warmth on his tongue.

He sank down to his knees. He pressed his forehead against the altar, and looked down.

The five bullets. Trembling, he took them out of his pocket and looked at them. Death! Joshua's death. Bearing his crown! Forging his life.

Love. Trembling, Alex felt it. And now he looked up.

Joshua was standing before him.

Alex stared up at him from his knees, holding his breath. Joshua stood next to the altar, his gaze on him.

"Are you loving, Alex?" asked Joshua, and Alex clenched his fingers around the bullets. Pain! Pain!

"Yes," he whispered. "I am loving."

"Do you love these?" asked Joshua, and he gestured around the church and up to the broken windows. The saints! The martyrs Alex had shot.

"Yes," he whispered, trembling, "I love these."

Now Joshua knelt in front of Alex, reached out to take Alex's hand, and drew his fingers between the buttons of his own shirt.

Alex stiffened, and Joshua hesitated.

"Let me," said Joshua, and Alex relaxed, and Joshua drew his fingers to the bullet wound over his heart.

Alex gasped, and now Joshua reached toward Alex's own chest.

"Let me," murmured Joshua, and Alex nodded. Joshua's hand grasped his chest, and agony seized Alex, and he contorted, and grasped onto Joshua's chest, and the brown eyes misted with Alex's pain, and Alex saw him.

"Will you love me more than all of these?" asked Joshua. "Whatever they may do to you?"

Alex clung to his gaze. "Yes," he whispered. "I will love you more than these."

Joshua smiled gently at him.

"Do you think you are only my slave, Alex Kensington?" he said. "You are not merely my slave. I have made you my friend. You have become my family."

Alex trembled, looking at him. "Brother," he whispered. "You are my brother."

"You carry my Light within you," said Joshua. "You have seen my cost. You have tasted it for yourself. Shine my Light! Carry the cost."

"I love you," whispered Alex, and his chest ached. He felt again for the bullet wound in Joshua's heart, and he continued. "I love you."

"And I love you," said Joshua. He grasped Alex's hand, and Alex stiffened. Love? Pain! Pain. "Receive my love," said Joshua. "Receive it, and pass it on."

"Pass it on," whispered Alex, and Joshua broke into a wide radiant smile, and then he was gone.

Tears filled Alex's eyes. "Love," he whispered. "I will love you, and be loved by you, and pass it all on, whatever the cost! Whatever the cost."

He rose to his feet and turned, and Mark Blake was standing before him.

Mark's gentle face smiled at him.

"You saw Joshua?" he asked, and Alex gazed at him, swallowing.

"I did," he choked. "I did. But...how did you know?"

Mark's smile widened.

The Price of Redemption

"Oh, don't bother asking him to translate," Tristan's voice floated over them. "He loves being cryptic. It's all a mystery to him, and he seems to prefer it that way!"

But Alex reached out to grasp Mark's arm, to search out his eyes.

"Did you see him?" asked Alex, and Mark's smile became sad.

"I did not," he said.

"Then how...?"

"I deduced it," said Mark, his eyes twinkling. "I heard his voice. Paul had to enter the story at some point."

"Paul?" asked Alex, and he looked up at the broken windows.

"Paul," repeated Mark. "The one who took the news to those who didn't yet know."

Alex gazed at him, tilting his head. "The missionary..." he murmured.

"It won't be an easy life, Alex," said Mark, laying a hand on his shoulder. "Beatings, hatred, rejection, jail...Paul was stubborn! He knew the race he was running. He knew his purpose, even if it would kill him."

Alex threw a hand over his mouth, and reached out to touch Mark's face.

"I can see!" he whispered. "I can see."

He turned away from Mark, and walked around the altar to the space between the altar and the cross. Here his father's body had lain, shot. Alex looked down at the spot: his father's blood was still marking the carpet. A cold fist clenched around his heart, but then he looked up at Jesus on the cross, at the spear wound in his side.

He took a deep breath, braced his own side, and looked back to the position of his father.

"Gone..." Mark's voice murmured beside him. "The Curse has gone."

"Will the demon always haunt me?" asked Alex "A thorn in my side? Always tormenting me?"

"Peace," whispered Mark over him. "Peace be with you."

Alex grasped his hand, and took a deep breath. His pain was easing, and he looked up through the jagged windows to see the sun shining directly into the Church.

"Peace," whispered Alex. "At last, a chance for peace." And he gathered the bullets back into his pocket, bowed toward the cross, and walked back down the aisle and out of the church.

Chapter 30

THE PRISON CELL

James Lester sat in jail. His cell was small – he felt the white walls pressing in on him on all sides. Agitated, he hovered on his feet, pacing backwards and forwards before the bars, like a caged animal.

A guard was on the other side of the bars.

"You have a visitor," he said.

"Like shit," whispered James, wrapping his arms around himself, and then the guard opened the bars, and Rachel was walking into his cell.

James stared at her. Too close!

He stepped away from her, and shrank back against the wall.

"What are you doing here?" he asked, and she pulled out his stethoscope from her pocket.

"I brought this," she said.

He grasped around his cell, clutching for his few items. He found her smaller stethoscope, and threw it at her.

"Here!" he said. "What use have I got for this now?"

She caught her stethoscope, fiddled with it, and laid it on the ground. She stepped forward, and laid his stethoscope on the ground at his feet.

"Here," she said, and he reached down to his own stethoscope, his body stiffened, and he threw it back at her.

"No, you bitch!" he said. "You put me here! I'm not accepting your peace offering!"

But then, suddenly, she was seizing his body.

Shocked, he wrestled against her – arms? Arms? He started to panic.

"Don't!" he cried. "Don't!"

"Hold on," said her voice over him, and he felt his voice lifting to a scream, but still she was holding him! Still her arms were tightly around him!

"Don't," he pleaded, but her arms didn't move.

"Cry," whispered Rachel. "Cry, for all your life."

"No," he whispered, hiding his face in her neck, clinging to her. "Please, no."

Her arms tightened around him, and suddenly he remembered other arms: a mother's arms…

"Seven," he whispered. "I haven't been held since I was seven."

Rachel's voice murmured over him. "I know," she said. "I know."

She was rocking him. He gasped. Trust her? Trust? He hadn't…he mustn't…and yet he was hiding in her arms; and yet he was clinging to her. Tears took him, and pain took him. The tide! The tide…

"Dive," whispered Rachel. "Dive under the wave."

He faced the onslaught. He dove under it, and she held him.

He took a deep breath. How long had it been? He didn't know. She was still holding him. He stepped away from her, and looked into her eyes. She was crying.

"I don't understand," he whispered, and she smiled through her tears.

"I know," she said. "That's okay."

He gazed at her. Then he reached down and took his own stethoscope from her hands.

He stared down at it: cardiology grade. His career was gone! His hands trembled.

"Lost," he whispered. "I am lost."

"I know," said Rachel gently "But I am here."

He looked up at her, at her pretty face. He held onto his stethoscope. He glanced around the walls of the cell. They weren't crowding in any more; somehow he could accept them.

"Prison," he muttered. "Everything is stripped away."

"Yes," murmured Rachel. "It's horrible."

James frowned, and then looked up at her. "You've been to prison too?"

Rachel shifted on her feet, holding his gaze. "In a prison of sorts," she said. "Home detention."

James gazed at her, and then he gestured to the floor.

"Welcome to my palace," he said, and Rachel smiled. She crossed her legs, sitting on the floor, and James sat next to her.

He stared down at the ground. He stared into his own hands. He reached out, and picked up her stethoscope.

"So you're working again?" he asked.

"In the Hutt," she said.

"Oh," said James, and he smiled sadly. "I think you'll like it there."

Rachel smiled sadly back to him. "I had this patient," she said. "I heard another mid-diastolic murmur with your stethoscope…"

"Don't talk to me about patients," whispered James, and he closed his eyes tightly. Rachel's hand was on his arm now, he could feel it.

"Sorry," she said, and he shrugged.

"Don't say sorry," he said.

"I mean," she said, and now she hesitated, and he looked up into her face as her eyes clouded with tears. "I mean, I'm sorry for pricking your pain."

James gazed at her, and then he looked back down at his own stethoscope.

"My pain," he murmured.

"Morphine," whispered Rachel, and James turned his head away from her, feeling his face contort.

"Your words are like poison arrows sometimes," he said, and Rachel shifted alongside him.

"I know," she whispered. "I know."

"But it's not…" He hesitated, and then made himself continue. "It's only because…"

He dared to look at her; dared to steadily hold her gaze. She was in pain! She was in pain because she knew she was causing him pain.

"It's only because…" Now he took a deep breath, and faced her. "It's only because I want you to think well of me."

And now he looked quickly away.

She was reaching out a hand to him. He looked at the hand.

"The truth hurts like hell sometimes," whispered Rachel, and he looked back up to her face. "I understand that," she said. "I do understand it."

James gazed at her. "You use truth as your weapon," he said.

"But not to destroy," said Rachel quickly. "You must understand that about me, I'm not using the weapon to destroy."

"No," murmured James, tilting his head, studying her. "Not to destroy the person, to remove the corruption. Always, always, to remove the corruption."

"I am a surgeon," said Rachel. "The scalpel hurts! But I don't want it to hurt. The cut bleeds! But I don't want it to bleed."

Her hand was still offered to him. He gazed at it.

"I told you that you didn't want a brother like me," he said. "I told you that kind of love would kill you."

"I know," said Rachel. "You told me, and I said, 'So be it.'"

In wonder James gazed at her. "'Amen'?" he asked. "You would finish all of this with 'Amen'?"

Rachel broke into a pretty smile, and she shrugged her shoulders.

"Love," she said. "It does crazy things sometimes."

He found himself smiling with her; he found himself reaching to take her hand.

They were touching. He trembled. He swallowed, and then drew his hand away.

"Masterton," he said spontaneously, and she frowned quizzically at him.

"What?" she asked.

"Masterton," he said. "I'm from Masterton."

He rose to his feet, and wandered over to the bars, and leaned against them; and she joined him, at his side, and also leaned against the bars, and he thought she just might be able to press herself through...

Chapter 31

LIGHT

John stood in Saint Peter's Cathedral. He looked up to the white altar, with the silver chalice and silver plate sitting on top. He looked beyond the altar, to the image of Jesus on the cross. He looked overhead, to the broken windows. They had been repaired!

He gazed at the new windows. There were images there, old and new: Jesus, Peter, John, Paul...

"What are your thoughts?" murmured Mark from behind him.

"Completion," said John, still looking at the windows. "Actualisation."

"Actualisation of whom?" asked Mark, and John glanced back to his gentle smile.

"You know of whom," said John, and Mark nodded, light in his eyes. The Bishop passed him, wandering up to the altar, and reached out to touch the linen.

"Christ incarnate," he said, lifting his eyes to Jesus on the cross. "Death to the old man; a new man in Christ."

"A little Christ," said John. "A member of Christ's household."

"A broken member," said Mark. "A broken lampshade."

"Life," said John, "out of death."

Mark bowed his head. "New life," he said. "A new kind of life."

John wandered up to the altar to stand alongside him, and reached out to touch the chalice of wine.

"But the cost!" he murmured gently to Mark. "The cost, of keeping the sanctuary open! The blood of the saints; the crucifixion of the redeemed martyrs. Was it worth the cost, my friend?"

Mark reached into a pocket of his purple robe, and pulled out a photo of Selena. His face contorted as he laid the photo on the white altar.

"For God so loved the world," he said, "that he gave his only Son, that anyone who believes in him might not perish but have everlasting life."

"The Gospel of John," murmured John.

"John 3:16," said Mark. "Family dies for family, the price doesn't come into it. She knew that – she knew it in the end."

"A sister dies so that a brother may be born?" asked John quietly.

"She's not dead," said Mark, looking at him. "You forgot the 'everlasting life' part."

John flushed and looked up at the stained glass windows, to the light shining through the glass: the colours, deep red, green, blue; the faces, the wind, the light…

"Everlasting life," he murmured. "The saints are still alive."

"The saints are still alive," repeated Mark, looking up with John.

"Without the resurrection," Alex's voice floated over them, "I am most to be pitied. The saints are still alive.[5]"

And now the young man was standing behind them, also looking up.

"What are you all looking at?" asked Tristan's voice from behind. "Why are you staring up, as if Christ is about to appear at any moment: as if God himself is contained in these windows?"

John glanced at Mark's wry smile, and at Alex's grin. He looked back at Tristan's affectionate smirk, as he strode up the aisle to stand with them.

"What are we looking at?" repeated John. "A glimpse of eternity. A taste of paradise."

"Paradise?" asked Tristan, looking up. "Any room for me?"

He reached out to lay a hand on Alex's shoulder, and Alex reached out to Mark's arm, and Mark reached out to grasp John's shoulder, and John reached out to the altar to take the photo of Selena and hand it to Alex.

Alex looked down at the photo in his hand. He trembled, under Tristan's hand. Then he took the photo into his own pocket and looked back up.

"Yes," he murmured to Tristan. "There is room for you. There is room for anyone who would search for the Light, and find it."

"Let there be Light," murmured John to Alex, and sunlight flooded through the stained glass into the Church, in a full array of colour, and Alex breathed in deeply, and his face lit up.

Chapter 32

ACTUALISATION

Alex stood on the steps of Saint Peter's. Across the street, behind the open iron gates, the Beehive and Parliament House stood at peace. Democracy was secure! Freedom had been established.

Behind him, in the Cathedral, Mark remained with John and Tristan.

Alex's eyes wandered across the streets of Wellington. The wind was blowing, and the rain was falling. It was cold. He breathed in the weather, and launched himself down the steps into the heart of the rain. He smiled.

Time passed – he didn't know how long. He walked, by instinct. He trusted. The streets unfolded before him, and soon he was at Oriental Bay.

A small group of people were meeting on the sand, in the rain. There were no army officers keeping guard. Alex wandered forward, and climbed over the retaining wall onto the sand.

Rau Petera was standing near the water, talking to the people.

Alex looked at him, and then walked up to him. He reached down for a stick, and poked five bullet holes in the sand.

Rau's warm face smiled at him. He reached for the stick, and gently drew a koru around the bullet holes.

Tears pricked at Alex's eyes. He smiled. He took the stick from Rau, and drew another koru, and another, and another, wandering across the beach – and then he threw the stick down, turned, stretched out his arms, and lifted his face to the sky, breathing deeply.

"It's finished!" he said. "It's done."

Rau stooped down to the sand to pick up the stick, and handed it back to him.

"No," he murmured gently. "It has only just begun."

"Only begun?" said Alex, and Rau's smile widened.

"Ae," he said. "Draw, Alex. Draw."

And he gestured to the sand.

Alex looked into his face and looked down at the sand. A stick? He threw the stick away. He knelt in the sand, reaching down with his bare hands, and drew the sand up into piles.

"Build," murmured Rau. "Build."

Alex quickly gathered the sand, shaped it, and formed a structure.

He rose up to his feet, and looked down at it. Rau stood next to him, also looking down. Now Alex reached for the stick, and he drew a symbol on the structure.

The cross, on an empty tomb.

"Ka pai," said Rau. "The old is made new, with every generation, with every people, with every heart."

"He saved my life," whispered Alex. "It is my tomb; it is his sacrifice."

"Go, then," said Rau. "Go, with the blessings of God the Father, and the Son, and the Holy Spirit. Go, and make his offering known to the world."

"I will go," whispered Alex, and he grasped Rau's stick to himself, and walked off the beach.

He walked down the street, and carried the stick. The wind blew on his face, chilling him, but he didn't care. The rain beat on his head, but he smiled.

He stood on the waterfront, facing the gale and choppy water of the harbour.

"Have your way," he whispered, and he took the stick and threw it into the depths of the water.

A wave rose up, high over the sand. He was not afraid. It crashed on the coast. He did not move.

Strength surrounded him – he breathed it in. He reached a hand into the icy water, and flicked drops back into the ocean.

"I'm ready," he whispered. "I'm here."

The stick floated back up on the sand. He looked at it, and reached out to grasp it. He smiled, drew it to himself, and set back down the street.

Saint Peter's was in front of him. He gazed up at the Cathedral. The old and the new were together! As one.

He laid the stick at the feet of the steps, and looked around himself. A symbol! He needed a new symbol.

"Understanding..." murmured Alex to himself. "Let those who have not yet had the chance gain understanding."

And he reached out, and grasped a blade of grass.

"A new kind of life," he whispered. "A new kind of growth."

And he turned, left the Cathedral behind, and moved out into the City.

Chapter 33

LIFE AFTER DEATH

Rachel sat in a café, in Lower Hutt. It was Sunday, lunchtime. John was sitting across from her, next to Alex, and Tristan was beside her.

A plate of nachos sat in front of them, alongside the deformed bullets Alex had lain on the table.

"I don't get it," complained Tristan affectionately. "Why have you got to bring out the bullets all the time? I'm trying to eat!"

Alex grinned at him. "You're army," he said. "I'm sure your stomach can hack it."

Rachel glanced up at John's lit eyes. He remained silent.

"Help me out here," said Tristan to Rachel, reaching to pluck a nacho from the pile. "I can't seem to keep my younger brother in line."

"All strength to him," said Rachel, smirking. "You're the older one, you can take care of yourself."

Tristan grimaced at her, and then reached to take up the bullets. Rachel watched him finger them.

"Five," he muttered. "I really hammered him."

"He was up to it," said Alex.

"If you're going to do it," said Tristan, "do it right."

"Death," said John. "The death had to be convincing..."

"...in order to prove the new life," finished Alex.

"Hmmm," said Tristan, still fingering the bullets.

Rachel studied him, and then looked back to John's quiet knowing smile.

"It's a curious thing," murmured Rachel, "that something as enormous as life after death would be entrusted to the word of a select few."

"And yet," replied John, "how else would word of it be passed on?"

"It's no different from science," muttered Rachel, "at the end of the day. One person's observation is passed on to all people."

"Yes," said John. "And the word of the truth of it is trusted."

"Yes," said Rachel, and she looked back to Tristan's face.

He was frowning slightly, looking down at the bullets. He was turning them over in his hands.

"Why didn't he give me a good telling off?" muttered Tristan. "It's the first thing I would have done, if I'd come back from being shot by my friend."

Alex reached over and took the bullets, and put them back into his pocket. There were tears in his eyes.

"Because he did it on purpose," he said. "He took the bullets for us, so he would die instead of us, so we could live."

Tristan's eyes were on him. "What kind of life?" he asked. "What kind of death?"

"A death of the soul," said Alex. "A new life for the soul."

Tristan's gaze passed over Alex's face. He smiled sadly. Then he rose to his feet.

"I still don't get it," he said, "but keep talking to me! I know that you will."

And he flicked a grin in Rachel's direction, and walked out of the café.

Alex's eyes turned to John, his face looking exasperated.

"How many times do I have to explain it?" he asked, and John smiled, and shrugged.

"As many times as you both are willing to discuss it."

"It's like he's wilfully trying not to understand," said Alex.

"No," murmured Rachel, and her eyes wandered after Tristan. "No, he understands it all right." And she rose to her feet, and wandered out to the street.

Tristan was lingering, on the side of the road. He smiled at her, and gestured down the street.

"Come," he said. "Let's talk." Rachel glanced back to John, and then shrugged.

"Okay," she said, and she followed him.

Tristan led her through the streets, and down to the Hutt River. Rachel shifted slightly on her feet. Did he still have feelings for her? But, no, there was no romance in his eyes.

He wandered down to the water, and gestured for her to follow. She joined him, at the water's edge.

He reached down for a leaf, and threw it into the water. She followed him, she did the same. Then he smiled at her, through wet eyes, and reached into his pocket.

It was his rifle.

Rachel stared at it, confused, and looked back to his eyes.

"I had the bullets checked," said Tristan, and Rachel stared at him.

"What?" she breathed.

"I had them checked," said Tristan. "To see if they matched my gun."

Rachel found herself holding her breath: evidence? One way or other?

"You tell me," said Tristan. "Do you want to know the truth? If you expect me to believe your version, are you willing to accept mine?"

Rachel stared at him, and straightened her shoulders, and swallowed.

"Okay," she whispered. "I'm willing to accept yours, if it is the truth."

"Good," he said. "Then I believe you." And he threw the rifle into the water.

Rachel stared after it, and then at his face. "What are you doing?" she cried, and Tristan shrugged.

"I believe you," he said. "I believe John, through you. I believe these bullets were the ones I sent into Joshua, and that he gave them to John."

"But why?" asked Rachel. "Why believe, if you have the truth?"

"I don't have the truth, Rachel," said Tristan. "I only have your word. I only have your character, behind your word."

"You said…"

"I said I had them tested," said Tristan. "The results were inconclusive."

Rachel gazed at him, and tilted her head, and laughed.

"A test?" she cried. "You were testing me?"

"Well, why not?" asked Tristan. "You people keep testing us!"

He broke into a wide grin, Rachel hit his arm, and now he grasped her hand and led her back up the hill to the road, away from the flowing waters.

Rachel wandered back into the café. The nachos were almost finished. Alex was in an animated conversation with John.

Tristan was easing himself back onto a seat, and Alex looked back up at him.

"Well?" he asked. "Got anything else to say?"

"Sure," said Tristan. "I believe you."

"What?" exclaimed Alex.

"I believe you," said Tristan. "I believe that, despite the best efforts of you and me, Joshua is, in fact, still alive."

Alex stared at him. Rachel laughed, and looked at John's smile.

"Well why didn't you tell me that before?" exploded Alex, and Tristan grinned at him.

"You never asked," he said. Alex slapped him on the arm, and Tristan wrestled with him. Rachel rolled her eyes and looked back to John, who was beginning to doze after the heavy meal.

Life, after death. Rachel looked over Alex's face: the young man who had almost been killed. She looked over the face of Tristan: the distraught murderer. She looked over John, at peace, resting.

It was finished. They were sorted.

###

Next in The Zeal Trilogy:

THE CRUX OF SALVATION

Rachel wants to save her brother. But the world is hurtling toward war...

Rachel Connor has qualified as a physician, but her brother's pain is haunting her. Locked in prison for murder, he carries the power of life and death in his hands. New Zealand has settled in an uneasy peace, but Rachel's father, the Prime Minister, sees the threat of a nuclear holocaust on the horizon.

Love is calling Rachel into the highest cost. The security of her home is lying in the balance. How far will she go to try to protect the world from the enemy within her borders? How much will she sacrifice to try to save her brother's mind?

The Crux of Salvation is the third in the *A New Kind of Zeal* trilogy, a spiritual and psychological suspense novel for people of all walks of life. If you enjoy compelling characters, powerful drama, and stories with a New Zealand flair, then you'll love Michelle Warren's books of hope under fire.

Connect with the Author,

MICHELLE WARREN

Michelle Warren was born in Wellington, New Zealand. She lives 1.5 hours away from Matamata, otherwise known as Hobbiton. She is glad to live in Middle Earth, and loves The Hobbit and The Lord of the Rings.

Michelle has visited many places, most notably of late Ghana, for which she is grateful for warm hearts and excellent cocoa beans.

Michelle writes spiritual psychological suspense, in which she expresses journeys into Christian spirituality. She seeks to provide a medium in which people of different perspectives, faiths or outlooks can be entertained and need not fear to tread. Michelle believes that friendship in the midst of our differences is vital and mutually beneficial, and so she seeks to write fiction representing and allowing for the coexistence of all.

In her newsletter, Michelle explores different challenges facing New Zealand and the world, exploring different human outlooks and potential.

Contact Michelle at **michelle@michellewarren.kiwi** or grab a free copy of her novel *Yeshua* and sign up to Michelle's Newsletter here: **https://BookHip.com/ZBSVHAX**

Books by

Michelle Warren

THE ZEAL TRILOGY

Available as ebooks, paperbacks and audiobooks.

A New Kind of Zeal

The Price of Redemption

The Crux of Salvation

Yeshua

ENDNOTES

1) Psalm 62:2 Paraphrased. Scripture taken from the HOLY BIBLE, NEW INTERNATIONAL VERSION ®. NIV ®. COPYRIGHT © 1973, 1978, 1984, 2011 by Biblica, Inc.®. Used by permission. All rights reserved worldwide.

2) 1 Corinthians 11:25 Paraphrased.

3) John 15:13 Paraphrased.

4) Paraphrased from Newton, John. Amazing Grace. 1779.

5) 1 Corinthians 15: 12-19 Paraphrased.

REFERENCES

Chapter Two

Kenneth Barker, ed. The NIV Study Bible New International Version.
Michigan: Zondervan, 1985.

Chapter Three

Kenneth Barker, ed. The NIV Study Bible New International Version.
Michigan: Zondervan, 1985.

Chapter Twenty-Five

Newton, John. Amazing Grace. 1779.

Chapter Thirty-One

Kenneth Barker, ed. The NIV Study Bible New International Version.
Michigan: Zondervan, 1985.

www.ingramcontent.com/pod-product-compliance
Lightning Source LLC
Chambersburg PA
CBHW050018180626
46810CB00002B/471